Also by Amelia Grey

THE ROGUES' DYNASTY
A Duke to Die For
Only a Duchess Would Dare
An Earl to Enchant
A Gentleman Never Tells
A Gentleman Says "I Do"
The Rogue Steals a Bride

Never a Bride
A Dash of Scandal
A Little Mischief
A Hint of Seduction
A Taste of Temptation

THE Rogue STEALS A BRIDE

AMELIA GREY

sourcebooks
casablanca

Published by Sourcebooks Casablanca, an imprint of Sourcebooks
P.O. Box 4410, Naperville, Illinois 60567-4410
(630) 961-3900
sourcebooks.com

Originally published in 2013 in the United States of America
by Sourcebooks Casablanca, an imprint of Sourcebooks.

Printed and bound in the United States of America.
OPM 10 9 8 7 6 5 4 3 2 1

This book is dedicated to my good friend Gene Duggan, who was kind enough to help me with the alfresco entertainment of Old London. Your insights were invaluable to me.

One

The affections are like lightning: you cannot tell where they will strike till they have fallen.

—Jean Baptiste Lacordaire

MATSON BRENTWOOD STOPPED DEAD IN HIS tracks.

It was a clear and crisp spring day, and the London street was busy with pedestrian, horse, and carriage traffic, but all Matson saw was the woman of his dreams walking straight toward him. She was tall, slim, and graceful, with a regal tilt to her chin. With every step she took, the flounces of her pale yellow pelisse fluttered like delicate leaves caught on a summer wind. From beneath her fetching short-brimmed straw hat, he saw ringlets of gorgeous red curls framing her beautiful face.

Matson had always been attracted to redheads.

He had attended more parties than he could count during the six months he'd been in London and was certain he'd never seen her before. She must have just arrived in Town for the Season.

She was flanked by a pair of older women who

looked so much alike they could have been book-ends. Though they each wore a different color, their dresses and bonnets were made from the same pattern. Matson knew at once they had to be sisters and maybe even twins, but his gaze didn't linger on the matrons. It was the younger lady who commanded his attention.

Matson couldn't help but think she must be the daughter of a powerful duke or an earl to have such severe-looking chaperones on either side. The lovely belle was at least half a head taller than her prim escorts, and they all carried fancy ruffled-and-beribboned parasols over their shoulders.

His pulse raced when the young lady caught sight of him. He bowed, as was custom, though an observant onlooker would note the restraint, as if he hadn't spent his life bowing in London streets. When he lifted his head, their gazes met once again, and she returned his smile. A slow throb started in his loins. There was a sensuous quality to her full lips, and an amusing twinkle in her eyes that beckoned him.

When she was only a short distance from him, Matson heard a man yell, "Stop that thief!"

A second later a lad of about eight or nine years of age rushed in front of the three ladies, shoving one of them aside and almost knocking her down. The incident slowed the boy just enough for the shopkeeper to grab the back of his tattered coat and stop him.

"You little bandit!" the portly merchant yelled and almost lifted the boy off the ground by the neck of his shirt. "I'll teach you to steal from me."

The young lady broke away from the two women at her side and rushed to the boy's aid.

"Put him down," she commanded. "That's no way to treat a child."

"I'll do no such thing," the man barked, his expression blazing with barely controlled rage. "It's the second time this week he's stolen a loaf of bread from me."

"He's holding nothing," she protested, her tone full of challenge.

"That's because the little imp threw it aside when I gave chase."

"He is probably hungry," she answered, continuing her defense of the street urchin whose face, hands, and clothing were smeared with grime and coal dust.

"Sophia, you must not get involved in this," one of her chaperones said breathlessly. "This is not our quarrel. We must go."

Sophia.

So now he had a name for the lovely young lady.

"Not yet, Aunt June. I'll not stand by and watch anyone this small be treated so violently." She turned to the man again. "Release him."

Matson admired the young lady's display of courage and determination to help the impish lad and was impressed by the way she took the bellowing trader to task. Obviously others were too. A small crowd was gathering around them to watch.

"He deserves far worse," the shopkeeper muttered without backing down on his firm stance.

"Not from you, he doesn't," she answered quickly.

Matson wasn't the kind of man to stand by for long and let the young lady take up for the lad all by herself. He wasn't very familiar with London streets, but in Baltimore, some shopkeepers put out baskets of stale bread by their door each morning where street scamps could help themselves without fear of punishment. It was the charitable thing to do, and it kept most of the youth from pilfering the fresh-baked loaves put out later in the day.

"I'll pay for the bread," Matson said, stepping closer to the group and reaching into his coat pocket for a coin.

The young lady gave Matson a grateful smile, and his stomach tightened with desire. There was something infinitely rewarding about aiding a pretty lady and receiving her gratitude.

"Such a nice thing to do for the lad," he heard one of her chaperones murmur softly.

"Hush, Mae," the other lady said. "This is not our concern. Sophia needs to stop this nonsense and come with us immediately."

"Oh, yes, of course you're right, Sister."

Matson looked back to the shopkeeper. "Take

this, and the bread will be more than paid for both days. Now do as the lady asked and let him go."

There was a moment of tense silence before the irate man turned the lad loose. "Yes, it's paid for today, yesterday, and maybe a bit more for times past," he grumbled, grabbing the coin with stubby fingers and squeezing it in his beefy palm. "But what will I do about tomorrow or the next day when he comes back?"

"I will not be here to help him." Matson peered down at the dirty-faced rascal, whose big, expressive brown eyes showed no fear. His calmness was unusual for one so young and in his predicament. That told Matson the lad was no stranger to trouble. He was probably used to being manhandled, and it obviously wasn't the first time he'd been caught helping himself to food he hadn't paid for.

"I'd say that's a good thing," the merchant said. "He needs to be taught a lesson."

The young lady bristled again. "What would you do? Thrash him? You are more than three times his size. He is only a hungry child."

"He is a thief," the man growled malevolently.

"Stop this," one of the aunts said sternly, taking hold of Sophia's upper arm. "I insist that we go now. This is not any of your concern and not a place you should be."

"Wait," she said.

"No, Sophia, June is right. We are drawing a crowd of onlookers. We must go now."

Sophia acted as if she hadn't heard her companions and didn't make a move to back down from the shopkeeper's angry glare and harsh accusation.

"Where is your benevolent spirit for one so young?" she asked the man as she tried to shake off June's tight hold on her arm.

"I suppose he robbed me of that too," the merchant shot back.

Matson didn't want to lecture anyone, but in this case felt he had to do more to settle this dispute. The trader was obviously looking for punishment for the lad to go with the payment Matson gave him, and Sophia was determined the child simply be set free.

Looking down at the boy's smudged but innocent-looking face, Matson said, "You may not be so lucky to have someone come to your aid next time. You'd best not try your hand at stealing again. If you need food—just ask for it. I'm sure this man would be willing to give you a job or two to do around his store to pay for some bread." He looked up at the merchant. "Do you agree?"

"I'll not be promising this scamp anything," he muttered and stomped down the walkway.

Matson returned his attention to the captivating young lady named Sophia. He was intrigued by her and attracted by the sparkle in her bright green eyes. He was downright tantalized by the dusky pink tint to her inviting lips. There was a faint sprinkling of tiny freckles that swept across the bridge of her nose and fanned her cheekbones. Matson had an instant desire to kiss his way over them. He knew her skin would be warm, smooth, and soft to his touch.

She fixed her gaze on his, and Matson's heartbeat leaped. His gaze followed the graceful curve of her chin, drifting down to the pulse in the hollow of her throat. She wasn't giving him smiles laced with promises or sensuous glances, but every cell in his body responded to her. He could see that, even though she'd boldly taken up for the lad, she was every bit a soft, feminine lady. Matson's body was making him quite aware of just how long it had been since a woman had truly interested him.

Suddenly, one of the older women gasped. Matson glanced down in time to see the boy swipe a knife across the strings of the young lady's reticule and grab it as it fell from her wrist.

The crested-hilt dagger the mischievous youngster used looked like Matson's!

His hand flew to his empty holder. How had the little bugger filched it from the belt around Matson's waist without his awareness? He reached for the rascal, but the only thing his hand closed around was air.

"You little cutpurse!" he called and took off after the artful thief, who was pushing, bumping, and tripping people in his haste to get away.

Matson had to slow down and sidestep bystanders

to keep from running them down. With ease, the boy took a quick, sharp right turn and deliberately toppled a large table that was piled high with breads, cheeses, and meat pies as he flew by it. Matson moved quickly to keep from taking a tumble himself as he jumped over loaves, kicked rounds of cheese, and stepped squarely into the middle of a savory pie. He heard a shopkeeper yelling from behind him, but Matson kept running. It was more important that he catch the lad than help the merchant with his ruined food items.

A few seconds later, Matson was gaining on the boy when suddenly the boy rounded another corner. Matson was right behind him, but pulled up short at the sight before him. He sucked in a deep, cold breath and caught the strong scent of fish.

It was market day, and every inch of Timsford's Square was covered with street vendors, shoppers, and merrymakers. Tables, carts, and stalls were filled with everything from meats, flowers, and spices to fabrics, trinkets, and embroidery samples. Hundreds of people were happily milling around in the festival-like atmosphere, looking, bartering, and buying from the wares available.

Matson let out a heavy sigh. Maybe he could have found the lad in the throng of people if the scamp had been the only child on the street, but to Matson it looked as if there were at least as many children as adults in the crowd teeming before him.

THE ROGUE STEALS A BRIDE 9

"Damnation," he swore softly, angry with himself for letting the little rascal outsmart him, and outrun him. He took off his hat and wiped his forehead with the back of his palm.

"Where is he? Where did he go?"

Matson heard the frantic voice beside him, and his attention jerked away from the square. He once again drank in the details of the red-haired beauty who had stopped beside him. Her chest rose and fell rapidly. The spring chill had colored her cheeks in a delicate rosy color, and her breath blew soft puffs of warm mist into the noisy air. Matson wanted to lower his mouth to her parted lips and mingle his own breath with hers.

In Sophia's haste to catch up with him, her bonnet had fallen off her head and lay on her back. Midafternoon sunlight streamed down and glistened on thick golden-red hair that looked as if it had been intertwined with shimmering tresses spun from gold. His stomach knotted in anticipation. He had an almost irresistible urge to release her lush hair from its combs right there on the busy street and bury his face in the silken torrent of lavish curls.

Matson mentally shook himself. He hadn't been so instantly attracted to a lady since he'd first met Mrs. Catherine Delaney when he was twenty years old. She'd had golden-red locks too. She had been the desire of his dreams for two years, but he hadn't thought about her in a long time.

Reluctantly, he tore his interest from Sophia's hair to concentrate on her features. Concern clouded her eyes, dulling the spark that had been there just minutes before. Obviously, she didn't like being bested by the lad any more than he did.

"I lost sight of him in the square," Matson said, unable to hide his frustration at being fooled by the youngster's wily escape.

A look of fiery determination flashed across her face. "I must find him."

"That's going to be difficult to do in that mob."

Her hands balled into tight fists. "I can't believe I was so gullible. I defended him and tried to help him."

Her troubled expression showed a hint of the sudden turmoil he heard in her voice. "We were both taken in by his innocent young face," Matson admitted. "He probably ran through the square at such a speed that he is way down one of the side streets by now."

"No, there he is," she exclaimed and took off running toward a child.

"Wait!" Matson called and ran after her. "That's not him."

Before he could reach her, she grabbed a young boy by the shoulders and turned him around. The frightened child looked up at her and tried to pull away.

"'Ey there, whatcha doing wid me son?" a large,

apron-clad woman called and started stomping toward Sophia.

"I'm sorry," she said, letting go of him and looking at the woman. "Excuse me. I thought he was someone else."

Sophia spun away from the kid and started searching the crowd again. Fearing what she intended to do, Matson tried to catch up to her, but before he could reach her, he saw her gaze light on another boy who looked like the thief.

She raced toward the lad and quickly turned him around. It was not the imp.

"Get yer hands off me boy," a woman yelled and shoved Sophia away.

Matson saw big trouble brewing if he didn't get Sophia away from the square. He touched her arm. "Miss, he's not here. We need to go."

She paid him no mind. Her gaze frantically searched the crowd again as her hands squeezed the fabric of her skirt. "He has to be here," she whispered earnestly.

"He's already gone. Come with me," Matson said, noticing that several men and women were slowly closing in on them.

"I can't leave. I must find him."

Matson sensed she had more at stake than just a purse with an embroidered handkerchief in it, but this was not the way to find her reticule. He took hold of her wrist and calmly said, "We'll return later, but right now you're coming with me." He started pulling her away from the crowd.

"No. Let go of me."

She tried to pry his hand from around her wrist, but he held tightly and kept walking.

"You don't understand. I must find him."

Matson didn't look back until he managed to get her a safe distance away from the square. When he let her go, she glared at him.

"Who do you think you are? You had no right to interfere, no right to touch me. Now, thanks to you, the boy will get away."

Matson grimaced. "Thanks to me? The boy had already run away. I was trying to find him too."

"Then why did you stop me from looking for him?"

Matson was determined to be patient. She was flushed, out of breath, and not thinking clearly. "Didn't you see the way most everyone in the crowd was staring at you? You were about to find yourself in big trouble for accosting their sons."

"Accosting?" she asked impetuously. "Don't be ridiculous."

"I'm not. You are. You were about to have several angry parents descending on you in an unruly manner."

Sophia gasped. "You make it sound like I was a madwoman out to hurt the boys. I only wanted to see their faces so I could find the thief."

"I'd like to get my hands on the cunning little devil, too. That was my dagger he made off with, along with your reticule."

Her brows lifted. "It was with your knife he cut the strings of my purse?" she asked incredulously. "Why would a gentleman such as you carry a weapon during the day? If you hadn't had the knife with you, he wouldn't have grabbed it and used it to steal my reticule."

Matson stared into her flashing green eyes. She was overwrought and looking for someone to blame. The gentleman in him wanted to let her pin it all on him without argument, but the man in him couldn't let her unreasonableness pass.

He said, "You aren't saying what the imp did is my fault, are you?"

"That's exactly what I'm saying." She quickly moistened her lips. "He didn't get the knife from me, and if it's yours, he didn't have it with him." Suddenly, she abruptly stopped talking and let out a long, shaky, sighing breath.

She squeezed her eyes closed for a moment. Matson couldn't help but think she was summoning some inner strength to compose herself. When her lashes lifted, her eyes were softer, calmer. Her expression was concerned and sad. Matson saw she had reasons he didn't understand for being so frantic to get her reticule back.

"My mother's brooch was in that reticule," she

whispered. Her attention strayed back to the teeming square. "I must get it back."

"I'm sure your mother will forgive you for losing it. It wasn't your fault."

She lowered her lashes again as if shading her eyes from something she didn't want him to see, and shook her head. "You don't understand. It's not a question of that. My mother died years ago."

Her voice was clotted with emotion and hampered by erratic breathing. Matson saw a flash of anguish in her eyes, and his annoyance with her vanished.

"I'm sorry," he offered softly.

Desire to draw her to his chest and soothe her grew inside him. He wanted to feel her soft, pliant lips beneath his in a tender, comforting kiss. If he hadn't been so enthralled by her loveliness, patting himself on the back for stepping up and handling the situation, the boy would never have made his escape.

As if resignation had settled in, she lifted her bonnet back onto her head, and her hand knocked a loosely pinned comb from her hair. A silken torrent of red curls fell over her right shoulder, caressed her neck, and tumbled down her breast. Everything inside Matson grew taut with restraint. His fingers itched to trace one of the curls and then slowly wind its softness around his finger. His knuckles wanted to brush across the fullness of her breast, where the curl lay on such a sweet pillow.

Suddenly, the shrill sound of a frantic lady's voice sliced through the air as if it were an icicle. "Sophia!"

Matson and the young lady looked behind them, and Matson saw her two chaperones, holding onto their hats and parasols, rushing toward them.

One lady outran the other and stumbled to a halt beside them, her face punctuated by a chaffed ruddiness. Clutching her hand to her chest and breathing hard, she said, "What is this? What is going on here?"

The chaperone may have been older, but she was not a dunce. Matson felt her question was more of a silent accusation. It was as if she had read his mind in the keenest way, making him wonder what her own romantic trysts had been when she was younger.

"We're trying to find the boy, Aunt June. You know my mother's brooch was in that reticule."

"Yes, yes, I know that. Here is your parasol. Open it quickly. The sun is very bright today. And do fit your bonnet on properly, my dear."

"Sophia," the other lady gasped, inhaling deeply when she skidded to a stop beside them. "Thank God we caught up to you. We were so worried to see you racing off like that to heaven knows where."

"The boy ran in there, Aunt Mae," Sophia said, pointing toward Timsford's Square. "I must find him."

"Oh, but you can't do that. Come, we'll go to the authorities and let them handle this."

"That's just what I was going to say, Sister," June added. "Why, trying to find that ruffian in so large a crowd would be like looking for a needle in a haystack."

Sophia gave Matson a determined glance before turning her attention back to the women. "Perhaps it is, but you know me well enough to know that doesn't mean I'm not going to try."

"Oh, Sophia, for once in your life be sensible."

Now that the chaperones were so close to him, Matson could see that they must be twins—Mae and June. They had the same color of hair, eyes, and complexion, as well as the same facial features. Being a twin himself, Matson knew how rare it was to see identical adults. Even when he and his brother were youngsters, they seldom came across another set of twins.

But Matson and his brother Iverson had been more than mere oddities because their faces were indistinguishable from each other when they'd arrived in London last fall. They had the misfortune of being the spitting image of the older, well-respected Sir Randolph Gibson, and they didn't resemble their legal father at all. Months later, the gossipmongers were still talking about them being Sir Randolph's by-blow, a poet had written a slanderous parody about them, and wagers concerning their parentage were still offered at White's and other gentlemen's clubs throughout London.

"Ladies," Matson said, bowing, "pardon me for interrupting, and permit me to introduce myself."

"Absolutely not," June said, seeming horrified that he'd even spoken to them.

"Sir, we can't allow you to do that," Mae added, moving to stand between Matson and Sophia as if she feared he might pounce on the young lady. "We know nothing about you."

Matson watched the shifting emotions on Sophia's face. It looked as if she didn't want to remain quiet and adhere to the women's commands, but she didn't want to take them to task and be disrespectful to them in front of him either.

"He's looking for the boy, too, Aunties. We know what he looks like. The authorities will not."

"It doesn't matter, my dear. As of here and now, this is no longer our concern."

"Of course it is," Sophia protested again.

"We'll give the authorities a detailed description of the lad. June is right, and we must listen to her. We can't allow just anyone who happens to be on the street to introduce himself to you."

"Come along, Sophia," June said and then made an odd clucking sound before saying, "We have much to do if we are going to have any hope of finding your purse."

Matson watched in surprise as, in tandem, the matching sentinels hooked their hands around the young lady's elbows, turned her around, and marched away with her, the ribbons hanging from their parasols fluttering in the breeze.

Matson had no idea who Sophia was, but he wanted to know.

She was beautiful. She was delectable. She was provocative, inviting, and intriguing. Most captivating of all was the small flare of vulnerability he witnessed when she told him the brooch was her mother's. She had covered the weakness quickly, and he liked the fact that she wasn't going to let it keep her from going after the cutpurse. That is, until the two *soldiers* came along and waylaid her.

Matson watched as the three rounded the corner and disappeared from view. He smiled to himself and wondered which gave the other more trouble: the chaperones or Sophia. He chuckled to himself and thought perhaps the twins. They were definitely *double trouble* for the young lady.

He spoke softly to himself: "What man wouldn't be instantly drawn to her?"

She couldn't be engaged or married. If she had a husband, she wouldn't be so carefully watched by her aunts. He'd learned years ago with Mrs. Delaney that there were some boundaries a gentleman shouldn't cross, and pursuing an engaged or married lady was one of them.

But what if she was a powerful duke's daughter, as he had suspected when he first saw her? Would the second son of a viscount be a welcomed suitor, especially a son who'd gone to America, made his fortune, and had only recently returned to London and the polite society to which he'd been born?

Matson snorted ruefully and shook his head. He had another strike against him too. He was very obviously the son of Sir Randolph Gibson, a man who was not his legal father. That gave Matson more pause than the prospect of the lovely Sophia having a fiancé. Fathers could be damned difficult about their daughters.

Especially powerful fathers.

His oldest brother, Brent, was testament to that.

The first thing Matson had to do was to discover who she was.

He placed his hat back on his head and looked out over the packed square. No, the first thing he had to do was find the boy and take back the reticule and dagger. Returning the beloved brooch should win him favor with the young lady and perhaps her father too.

Two

Nothing so much prevents our being natural as
the desire of appearing so.

—François de La Rochefoucauld

SOPHIA HART STOOD WITH HER TWO AUNTS AND
her guardian, Sir Randolph Gibson, in the crowded
ballroom of the Great Hall and looked at the faces
of all the gentlemen on the dance floor. She was in
a quandary.

How was she going to fulfill her promise to her
father? Even though it wasn't in her nature to be an
obedient or submissive daughter, she didn't regret
making her vow to him. It was the right thing to
do then and now, but until she had arrived at her
first ball and seen the sheer number of gentlemen
present, she had no idea how difficult that promise would be.

It wasn't very late in the evening, but the
large, opulent room was crowded, hot, and loud.
Candlelight from the magnificent chandeliers
bathed everything in a golden glow. The dance
floor was centered in the middle of the room, and

the host of people stood around it, talking, laughing, and whispering.

She'd arrived at the Great Hall over two hours ago, and already she'd encountered more gentlemen than she could remember. Much to her aunts' and Sir Randolph's excitement, she had been presented to an earl, two viscounts, five barons, and more than a dozen other eligible gentlemen. The problem was she couldn't envision herself spending the rest of her life with any of them.

Her aunts had done well in preparing her for her first ball. Because of her father's illness and then his death, she'd missed the past two Seasons and had already turned twenty. They were all eager for her to make a match before the spring parties ended, and be a bride before the fall chill set in.

Mae and June had seen to it that the year she'd spent mourning her father was productive. All her gowns, wraps, headpieces, and shoes were elegantly styled in the latest fashions. Before he fell ill, the settings of her pearls, emeralds, and sapphires had been handpicked by her father and had been tucked away in the safe, waiting for her first Season to begin.

From her birth, it seemed, she had been groomed for this. Her dance instructor had sung her praises, delighting in how light she was on her feet. She had been well tutored in writing, reading, and sums, as well as the finer things ladies were supposed to excel in, such as painting, embroidery, and playing the pianoforte.

Sophia had endured many lessons on how to properly manage a large household with up to twenty staff. Nothing in her dowry, education, or her trousseau was lacking, and as far as her father, Sir Randolph, and her aunts were concerned, there was no reason she couldn't tempt a titled gentleman to offer for her hand. To them, her great fortune, which Sir Randolph was currently in charge of, was just an added enticement to her many personal accomplishments.

A month ago, Sophia and her aunts had arrived in London and had settled into Sir Randolph's comfortable but eccentrically decorated town house. Everything possible had been done to ensure that Miss Sophia Hart, heiress to Shevington Shipping Company, would keep the vow she had made to her father on his deathbed and become the bride of a titled gentleman. Now, actually settling on the man and getting him to offer for her hand was up to Sophia.

The wealth or title of the man wasn't important to her, but that he allow her freedom to continue to have a substantial say in how Shevington Shipping was managed mattered a great deal, so Sophia had to be careful whom she chose. She couldn't turn her back on what she had promised her father; as Sir Randolph had said many times: a person was only as good as their word. She would keep hers.

All the preparation that went on before her arrival in London had been easy compared to the task at hand now. Her first two hours at the ball were a series of one introduction after another. Sir Randolph had paraded her around the room, making sure she met everyone who was there at the time. She found out only tonight that Sir Randolph had not told one soul that he had become the guardian of a young lady little more than a year ago. Everyone was surprised and clamoring to meet her. It truly wasn't remarkable or unusual for an older, well-respected gentleman to become the guardian of an heiress. She could only assume the whispers behind fans and hands were because Sir Randolph had never married and had no children of his own.

Her father and Sir Randolph had been business partners in several shipping ventures and good friends for many years. Sophia had always known Sir Randolph was the only person her father would trust with her future. Her father wanted her to have what his lowborn social standing could never achieve for her, even though he'd beaten the odds, considering his impoverished upbringing, and become a very wealthy man. He'd wanted her to marry a titled gentleman.

She had no doubts that Sir Randolph could see her properly wed, but she had many doubts concerning his ability to oversee her fortune. Unlike her father, who had worked hard and developed his business empire from shrewd dealings over many years, Sir Randolph had inherited his wealth. He had little knowledge or interest in the finer details that kept a business thriving.

Since Sophia was an only child, her father had indulged her and allowed her to learn far more about his shipping business than most would consider appropriate for a daughter. Long before his death, he'd allowed her to go over the account books with him and help him make decisions concerning companies, cargo, and countries that were eager for fabrics, spices, gemstones, and a host of other things from India and the Orient. Sir Randolph was much too willing to leave many details and decisions up to the solicitors and Shevington Shipping's primary manager, Mr. Edward Peabody.

A rotund gentleman no taller than Sophia approached them. Sophia was well acquainted with the procedure and smiled all through the complicated introductions and curtsies while she and her aunts were presented to the robust Earl of Bighampton.

"You two look so much alike, you must be twins," Lord Bighampton said to one of her aunts, causing them both to beam.

"Yes, we are," June said.

"That's just what I was going to say," Aunt Mae

added, smiling sweetly at the man. She opened her fan and started slowly fanning herself. "We are twins, my lord, though we were born on different days."

"And different months, too," June quickly inserted.

"I'm sure that is quite uncommon," Lord Bighampton said, seemingly a bit taken aback by the comment.

"Not really. You see, Mae was born just before midnight on May thirty-first, and I was born just after midnight on June the first."

"That's why our mama named us Mae and June," Mae said, finishing the story for her sister.

"We think it's an exceptional story indeed, and we do seem to attract attention wherever we go."

"It's been that way all our lives," Mae added.

"I'm sure that's true," the earl said drily, making no show to hide how uninterested he was in the aunties' account of their birth.

There was nothing her aunts liked better than telling the story of their birth, and they told it often. While her aunts were keeping the earl occupied, Sophia let their chatter and the roar of the large and crowded room fade from her thoughts. Once again, her gaze flitted across the face of every gentleman in the room.

Off and on all evening, she had scanned the crowd for the gentleman who had tried to help her with the little thief she'd encountered a few days ago. She'd wished a thousand times since then she'd defied her aunts and had gotten his name before they whisked her away. If she had, she would have been able to send him a note to thank him for his willingness to aid her. She knew she had acted too hastily in the square when she was looking for the boy, but at the time she couldn't do anything else. She couldn't let herself admit that the lad had gotten away. Thoughts of having lost the brooch always caused a pang of angst in her chest, but she refused to give up hope or faith that it would be returned to her. It was the last tangible thing she had of her mother's.

The constable had quietly listened to her story and description of the lad but didn't leave her with much hope of recovering her treasured item. He insisted that London had many young ruffians and pickpockets roaming the streets, looking for mischief. But just this afternoon an idea had come to Sophia that she would put into action tomorrow—if she could talk Sir Randolph into letting her do it. She couldn't continue waiting on the authorities and doing nothing to help find the brooch.

Thinking of that afternoon reminded her of the exciting and delicious feelings that tumbled in her stomach when she first noticed the gentleman who'd helped her. She'd never seen so young a man wear a beard. For a moment she wondered if one could call the narrow line of closely trimmed hair that bordered the outside of his clean-shaven cheek, along his jawline, and across his chin, a beard. It certainly wasn't much of one, but what little there was made him appear so devilishly handsome—just how she envisioned a rogue or rake of the highest order would look. Her heartbeat had raced at the sight of him chasing after the boy, dodging people, smashing pies, and jumping over tumbling loaves of bread.

She'd tried every argument she could think of to get her aunts to take her back to the square to look for the lad, hoping she might see the man again too, but the aunties would have none of that. They insisted there was no way they would risk even a breath of scandal touching her name. They had worked too hard to help keep her reputation pure and unblemished, and a brush, no matter how slight, with the unsavory side of life was not in the best interests of her future.

The earl faced Sophia, and she realized he was talking to her, so she smiled.

"When the music resumes, Miss Hart, would you give me the pleasure of a dance?"

"Yes, thank you, my lord."

"Good. I shall return for you later." He nodded to her aunts and Sir Randolph before walking away.

"And with his leaving, I think I shall bid you ladies adieu and take my leave as well," Sir Randolph said.

"Surely not, Sir Randolph," June said.

"It's growing late, Miss Shevington, and I've already introduced Sophia to far more gentlemen than she can possibly dance or converse with tonight."

"Sir Randolph, are you sure?" Mae asked.

He nodded. "My duty for this evening is done."

"Well, I don't think you should leave Sophia just yet, Sir Randolph," June added tersely. "There is much more that needs to be done for her."

"Then you do it, Miss Shevington. I'm only her guardian. You and your sister are her chaperones. I trust you can keep her safe. Unless for some reason you don't feel capable, and if that's the case, I'll make other arrangements for her."

"No, no, of course not," June hurried to say.

"Someone other than us to watch after Sophia," Mae added huffily. "Absolutely not. Her father would rise up out of the grave."

"Besides, we'd never hear of it, either," June added.

"Then I suggest you do your jobs, and I'll do mine."

Sophia cleared her throat to cover her laughter. It wasn't often anyone got the best of her dutiful aunts. Sophia had already known Sir Randolph well when he became her guardian. She had always looked forward to his visits with her father. But even so, the more she saw of him, the more she liked him. She considered him dapper, dashing, and quite a handsome fellow for his age. He was tall and robust, with thick silver hair and an almost mischievous twinkle in his blue eyes that always made her smile.

"Of course we will," June said in a more conciliatory tone. "You'll find no fault on our account. But before you go, tell me, do you think she pleased the patronesses of Almack's?"

Sir Randolph looked at Sophia and smiled. "She would please anyone, Miss Shevington."

"How can one know?" Mae asked. "They were so dour-looking when they spoke to her."

"They are always dour. It is their job to intimidate, discriminate, and irritate. They are supposed to do it well."

June pursed her lips and seemed to study over what he'd said. "So there is really no way to tell if she will be getting her vouchers?"

"Aunties, please," Sophia said, "don't overburden Sir Randolph about such matters and with so many needless questions. We shall know soon enough if I'm to be allowed entrance into the hallowed grounds of that establishment. I'm certain I shall live quite well even if I'm not."

Mae gasped and quickly looked around her. "Mind what you say, my dear, you never know who is listening."

June gave a worrisome cluck with her tongue. "And this is so very important, my dear. It's such a coveted honor to be allowed entrance. It will increase your possibilities to make an excellent match."

Sophia turned with a smile to Sir Randolph. "I have no doubt that I shall be fine with or without the prized tickets, don't you agree?"

He smiled and nodded.

"Aunties would keep me here all evening if they could. In fact, I'm quite ready to quit this place myself."

"Oh, but you can't," June said. "You promised Lord Bighampton a dance, and at least two or three other gentlemen."

"And I shall honor my commitment to each one of them, Auntie. I said only I'm ready to go, not that I will."

"Well, Sophia," Mae added, "if you think this has been a long night, just wait until the Season is in full tilt. You'll be attending three or four different parties each night. Sir Randolph has opened many doors for you, my dear, and we intend to see you walk through each and every one of them, don't we, Sister?"

"Indeed we do."

Sophia turned to her guardian again. "And I do thank you for your attention tonight, Sir Randolph."

He patted her upper arm affectionately. "I have no doubt that gentlemen will start approaching me with offers for your hand tomorrow morning, but

I will refuse to see all of them. Just remember that when you choose to marry, Sophia, choose wisely."

"I shall, Sir Randolph."

Sophia knew exactly what she needed to do. A titled gentleman would satisfy her debt to her father and give her the redemption she sought, and a gentleman who would allow her the freedom to make decisions in Shevington Shipping would satisfy her. Her father had never once mentioned that she should marry for love, affection, or even respect, so those things needn't be considered. The only thing that had mattered to him was that she have the one thing his wealth was unable to give him: a title. And the only way she could achieve that high honor was to marry a titled gentleman and become his countess or his duchess.

There were times when she couldn't believe she'd given her father her word that she would fulfill his wish for her. But it had been at the height of his suffering, and she had hoped in some way it might ease his pain and maybe save his life. And in doing that, give her the release she needed for what she'd cost him when she was seven years old. She had always been rash, impulsive, and had acted before she gave due consideration for the consequences of what she was doing. That behavior must be her nature, because she was still prone to speak and act before she thought.

"Oh, wouldn't it be simply divine if she married

someone like that handsome Lord Bighampton?" Mae said as Sir Randolph walked away.

June gave her sister an odd look. "What are you speaking of, Mae? You know it matters not if he's handsome as long as he's titled."

"Yes, of course you are right, Sister, but Lord Bighampton just happens to be both."

Sophia didn't want her aunts to get into an argument, as they were prone to do at times, so she said, "Aunt June, could I trouble you to get me a cup of punch? I feel in need of a little refreshment before the next dance begins."

"Why, of course, my dear. It's no trouble at all."

"I'll go with you," Mae said.

"You'll do no such thing," her sister admonished. "We can't leave Sophia alone. What would people think if they saw her standing all by herself at her first ball?"

"Of course, you're right. I don't know what I was thinking."

June walked away, and Sophia looked at her aunt Mae. Her dark green eyes were still watching Lord Bighampton with great interest. "Are you all right, Auntie?" she asked.

"Oh, yes, quite," she said without turning to look at Sophia. "I was just admiring how distinguished Lord Bighampton is. He's the most handsome gentlemen I've ever seen."

Sophia heard something that sounded like

wistfulness in her aunt's voice and saw a faraway look in her eyes. She wanted to dismiss those notions as ridiculous, but something stopped her. Sophia couldn't remember ever seeing either of her aunts as contemplative as Mae was. And while the earl was not a horrible-looking man by any standards, Sophia didn't consider him handsome. The stranger who'd helped her with the young lad came to mind. Now he was a handsome man.

Sophia smiled. "I do believe you are enchanted by the earl."

Mae gasped and started fanning herself with her hand-painted fan. "Who? Me? Don't be ridiculous. Certainly not."

"Auntie, it's all right if the man is pleasing to your eyes."

"Well, of course, I know that. And he is. I think he will be a perfect match for you."

"For me?" Sophia shook her head. "He is an earl, and I will consider him, but I'm not sure he would be the right person for me. You know, Auntie, he's the perfect age for you."

"Me?" Mae fanned herself faster. "What's gotten into you, child? I'm way too old to make a match."

"Nonsense. You can be too young to marry, but you cannot be too old."

"I suppose that could be true if you've been married before. Widows often remarry, and more than once." Her attention drifted back to Lord

Bighampton. "But marriage is not for spinsters like me. I let my chance at marriage and a family pass me by, and now it's too late for this dried weed on the shelf."

The ring of wistfulness returned to her aunt's voice, causing Sophia to say, "Oh, piffle. Who says it's too late? Those old hens in Polite Society? The eager mamas who don't care what they have to say or do to get their daughters vouchers for Almack's? They don't know everything."

"Yes, they do. And besides, June wouldn't like it either."

"It doesn't matter," Sophia argued. "She can't tell you what to do, can she? You're the oldest. You were born first, right?"

"Here's your punch," June said, walking up to Sophia and Mae. "And yes, she was born first. Now, I just heard the music will start again shortly, Sophia, so drink up."

Sophia took the punch cup and took a long sip.

"Sophia, please," June said, "you might be famished, but we don't want anyone seeing you drink as if you were a dock worker at a local tavern. Take small, ladylike sips."

Her aunt continued to talk, but Sophia didn't hear what she said. Over the rim of her punch cup she had caught sight of the gentleman who had tried to help her catch the boy thief. She slowly lowered her drink and stared at the man.

He was superbly dressed in an evening coat that fit perfectly over wide, straight shoulders. His shirt was stunningly white beneath a red quilted waistcoat, and his neckcloth was superbly tied. Black trousers covered strong-looking legs spread far enough apart to lend a touch of arrogance to his stance. Everything about him spoke of power, privilege, and wealth, and her body and her mind were completely aware of him.

She could tell that he was slowly searching the room, and for a heartbeat she wondered if he might be looking for her.

Three

Chance is always powerful. Let your hook be always cast; in the pool where you least expect it, there will be fish.

—Ovid

SOPHIA'S BREATHS DEEPENED. HER LAST SIP OF punch went down hard as she stared at the stranger. Out of the corner of her eye she saw someone approach her aunts and start talking to them, but she couldn't take her gaze off the gentleman she'd met on the street. He was still slowly scouring the faces of everyone on the dance floor.

"Sophia." June lightly touched her shoulder. "You were just presented to Lord Snellingly, my dear. What do you say?"

Quickly diverting her attention from the man she'd been watching, Sophia looked up to see a tall, thin man with a large pointy nose smiling down at her. Her gaze was drawn to his collar and neckcloth. Both were unusually high, completely covering his neck and causing his head to tilt back. It looked woefully uncomfortable to

Sophia, and she'd be surprised if the dear fellow could breathe properly.

She curtsied and said, "It's a pleasure to meet you, Lord Snellingly."

He returned her smile with an ear-to-ear grin. "No, no, Miss Hart, it is always a gentleman's pleasure to be introduced to such a beautiful young lady as yourself."

The earl moved so he was standing right in Sophia's line of vision, so she stepped a little to one side, hoping to find the handsome stranger whom she could no longer see. Lord Snellingly moved too, and right in her line of sight again. "That's very kind of you to say, my lord."

"Your story is such a fascinating one."

She studied on that comment for a moment and realized she had no idea what he was talking about. "In what way?"

"Well, everyone knows and respects Sir Randolph, and no one had a hint from him that he has been your guardian for over a year. He kept knowledge of you secreted away from us."

"There was really no need for him to mention me. I couldn't come out into Society until my period of mourning was past."

His eyebrows lifted, and he laid a hand over his heart. "It's never easy to lose a loved one, is it?"

"No, never," she answered, not wanting to think about having lost her father or her mother.

"Tell me, Miss Hart, do you enjoy reading poetry?"

Sophia was surprised he went from one subject to the other so quickly, but answered, "Yes, of course, I read poetry."

"Splendid." He sniffed into the lace-trimmed handkerchief he held. "I've found it can be very comforting, no matter the troubles that tear at a tender heart. And tell me, do you write it?"

"I'm not very good at writing poetry, I'm afraid," she said, moving a little to the left again in hopes of catching a glance of the stranger, but once again the earl moved when she did. "I do give it a try from time to time."

"Excellent to hear." His smile broadened, and he clasped his hands together in front of him. Layers of lace cuffs spread across his chest. "I am a member of the Royal Society of Accomplished Poets."

"I'm sure that's a great honor," Sophia said.

"Indeed it is. I'm told I'm a dramatic poet. Perhaps I can stop by your house tomorrow afternoon and share some of my latest verse with you."

"We would be honored for you to do so, Lord Snellingly," June said, "but not tomorrow. Perhaps in a couple of days it will be fine. This is Sophia's first ball, and we would like for her to attend one or two more before we start allowing gentlemen to call on her. You do understand, don't you?"

"Yes. Quite the thing to do, Miss Shevington. I completely understand."

"But we're so pleased that you want to share your poetry with her," Mae added. "I'm certain it's truly inspiring."

"Why, yes, Miss Shevington, it is," Lord Snellingly said.

He turned his attention back to Sophia. "I'm also aware of a young ladies' poetry society. I'm certain I can get you an invitation to join, if you would like to be considered."

Writing poetry was not something Sophia wanted to do. In fact, it would be torture. She wanted to write business letters to Shevington's suppliers and negotiate contracts for better terms on their shipping fees. But she kept all that to herself, smiled pleasantly, and said, "It's certainly something I'll ponder. Thank you, Lord Snellingly."

"Miss Hart, the shade of your green eyes reminds me of a meadow that has just been washed by a spring rain." The earl then turned to June. "With your permission, I'd like to claim a dance with Miss Hart later in the evening."

"She will be delighted."

"Good. Now I shall find a quiet corner and write a few lines of poetry just for you, Miss Hart."

Finally Lord Snellingly smiled at Sophia, bowed, and walked away. Sophia immediately searched for the stranger. She wanted to talk to him but knew her aunts would never allow it unless someone introduced them, or unless she managed to get away from her aunts' watchful eyes.

"Oh, Sophia," Mae said, watching the earl walk away, "don't you think he is divinely handsome? He's so tall, so regal, and a poet too."

Sophia had barely looked at the man. She didn't think she'd ever seen a gentleman wear that much lace on his cuffs or one who thought so highly of his poetry. But not wanting to take issue with her aunt, she simply said, "Quite handsome." She took a sip of her punch, and then added, "I think I'll make a visit to the retiring room. Do excuse me."

"I'll go with you," June said.

"Please, Auntie," Sophia said, giving the empty cup to her. "Please allow me to at least do this one thing by myself. I remember how to get to the room, and with so many people here, I can assure you no harm will befall me before I can return safely to your side."

June's eyebrows rose disapprovingly. "I don't like the idea of you being alone. Don't you agree, Mae?"

"How can I be alone?" Sophia asked, frustration mounting. "There are more than two hundred people here."

A wrinkle of concern creased Mae's brow. "I suppose we could allow her to go alone once in a while. We don't want to be accused of smothering her." She turned to Sophia. "But do not allow any of the gentlemen you have met to entice you to take a walk in the garden with them."

Excitement suddenly danced inside Sophia at the thought of having a few moments alone. "That is an easy promise to make."

"Nor for a walk on the terrace, either," June added.

"Another promise," Sophia said and turned from her aunts before they could come up with another excuse or change their minds.

Sophia searched the faces for the gentleman as she slowly threaded her way through the people to the other side of the room. He had moved from the area where she'd last seen him. She reached the exit doorway and paused. Another slow perusal of the people told her he was nowhere to be found. She exited the noisy room, continuing to look for him even as she walked down the corridor, but it was as if he'd disappeared. Disappointment stung deep in her abdomen. She'd wanted to talk to him.

She made her way down the first long corridor that would, after a couple of turns, eventually lead her to the ladies' retiring room at the back of the Great Hall. She turned another corner and felt someone ease up beside her.

Her pulse quickened in anticipation. She turned and saw it was the stranger.

"Sir," she said softly. She stopped and inhaled deeply, trying to calm her racing heartbeat. "I've been looking for you."

A touch of a smile played at the corners of his mouth, making him even more handsome than she'd remembered. He was obviously pleased with her words, and her heart fluttered at the prospect.

"If that's the case, I don't know how you missed me. I've gone back to the square for the past several days, searching for you, hoping you would return. I've searched for you at all the parties I've attended this week."

She smiled. "I meant I was looking for you tonight."

"Good. I was beginning to think I had imagined you the other day and you weren't real after all."

His words made her feel good. Maybe he hadn't been completely put off by her rash behavior that afternoon. He lifted his chin a notch, and she looked into intriguing dark blue eyes. They had the power to hold her motionless. Suddenly she felt uncharacteristically flushed and out of breath.

"My aunts won't allow me to return to the square. They now deem that street unsafe and refused to accompany me there."

He cocked his head back and laughed quietly. "Don't they know that footpads and urchins can show up on any street?"

"I tried that argument and several others. None of them worked. This is the first party I've attended since we arrived in London. I wanted to see you and apologize for my behavior in that square," she said softly. "I know you were trying to help. I just didn't want to believe that the lad had gotten away."

"It's understandable." He nodded. "Being robbed would upset anyone."

"Yes, but that doesn't excuse my desperate attempt to look at the faces of every lad in the square or to blame you for the boy's theft. I would have sent you a note to thank you for helping me, but I didn't know your name."

"Do you know it now, Sophia?"

"No, how could I? But you know mine."

He nodded. "And your aunts', Mae and June, from our conversations on the street."

"That's right. You heard them call me Sophia, and I, of course, said their names."

"How long have you been in Town, Sophia?"

Her pulse jumped again. She loved hearing the whispery way her name wafted past his lips. It was especially provocative because he should never be so forward as to use her first name.

"A month," she answered.

"I find it refreshing that you've been in Town more than a fortnight and you don't know who I am."

She gave him a curious smile. "That must mean you are a very important gentleman, if you expected that I should know who you are."

His gaze swept up and down her face, causing her skin to prickle deliciously. Sophia felt her breath catch again. She realized she was staring at his lips with what could only be described as desire for him filling her. When had she ever looked at a man's lips and wondered what it would be like to have them brush across hers?

She sensed that same powerful strength in him that she felt at their first meeting, and it drew her. Clearly he wasn't going to admit to anything about what kind of man he was, and she liked that about him too. She was drawn to this stranger in a way that was exciting, and yet a little frightening, too.

"Your silence tells me that you must be the most talked-about rogue in London."

A teasing grin lifted one corner of his mouth. "Would you be horrified if that were true?"

Sophia's abdomen quivered deliciously. "No, but I don't know that I would believe it."

"Then I'll leave you to find out anything you may want to know about me."

"I never back away from a challenge."

"I like that. I'm glad I issued one."

He was clever, and that pleased her. "Tell me, on your trips back to the square, have you seen anything of the lad?"

"No. What have you heard from the authorities?"

She shook her head. "I've heard only excuses and platitudes about how diligently they are working to recover my brooch. I still can't believe I thought he was a hungry little boy, when he was a crafty little pickpocket."

"He probably *was* hungry, and we were both fooled by his innocent manner."

His words were sincere, and she appreciated them. "I haven't given up hope I'll find him and the brooch."

"There's no reason ever to give up hope."

She gave him a grateful smile. "I am glad you are out searching for him each day. I would be helping you if I could manage to slip away from my aunts."

He smiled and leaned in a fraction toward her. "I take it you aren't spoken for."

Pleasant warmth tingled across her breasts, alerting all her senses. His implication was clear, and it made her knees weak. "No," she said quickly, and then realized she might have sounded a little too eager, so she added, "Are you?"

He shook his head. "I was thinking that you must be related to the king to have two such stern chaperones watching your every move."

She laughed lightly. "My aunts take their responsibility a little too seriously."

He stepped closer to her. "Perhaps they have reason to. I can assure you every eligible gentleman in the ballroom tonight has his sights on you."

"I do seem to be an oddity tonight."

His eyes softened. "I would not characterize you as an oddity, Sophia."

He moved even closer to her, and warning bells sounded in her head. They were standing in a dimly lit corridor. Anyone could happen upon them at any moment and accuse them of planning a rendezvous, but not even the possibility of scandal caused her to step away from him.

"I think your aunts are acting like guards because they are afraid a handsome young gentleman might try to steal a kiss from you."

Her breaths came more quickly. "I believe that is exactly what frightens them."

"Does a stolen kiss in a darkened corridor frighten you?"

Did it?

She swallowed as her gaze swept down the passageway behind him. He reached up and let the backs of his fingers lightly caress her cheek, drawing her gaze back to his. Her chest felt heavy. Her lips parted slowly. Short, choppy breaths clogged in her throat.

"Is that fear I see in your eyes?"

She raised her chin. "No," she whispered, relaxing. "I have no fear of being kissed, only of getting caught."

He chuckled so softly she might have missed it had she not been so attuned to his every breath.

"That is not what I expected you to say."

"It is the truth. I've often dreamt of being kissed by a handsome stranger."

He gave her an almost imperceptible smile. "You've dreamed of it? Then let me make your dream come true."

Sophia's heartbeat quickened. Should she let this man be the first to kiss her? "Yes," she heard herself whisper.

He placed his hands under her chin and tilted her head up. She caught the invigoratingly clean scent of shaving soap on his fingertips. Slowly, he bent his head. She parted her lips slightly, and he gently pressed his lips to hers. It was barely a touch, really just a teasing brush of his soft, moist lips against hers, but enough that her insides went warm with yearning for more. A delicate fluttering started in her chest.

He lifted his head, smiled as he took a step back, and said, "Did the kiss measure up to your dreams?"

Her breathing was unsteady, but she managed to say, "In all honesty, sir, I must say it far surpassed them."

He smiled. "Reality is usually much better than a dream, isn't it?"

She swallowed hard. "Heavens, yes. Thank you for giving me my first kiss."

"Your first? Really?"

"Yes," she answered, wondering why he seemed so surprised.

His eyes narrowed for a moment as if indicating he wondered if he should believe her.

"Not even a buss on the cheek from a distant cousin?"

She shook her head.

"Well then, perhaps I should give you another."

She moistened her lips. "Perhaps you should."

"Good evening."

Sophia turned and looked down the corridor to see a tall, lanky gentleman with unusually big eyes walking toward them. Sophia had been introduced to Lord Waldo earlier in the evening. Sir Randolph had made a point of telling her later that Lord Waldo was the younger brother of the *unwed* Duke of Rockcliffe, but that the duke was a man she could not encourage. The duke was known to cheat at cards and, according to Sir Randolph, that made His Grace an unacceptable match for her.

"Good evening, Miss Hart, Mr. Brentwood," the man said.

Brentwood?

Sophia felt as if her heart slammed against her chest. She tried to hide her shock at hearing his name but wasn't sure she had.

Could her handsome stranger be one of the Brentwood twins? The gentlemen who were connected to Sir Randolph by a long-ago secret love affair and slanderous gossip? The twins she'd heard about for years? He had a thin beard and much darker hair, so she hadn't seen the resemblance to Sir Randolph that the scandal sheets had talked about. Now that she knew who he was, she could see a resemblance.

As Lord Waldo neared them, Mr. Brentwood whispered softly enough so only she could hear, "I think we can declare that Lord Waldo just introduced us, Miss Hart."

Sophia searched his face. He gave no indication that hearing her name told him she was Sir Randolph's ward. Surely that would have at least caused his eyebrows to go up in recognition.

She cleared her throat and just as softly answered, "I believe you are right, Mr. Brentwood, and we can thank the angels watching over us that he didn't witness our kiss."

"Indeed we can."

Sophia searched her mind for things she'd heard about the Brentwood twins and their shipbuilding company while she'd lived with her father in Baltimore where he took treatments for his lungs. At the time, Sophia wasn't old enough to attend the parties and balls, so she had never met either of the brothers, but she had read plenty.

She knew the twins had been very successful in their business strategy. To the public, it appeared that one twin was more aggressive and daring in his approach to business dealings than the other. But according to what Sophia had gleaned from her father's assessment of the brothers and from what she'd read, it was the more even-tempered twin, the one who was slow to act, who had been the success behind the business. Her father had considered Mr. Matson Brentwood a reasonable, approachable, and resourceful gentleman who efficiently and successfully made all the decisions.

The twins had only recently moved to London, and the stir they caused was still being felt. Even their older brother, who was a viscount, had caused a big scandal when he'd been caught in the park with a duke's daughter late last year. Everything must have worked out for the viscount, because Sophia read not long ago that he and the lady had married.

Sophia continued to stare at Mr. Brentwood. So which twin did she have standing before her now: Mr. Matson or Mr. Iverson Brentwood?

"Lord Waldo," Mr. Brentwood said coolly as the man stopped in front of them.

"Good evening again, Lord Waldo." Sophia greeted the man only a little more friendly than Mr. Brentwood had.

"I hope I'm not interrupting a private tête-à-tête here in this darkened section of the corridor."

"Not at all, Lord Waldo," Mr. Brentwood said.

"Ah, wonderful. I'm glad I found you, Miss Hart. I was having a conversation with a couple of gents a few minutes ago, and we decided Sir Randolph was the only one who could answer a question for us and settle a bet we have going. Do you happen to know where he is?"

"I spoke to him not ten minutes ago," she said. "I'm sorry, he's already gone home."

"Home, you say? Well, I won't be getting the money on my wager tonight, it seems. Would you mind mentioning to him that I'm looking to ask him a question about the hot air balloon venture he was involved with a year or two ago?"

"Yes, of course," Sophia said, knowing all about Sir Randolph's failed attempt to garner investors to open a hot air balloon travel business, and his many other endeavors that never seemed to come to pass. "I won't see him again tonight, but I'll be happy to do that for you tomorrow morning."

Sophia glanced at Mr. Brentwood. His blue eyes had darkened intensely, as if a shadow had crept in front of them. The easy smile had left his lips, and a wrinkle had formed between his brows. She had a feeling he now knew exactly who she was.

"Are you related to Sir Randolph?" Mr. Brentwood asked in a low voice.

There was an uncomfortable edge to his voice that she hadn't heard before, and tightness around his eyes. No doubt it was the mention of the man rumored to be his father that had changed his disposition. She knew finding out *his* name had surprised *her*.

"No," she answered, thinking he must have just arrived at the ball when she saw him if he had not heard that she was Sir Randolph's ward. "We're not related by blood. He's my guardian."

"You look surprised by that, Mr. Brentwood," Lord Waldo offered.

"Do I?" Mr. Brentwood said quietly, though his gaze never left Sophia's face.

"I thought so, but perhaps not. As I'm sure you know, Miss Hart and Sir Randolph have been the whisper of the party all evening."

Mr. Brentwood's intense gaze focused on Lord Waldo. "You know what my brother and I think about gossip, don't you?"

Lord Waldo cleared his throat and took a step back. "Yes, quite right. Well, thank you, Miss Hart. Mr. Brentwood."

As Lord Waldo walked away, a shivery feeling stole over Sophia, and her heart raced. "Which twin are you?"

"Matson," he said. "It's too bad Lord Waldo took the challenge out of finding that out."

"You and your brother are the twins who have caused Sir Randolph so much grief."

His shoulders stiffened. His forehead creased, and his face drew into a frown. "What? Did you say we caused him grief? That's the most laughable thing I've heard in weeks, Miss Hart. Just how did we do that?"

She swallowed uncomfortably. "You came back to London. He and your parents had worked out a plan to keep you and your brother in Baltimore so no one would ever know that you are his sons."

Disbelief shone in his eyes. "He worked out a plan with my parents?"

Sophia realized she had started on a subject that was obviously very raw to Mr. Brentwood. "You didn't know that?"

"Not that Sir Randolph was a party to the plans. My parents were already deceased when I learned of the affair. I'm wondering how you know more about my past than I do."

"I'm sure I don't, and I don't think I should say anything more about this."

"It's too late to play the innocent, Miss Hart."

She lifted her chin slightly. "I'm not playing anything. How could I have known that you didn't know? Sir Randolph was my father's best friend for many years. He told my father everything."

"Everything? Are you telling me he told your father about his affair with my mother?"

"Well, I have no idea exactly how much he told Papa. I only know that he never wanted you to know what had happened between him and your mother, and...and..." She stopped and sighed in dismay.

"What?" he asked, stepping closer to her once again.

"That you resemble him, which I don't think you do. I mean, not very much, anyway."

"And why did Sir Randolph tell you this?"

"He didn't tell me, and neither did my father.

I accidentally overheard their conversation one night."

"Accidentally?" His brow wrinkled into a frown. "Are you sure about that?"

"All right, it wasn't accidentally," she confessed. "When I was younger, I would often slip out of my bedchamber after the nurse went to sleep and sit outside my father's book room. I enjoyed listening to him and his guests' conversations. I've always been inquisitive, and my father never could rein in my penchant for wanting to learn and explore."

"Perhaps he should have."

"To his credit, he did try. When I was about nine or ten, I fell asleep outside his office, and he came out and found me. He wasn't happy, I assure you, but he understood my innocent curiosity."

"No, he indulged it. Tell me how innocent curiosity and deliberately listening to a private conversation go together, Miss Hart."

She ignored his cynical-sounding question and continued with her thought. "I said it wrong earlier. I didn't mean to imply that you and your brother had personally caused Sir Randolph grief. But I assure you, Mr. Brentwood, he was very distressed when that horrible parody came out in *The Chronicle*."

"Then try to imagine how my brother and I felt about our mother's good name being smeared across the newsprint."

A blush of heat crept up her neck and into her cheeks. "Yes, of course you were upset and rightly so. As I said, I didn't mean to imply that you were not. I spoke without thinking," she confessed. "I'm sure you were made ill over the light it cast on her."

"Even that puts it mildly, Miss Hart."

"I know that Sir Randolph has searched all over town for the dreadful man who wrote that story, but he hasn't found him yet. He intends to see to it that poet doesn't write another word of that story."

Soft feminine giggles sounded behind Sophia, and she turned to see two young ladies walking toward them.

Sophia took a step away from Mr. Brentwood and cleared her throat before they both greeted Miss Matilda Craftsman and Miss Jessica Slant. When the ladies stopped beside them, it was clear Miss Craftsman had eyes for no one but Mr. Brentwood. She was a lovely, petite young lady with dark brown eyes. Her skin was a beautiful olive shade and so flawless she looked more like a painting than a real person. She had just the kind of complexion Sophia had always wanted, but with her smattering of freckles would never achieve. Miss Slant was lovely, too, with her gorgeous blonde hair and a smile that would turn any gentleman's head.

A prickle of envy washed over Sophia, but she quickly brushed it away. She had settled in her mind years ago that there was nothing to be done about her red hair, white skin, and freckles.

Miss Craftsman immediately turned the back of her shoulder toward Sophia and said to Mr. Brentwood, "I hope we didn't interrupt a private conversation."

"Not at all, Miss Craftsman. We were just getting to know each other. Isn't that right, Miss Hart?"

"Yes," Sophia said, keeping a smile on her face. "And we found we have many things in common, didn't we, Mr. Brentwood?"

"More than we could imagine."

"But now I must get back to my aunts," Sophia said, making sure she made eye contact with the ladies before settling her attention on Mr. Brentwood again. "Thank you for your help, Mr. Brentwood. You will let me know if you hear anything about the lad we were discussing, won't you?"

"You can depend on that, Miss Hart."

"Good evening, Mr. Brentwood, Miss Craftsman, Miss Slant."

Sophia turned and headed down the corridor. She heard Miss Craftsman ask about the lad she had mentioned, but she didn't hear Mr. Brentwood's response.

Sophia wondered how her apology to Mr. Brentwood ended up with them quarreling about Sir Randolph and the swirling rumor of the twins' birth. She squeezed her hands into fists.

Why couldn't she have just been nice and batted her eyelashes at Mr. Brentwood the way Miss Craftsman and Miss Slant had?

But she knew the answer to that.

Four

Man is only miserable so far as he thinks himself so.

—Jacopo Sannazaro

"DAMNATION," MATSON MURMURED UNDER HIS breath after nicking his chin with his razor.

He leaned in closer to the mirror and splashed water on the cut. It was hell shaving every morning now that he'd grown the fine, half-inch line of beard along the edges of his chin and jaw, but he just couldn't abide the thought of letting his valet shave him. Now that he was back in England, it was the gentlemanly thing to do, but Matson had lived in America too long to return to all of the rules and traditions of his birth land.

It took a steady hand, but with concentration he closely trimmed the blasted beard. He would keep the offending facial hair because it pleased him that he no longer looked exactly like his twin brother, and he was damned pleased he no longer resembled a much younger Sir Randolph Gibson.

Matson shook his head and sighed as he stared

at himself in the mirror and asked, "Did you really kiss that man's ward last night?"

He nodded to his reflection and added more soapy lather to his neck. That wasn't his smartest move, but how was he to know who she was?

It irritated the devil out of him that Miss Sophia Hart knew there had been an affair between his mother and Sir Randolph. Most Londoners suspected it but had no way of knowing for sure. Sophia had heard the story from the man himself.

And by eavesdropping.

He couldn't hold that against her, though he would like to. It was human nature to be curious, and most children deliberately listened to their parents' conversations at some point during their childhood. If fate had been only a little kinder to him and allowed him to be the one who had overheard his parents discuss that bit of useful news, he'd be a much happier man today. He needed to see Sophia and find out what else she knew about his life that he didn't know.

His stomach convulsed every time he thought about the lovely and intriguing Miss Hart being connected to Sir Randolph in any way. At the time, he thought a taste of her sweet lips on his would be worth the risk of getting caught, but not anymore. So why was he letting her get under his skin like a burr under a saddle blanket?

Because something about her appealed to him.

"Something?" he looked in the mirror and asked himself. "Everything," he answered.

From the moment he saw her walking toward him, she radiated confidence, and he found that extremely attractive.

"Damn fate," he whispered and dipped his blade into the bowl of foamy water.

Years ago his father had sent him and his brother to America, expecting them to make their home there and never return to claim the heritage they'd been born to. He and Iverson didn't know why their father had insisted they start Brentwood's Sea Coast Ship Building Company. In England it was unheard of for sons of a titled man to manage a business, but no one gave such a task a second thought in Baltimore. For most men in America, it was the way things were done. You made your own way in life, and you didn't live a life of leisure because you had a generous allowance from your father's entailed estates.

At first, he and Iverson had felt as if their father had placed them in exile. Even though they had been given the money to start the company, it hadn't been easy to accomplish anything in the new country. Because of continued tensions between the Americans and the British Crown, Iverson and Matson did their best to hide their aristocratic British roots. But they were Englishmen through and through, and over time, the new country couldn't compete with their homeland. Their parents had died, and the twins had gotten older. Moving their business to London seemed to be the right thing to do, since it was past time they settled down and started looking to make a match.

Only after they had decided to come back did their older brother tell them the truth behind the reason they had been sent to America in the first place. When they grew up looking exactly like Sir Randolph Gibson, their mother had been forced to admit to an affair with the man. Matson's parents' hope was that the twins would stay in the new land and never return to learn of their mother's betrayal of their father.

Matson hadn't believed the story himself until he saw Sir Randolph for the first time last autumn. Hence the recent closely trimmed facial hair that took an enormous amount of time in the mornings. He didn't actually like the attempt at hiding his looks, but he would do anything to help Londoners forget that he was Sir Randolph's by-blow.

After rinsing the last traces of soap from his neck and face, Matson picked up a cloth to dry his skin. He was examining his handiwork in the mirror when he remembered Miss Hart telling him that Sir Randolph had been grieved by the parody that had been written about the three of them. How gullible did she think he was? He wadded the towel and threw it on top of his shaving chest.

Matson had to hand it to her. That young lady had more nerve and audacity than was common in most young ladies, which was another reason for him to completely dismiss her from his mind as he had Mrs. Delaney all those years ago.

Now if he could just do that, Matson would be fine. So far, he hadn't been able to. Both times he'd seen Sophia, Matson had the same eager sensations gnawing at him as he'd had when he'd first seen Mrs. Delaney.

He'd met the married woman at the first party he attended in Baltimore. She was the most beautiful woman he'd ever seen. When she spoke to him, his twenty-year-old heart fell in love with her. He always sought her out for a dance or to talk to her at every event he attended. He now knew she must have suspected his feelings for her, but she never hinted that she did. Her husband wasn't as gentle with Matson's young feelings. Mr. Delaney wasn't long-winded about it. He simply walked up to Matson one evening and said, "Brentwood, stay away from my wife." It wasn't a subtle hint, and Matson had no problem getting the message.

Matson blew out a laugh and rocked back on his heels. The color of Mrs. Delaney's and Sophia's hair and eyes weren't the only thing they had in common. They were both off limits to his primal desires and tender affections.

Matson finished dressing and hurried down the

stairs. He'd already alerted his cook that he wouldn't be taking breakfast, and for Buford to have his carriage brought around, but things seldom went off as easily as he planned. With his hat, gloves, and coat in his hands, he opened the front door and saw the bulky Mr. Littlebury ambling up the footpath.

His hope of getting to his brother's house this morning to give him the news of Miss Hart's arrival before he read about it in the gossip sheets was fading fast. Matson needed to hear what Mr. Littlebury had to say.

"Ah, Mr. Brentwood, looks as if you were just going out. So glad I caught you."

Matson stepped back inside and held the door for his courier to enter. He laid his coat, hat, and gloves on the side table and said, "Yes, Mr. Littlebury, come in. I've been waiting to hear from you. I hope you have good news today."

The short, hunch-shouldered man stepped into the vestibule and took off his hat. "Good news? I'm afraid not."

"That's not what I wanted to hear," Matson said, unable to keep irritation out of his voice.

A wrinkle formed on the man's brow. "I know, sir, but I couldn't find the Duke of Windergreen. Believe me, I did my best. He wasn't at his estate, which I went to first. I was told he would be at the Duke of Rockcliffe's home, but by the time I arrived there, he had already departed. And, of course, they wouldn't tell me if he had left for London or some other destination. I arrived back in Town late last night, and first thing this morning I was at his door in Mayfair, asking if he'd returned. I was told he was not in residence. I thought it best to come back and receive further instruction from you."

Why is the man nowhere to be found?

If Matson didn't know better, he'd think the Duke of Windergreen was hiding from them. But Matson couldn't take his frustration out on Mr. Littlebury. Obviously the man was doing all he could.

Matson and Iverson had had a hell of a time securing warehouse space for their shipbuilding company when they arrived in London late last summer. When they first tried to rent space near the docks, their oldest brother, Brent, was in deep trouble with the powerful Duke of Windergreen. The duke had let it be known throughout London that he didn't want the brothers finding space to lease.

The twins thought they had outfoxed the duke when they found a company that was willing to go against His Grace's dictate not to lease to them. It was a couple of months later when they discovered they were the ones who had been outwitted. The company they were leasing from was owned by Sir Randolph Gibson. He was the last man on earth they wanted to be indebted to for space.

Now that Matson's older brother had married the duke's daughter, the twins were certain His

Grace would recant his edict and give the word they could lease space from another company and get out from under Sir Randolph.

If they could *find* the duke!

One of Mr. Littlebury's eyes twitched nervously. "I'm sorry for failing you, sir."

"It's not the news I wanted to hear, but it's not your fault the man is on the move. Keep checking on him each day and the minute you hear the duke is back in London, find me or my brother."

"Yes, sir."

———

A few minutes later, Matson strode past his brother's valet and into Iverson's house. If Iverson said he didn't want to be disturbed, that meant something was afoot. Wallace rushed past Matson and down the corridor ahead of him, insisting that Matson stop. Matson kept going. None of the three brothers had ever stood on ceremony with one another, much to the chagrin of all their staff.

Wallace was trying to announce Matson when he walked through the doorway of his brother's book room and said, "What's this trying to keep your brother out? Wallace was giving me such a hard time about seeing you, I was beginning to believe you had a woman in here with you."

Iverson turned from the window where he stood

and grunted a laugh. "That would definitely be a reason to keep you out."

"But I see you have something almost as powerful as a woman. Wine when it's hardly half past nine."

"Oh," Iverson said, and walked over to his desk and put the glass down.

That didn't sound good. "What's the matter?" Matson asked, even though he was fairly certain he knew the problem was Miss Catalina Crisp. Iverson had been in a stew about the lady ever since they'd met.

When Iverson remained thoughtful and silent for longer than he should have, Matson added, "Did you empty your pockets at the card table last night?" He asked this to give his brother an out.

"I came close," Iverson said.

Matson knew Iverson too well. A card game was not the reason he had a glass in his hand so early in the day. But he also knew he wouldn't get any information about the lady who'd stolen Iverson's heart.

"Now that you are here, make yourself comfortable, and tell me what you've heard from our courier."

Matson took one of the upholstered chairs, and his brother lowered himself into the chair behind his desk. Their warehouse problem wasn't the reason he'd come over, so Matson said, "I can make that quick. I just spoke to the man. Apparently the duke is not at his estate, nor is he at any other place where Mr. Littlebury was told the duke might be. Unfortunately, it was as if the courier had been sent on one fool's errand after another."

"That's not good news, Brother."

"No, that's why Mr. Littlebury came back here for further instructions. He was told the duke would be in London in time for the first party of the Season. The docking fees and all other monies are paid on our ships, so we have a little time to wait for him to return to London and hopefully get us out from under Sir Randolph."

"Then we're in good shape for now."

"Yes, on that count, but I have more news I'm guessing you haven't heard, since you didn't mention it the moment I walked in."

"What?"

"Don't look so cheerless. This might not be bad news."

"In that case, I'm all ears. What is it?" Iverson asked.

"Sir Randolph Gibson has just become a father again."

"What!" Iverson jumped from his chair, knocking it backward with a loud bang.

Matson rose too. "Well, not a father in the true sense of the word."

"Spill it out, Matson. Tell me what you know about this."

"Sir Randolph arrived at a party last night

escorting Miss Sophia Hart. She is the daughter of an old friend of his who died last year. Sir Randolph is now her legal guardian and charged with the task of seeing her properly wed."

Iverson relaxed and looked a little more intrigued by the news. "You saw her?"

"Yes," Matson said, averting his eyes from Iverson's. He liked the idea of being the one to break the news to Iverson, but he didn't want his brother reading too much into what he was saying. It was best no one knew just how fast Miss Hart had set his heart to racing.

"She's lovely?" Iverson asked.

"Mmm. She's fair," Matson answered, knowing the moment he uttered the lie that Iverson would know he wasn't speaking the truth. Being twins, they had always had a special bond, and often it was as if one knew what the other was thinking. It had always been difficult to hide anything from each other.

"Really? Just fair, you say?" Iverson asked, encouraging Matson to say more.

"Yes," Matson confirmed. "The good news is her arrival in London now assures us that we are old gossip. London finally has someone new to talk about. Everyone flocked around her as if she were a queen who had invited their full attention."

"And had she?"

"What?"

"Invited attention?"

"She's Sir Randolph's ward. How could she not? No doubt she will be all the rage now, and I for one am happy to turn that unappealing position over to her."

"So you were introduced to her?" Iverson asked.

More than once, Matson thought, but he said, "Yes. Actually, I'd met her before, in passing, but didn't know who she was."

"Hmm, tell me exactly how one goes about meeting a young lady in passing."

Matson knew he'd said too much.

"It's a long story."

His brother smiled. "I've got time."

Matson smiled too. "But I'm not talking."

"At least tell me what you thought about her."

That's the damned trouble. I've done nothing but think of her.

"She has red hair," Matson said, not wanting to disclose to his brother any of the feelings Sophia Hart stirred inside him.

Iverson nodded. "Mmm. That can be harsh. Golden, brassy, or that rusty shade of red?"

"Golden."

"And was her skin the color of warm alabaster?"

"Yes, you blasted nuisance," Matson swore as he picked up a pillow from the chair and threw it at Iverson.

His brother dodged the pillow and laughed.

"Next time I'll leave it to you to find out all the latest news on your own," Matson said before walking out the door.

Matson shoved his hands into his gloves as he walked toward his carriage. For a twin brother, Iverson could be such an annoyance at times. Ever since Mrs. Delaney, there was nothing Iverson liked better than teasing Matson about his penchant for lovely ladies with red hair.

"To Timsford's Square," he told his driver and then climbed in the coach and settled against the plush velvet seat.

He couldn't seem to stop himself. He'd been back to the square every day since the little imp had made off with his dagger and Miss Hart's purse. He liked to tell himself the reason he was so bent on finding the lad was because he didn't want the bugger to best him. And it was a damned expensive knife, but it was more than either of those two things. Even though it irritated the devil out of him that Miss Hart was Sir Randolph's ward, Matson wanted to get her brooch back for her. It didn't seem right that she had lost an item that had belonged to her mother to a street urchin who saw its value only in terms of money and not as a precious treasure.

He'd find the brooch for her, and then he'd consider himself done with her.

Completely.

For good.

Forever.

But only after he stopped by for a visit later today to find out what else she knew about his past.

Five

Wise men never sit and wail their loss, but
cheerily seek how to redress their harms.

—William Shakespeare

"Sophia, please do try to be still and stop
fidgeting. Mrs. Franco will never be able to get your
hem the right length if you keep squirming like a
worm in hot ashes."

"Sorry, Aunt June," Sophia said, looking down
from the seamstress stool she was standing on.
Being still for so long was next to impossible to
do. "Honestly, I don't know why we are doing this.
I already have more clothing than I can wear this
Season, and next year you'll just want to make
new gowns."

"Of course we will," June said as she studied a
piece of lace. "You'll be a new bride by then, and
you'll definitely want to be fashionably dressed for
your husband. Now, you'll find it much easier to be
still if you aren't talking so much."

Sophia squeezed her hands into fists and held
them tightly by her sides, hoping to force herself

to remain still. She centered her attention on the window in front of her. The panes were framed with a strikingly bright shade of red draperies. Each velvet panel was tied back with large gold-corded tassels, exposing fancy lace covering the panes. Looking out at the gray, windy day made her realize it was possible to be sad, happy, and angry at the same time.

She would always be sad when she thought about losing her mother's brooch. She would always be angry at the lad who stole it from her. But other, happier feelings and emotions crowded inside her as well. She would always remember her first kiss, brief as it was, in the dark corridor last night. She had never felt anything like the thrilling sensations that had rippled through her when Mr. Brentwood's lips touched hers. It was exhilarating and breathtaking to be kissed by a gentleman whose name she didn't know at the time.

Sophia closed her eyes and remembered the light caress of Mr. Brentwood's lips on hers. What a dashing and brave man he was to risk scandal to fulfill her dream. She wished the kiss had been longer, but now knew if it had, they would have surely been caught by the obnoxious Lord Waldo.

Disappointment was another emotion she could add to the other ones swirling inside her. Mr. Brentwood was easily the most intriguing gentleman she'd met since arriving in London, but it would not do her any good to daydream about him. He was not titled, and her oath to her father was far more important than her budding feelings for Mr. Brentwood. It was best for her to think about becoming the bride of a gentleman such as Lord Bighampton, Lord Snellingly, Viscount Hargraves, and the other titled gentlemen she met last night. Though none of them had stirred her womanly desires like Mr. Brentwood had.

But thankfully she had his kiss, her first kiss, to daydream about over and over again.

"Oh, excuse me, ladies."

Sophia turned at the sound of Sir Randolph's voice. He had walked into his spacious drawing room and was surveying the scene before him. Sophia watched his curious gaze sweep over the bolts of sarcenet, linen, and muslin that had been unrolled and strewn across the chairs, tables, and settees. The bundles of cloth were littered with various spools of lace, ribbons, and braided piping. Not only were Sophia and her two aunts in the room, but also Mrs. Franco and her two helpers, who were busily unrolling more trim for Sophia to choose from.

Sir Randolph couldn't hide his surprise that his orderly, eccentrically appointed drawing room had been turned into a dressmaker's shop. Being a confirmed bachelor, he would not be used to having three ladies take over his quiet house.

"Oh, Sir Randolph," June said. "It is so wonderful that you came in just now. We would love to have your opinion on Sophia's new gowns for the Season."

He backed up a step. "No, Miss Shevington, I'm not qualified to judge a young lady's wardrobe."

Mae picked up an ivory-colored gown trimmed with braided yellow ribbons. "Nonsense, of course you are. All gentlemen know what makes a young lady look beautiful and what doesn't. I think this should be the one she wears to Lord Tradesforke's party." Mae held the dress up against Sophia. "What do you think?"

"Dear me, Mae," June said, swiping a champagne-colored gown trimmed with pale green lace off one of the settees. "That sheer overlay doesn't have enough color, and it washes out all the pink in her cheeks." June marched over to Sophia and held the gown up to her face. "Look at this, with her hair and eyes, Sir Randolph. This is what she needs to wear to highlight the green in her eyes. Don't you agree?"

Sir Randolph looked from one aunt to the other and took another uncomfortable step back. "As I said, ladies, I'm not one to ask about a young lady's clothing. I didn't realize you had this—this going on in here today. I have some things to pick up from my book room, and then I'll be on my way out again."

"Oh, but please," June called to his retreating

back. "We didn't have time to report that after you left last evening, Sophia was presented to Lord Snellingly."

"And he has already asked to call on Sophia and read his poetry to her," Mae added.

"That reminds me," June said, turning to Mae. "We must see to it that Sophia works on her poetry this afternoon. I'm sure Lord Snellingly will want to read it."

Sir Randolph paid them no mind and kept walking.

That comment put Sophia in motion. "Yes, wait, Sir Randolph." Sophia stepped off her stool and started after him.

"Sophia, where are you going? Mrs. Franco isn't finished."

"I'm terribly sorry, Auntie, I won't be long. I must ask Sir Randolph something before he leaves again." She picked up a bolt of cloth and stuffed it into her aunt's arms. "I like this one. Would you mind picking out the perfect pattern and trim for it?"

June's eyes brightened. "Why, yes, of course, I'd love to."

"And I'll help her," Mae added.

"Thank you." Sophia smiled at both her aunts and rushed into the corridor. She saw Sir Randolph disappearing into his book room.

Sophia skidded to a stop when she made it to his open doorway. He was standing by the side of his desk, gathering papers together. "May I come in?" she asked.

He looked over at her and smiled. "You are always welcome to come in. What can I do for you?"

"I'm sorry we took over your drawing room and made such a disarray of it."

Sir Randolph laid the stack of papers back on his desk and chuckled lightly. "I have to admit I had no idea what it would be like to have three ladies living in my house. I've not been distracted by your presence, Sophia. I am enjoying having you here with me, and I'm happy to tolerate your aunts because it keeps you here."

Sophia smiled. "I know my aunts can create a fuss at times."

"Indeed."

"I enjoy being here, too, Sir Randolph, but if your privacy is invaded more than you can accept and we are too much of a bother, you can feel free to lease a house for us."

His eyes rounded, and he put his finger under his chin as if he were pondering what she said. "Now that's an idea." He paused, smiled, and that twinkle she often saw in his eyes appeared. "But I won't hear of it. No, your place is here with me until you wed, and here you shall be. Besides, I've grown quite fond of having you around and of not knowing what I'm going to encounter when I walk through the door each day."

"Thank you," Sophia said, appreciating his kindness and his humor. "I don't suppose you've heard anything about my mother's brooch from the constable today?"

He shook his head. "No. I would have told you immediately if there had been any news. I will keep my promise, you know that."

She nodded. "A couple of days ago, I thought of a plan that might help speed up this slow progress."

"What's that?"

"Keep in mind that I've taken the time to thoroughly consider this, and I believe it can work. I will need your permission and help to do it."

Sir Randolph shoved aside the papers on his desk and leaned a hip against it. He motioned for her to take a seat in the chair in front of her.

"You have me curious. Concerning what?"

"Finding the thief who stole my reticule and brooch," she answered, making herself comfortable on the chair.

Sir Randolph cleared his throat and crossed his arms over his chest. "No matter the plan, Sophia, that will not be easy to do. You were told how many young boys there are on the streets, looking to make mischief."

She inhaled quickly. "Yes, I've been told many times the past few days, as you well know, but will you please hear me out?"

He nodded.

"I remember quite well what the boy looks like. I will never forget his innocent-looking face, but my aunties won't allow me to go back to the square and search for him."

"They are correct in that," he said with seeming unconcern and went back to shuffling the papers on his desk.

"I don't agree, although I have been forced to concede that point, since my aunts won't let me go to Timsford's Square." She paused. "I would like to go to Bow Street and hire a runner to scour the streets for me, pick up all wayward boys he can find, and bring them here for me to have a look at them."

His eyes widened. "Sophia, you can't be serious."

"Oh, don't deny me this, Sir Randolph, please." She scooted to the edge of her seat.

"But that is not a plan," he admonished. "It's madness."

"No," she argued firmly. "The shopkeeper said the lad had stolen bread from him before, so it's obviously the area near where he lives. I know he is still out there, continuing his mischief, and that he can be found, but no one will let me go look for him."

"That is because you are a proper young lady."

"Who has been robbed," she protested.

"No matter. It would be unbecoming for you to be out searching for a thief. Besides, what if he has already sold your reticule and brooch and now he and his family are living happily off the money he received for it?"

Sophia frowned. "I've thought of that possibility. That's why I drew a picture of it for the constable so he could have someone check all the shops in town. And what you said may very well be true, but I won't ever know if I don't try. If I find him and he has already sold the brooch, you know I will pay whatever is necessary to get it back."

"Sophia, I don't want to see you do this to yourself."

She rose and stood before him. "Then help me. I must do something! If you won't let me go searching for the child, then let me pay someone to look for him, let me put a notice in the newsprint about a reward for the return of the brooch."

"You don't really think the footpad who stole your purse can read, do you?"

Sophia squeezed her hands into tight fists and sucked in a deep breath. "Probably not, but you must allow me to do something. You know what that brooch means to me."

"I do." Sir Randolph sighed. "All right, I'll make some inquiries on Bow Street and see whom we need to contact to do something more than is being done now. But I don't want you thinking this will be an easy process."

"I know." She heaved a sigh of relief, gave him a quick hug, and then backed away, smiling. "Thank you."

"There's one more thing," he said. "Even if we are never successful in finding the brooch, you have your mother's memory in your heart. You will never lose that."

Sophia's chest constricted. She batted her lashes to force back the tears that leaped into her eyes and threatened to roll down her cheeks. He was right. She had memories of her mother humming a melody while softly brushing Sophia's hair. She would always hold them dear. But it was so much more meaningful to have something she could hold in the palm of her hand and touch.

"If that proves to be the case, I will accept it. At least I'll know I didn't give up without a fight." She swallowed hard and clasped her hands together in front of her, forcing sad memories to the back of her mind. "There's more I'd like to discuss with you."

Sir Randolph grunted a laugh. "That doesn't surprise me. What is it?"

"I was wondering when Mr. Peabody was going to bring Shevington's account books for us to go over."

"The account books?" he questioned, looking as if he had no idea what she was talking about. "I really don't know. How long has it been since he was here?"

Sophia knew. "He hasn't been to London since I arrived. The last I saw him was when the two of you came to the Cotswolds, which was six weeks ago. Would you mind asking him to bring them to London so we can have a look at them?"

Sir Randolph unfolded his arms and walked behind his desk. "I didn't realize it had been that long. I'll send him a letter and ask him to come to London next week, but I don't think it's necessary, Sophia. Mr. Peabody seems to be doing a fine job. Your father trusted him."

After their return from Baltimore, her father knew there would be no recovery for him, and a relatively slow death from his lung condition. She asked if she might be allowed to do most of the paperwork, help in decision-making, and let her father sign everything. At first he was reluctant, but finally agreed when Sophia reminded him that she needed to know enough about the company to ensure that her guardian and trustee, and later her husband, took proper care of the shipping empire her father had built.

"Oh, I believe Mr. Peabody is doing a good job, too. Papa always said we should trust the work and words of every employee, but then we verify what was said and that the work was accomplished."

Sir Randolph placed the documents he'd collected in a binder and tucked it under his arm. "Quite frankly, Sophia, with Mr. Peabody's office in Southampton, I find it difficult to remember to ask him to make the trip over here."

"I agree, which brings me to my third request."

The old man's eyes squinted as if he were looking into the sun. He took the binder and laid it back on his desk. "How many requests do you have for me today?"

She smiled guiltily. "One more, I promise. I know my father used Southampton for Shevington's offices for years because it was such a busy port, but I think we should move them here to London." She hurried on, not wanting to give him time to tell her all the reasons why they shouldn't. "It would be ever so much easier for us to keep a watchful eye and know what is happening in the company. If I'm remembering correctly, we own some space down at the docks. We could move our offices there."

His gaze searched her face, and once again he leaned a hip against his desk. "We could, except for the fact that I leased that space last fall."

"Oh." She thought for a moment. "That shouldn't be a problem. We'll just tell whoever has it that we need it and want to buy them out of their lease."

Concern etched across Sir Randolph's face. "I'm not sure we can do that, but I suppose it's something I'm willing to look into. I have heard that our tenants are looking for other space to lease."

"Oh, that's wonderful," she said confidently. "We'll write them a letter informing them that we are giving them a month's notice, and for their trouble, we'll pay six months of the lease on their new space."

"Hold on there." Sir Randolph grunted a laugh. "I'm not sure we need to be that generous. Your papa was right. You certainly have a way of taking things into your own hands and wanting to get things accomplished quickly."

"I don't mind being generous to get the business moved here. And it's the least we can do for upsetting them. And I really think we need to have Shevington's offices right here in London." She waited, but Sir Randolph didn't say anything. "Why are you hesitating?"

"I was just thinking that perhaps it might be a better idea for us to wait and let your husband make these kinds of decisions about where the business is located. Where the offices are may not matter, because as your father cautioned you many times, your husband may not be as accommodating to you as your father and I have been."

"That is why I will be very careful whom I marry, Sir Randolph. I will marry a titled gentleman to please my father, but I will marry a man who is forward thinking to please myself."

Sir Randolph smiled indulgently. "Just today I received notes from Lord Bighampton and Viscount Hargraves, asking to see me. Snellingly was waiting at my club for me, and I won't even mention the gentlemen who aren't titled and have tried to have a word with me today about you. You could marry tomorrow, if you were so inclined."

"Heavens no!" Sophia felt a tug at her heart. "I must have more time to scrutinize the gentlemen." She breathed in deeply. "Papa knew I was not content painting, sewing, and playing the pianoforte. I need more interesting things to do."

"Adding numbers?"

She smiled. "And subtracting them, too."

"And reading boring documents?" Sir Randolph offered.

"They aren't boring. They are stimulating." Her smile quickly faded. "After I marry, you will be forced to turn my inheritance over to my husband, but I can't bear the thought of never knowing what is going on with my father's company. I will be very careful in choosing my husband."

Admiration shone in Sir Randolph's eyes as he said, "I believe you."

"So you'll write the letter canceling the lease?"

He seemed to study her for a moment before saying, "Yes, but there is something about the lease you should know." He paused. "It needs to be handled delicately."

Sophia felt a sense of relief. It appeared Sir Randolph was going to let her do what she wanted. "Whatever it is, I assure you no one has a more delicate hand with correspondence than I do, Sir Randolph. I can help you word the letter so there will be no offense."

"I'm not so sure of that." He walked over and sat

down in his chair, suddenly looking tired. "It's the Brentwood twins who have leased Shevington's building at the docks."

"Oh, my," she whispered softly and retook her seat too. The handsome Mr. Matson Brentwood came easily to her mind. "Yes, I can see where this might be more delicate than I imagined."

"It could be. That remains to be seen. I know the twins, for obvious reasons, never wanted to lease from me, and as I said, I've heard they have continued to look for alternative space."

"Why did they lease from you?"

"They had no choice at the time. Nothing else was available to them, and quite frankly, at the time they didn't know I had anything to do with Shevington Shipping. I've heard they are still trying to obtain space from the Duke of Windergreen, which would make this work well for all of us. They should now be able to lease from the duke, since his daughter married their older brother."

"Yes, I remember reading about the wedding. I met him last night."

"Viscount Brentwood?"

"No, one of his brothers, Mr. Matson Brentwood."

"Ah," he said softly as he watched her face intently. "He must have arrived after I left. I didn't see him."

"He did, but I'd met him before. I just didn't know who he was."

His eyes narrowed, and his lips tightened. "How? Last night was your first ball."

"He's the man who helped us that day with the footpad. When he tried to introduce himself to us, Aunties snubbed him and shuffled me away as if they were afraid I might get the plague. Remember, we told you a stranger helped us, but only last night did I find out who he was."

"I see." Sir Randolph's voice softened. "What did you think of him?"

Sophia tried to sound natural, even though talking about Mr. Brentwood made her heartbeat speed up, her breathing increase, and her stomach quiver. "He's very handsome, and as I told you that day, he's a very engaging man."

"Yes, you said as much, Sophia. You don't fancy him, do you?"

She smiled, hoping it didn't look as false as it felt. "It would do me no good. He is not titled, and I am committed to keeping my vow to my father. But that is not the only reason he would not be the man for me, Sir Randolph. I remember the things I heard about the Brentwood twins when Papa and I were in Baltimore for his lung treatments."

He continued to look intently at her. "What exactly did you hear?"

"That the brothers used the scheme of good-twin and bad twin to their advantage in business dealings. Mr. Iverson Brentwood would take on anyone and everyone, remaining firm on his stand, arguing his point, and sounding tough and as strong as the hull of the ships they built. He would ask for more than they wanted. He never budged an inch on whatever the issue was at hand. Mr. Matson Brentwood would then come in behind him in a conciliatory and approachable way, willing to compromise for something less than his brother had insisted on. Papa said their strategy had worked to get exactly what they wanted almost every time."

"I heard that too."

"And that is why he would not be a good match for me, even if I hadn't made the vow. With his business shrewdness, I can't see him ever allowing his wife even to look at a ledger, and certainly not look over terms of a contract."

"You are probably right. I'll work on the letter to terminate the lease later today or tomorrow, and then let you take a look at it. Right now, you run along. I'm going to get out of the house so you and your aunts can finish your dressmaking duties in peace."

Sophia thanked Sir Randolph and walked out of the book room and promptly leaned against the wall in the corridor. She didn't know why, but her legs were weak. She closed her eyes and remembered the light brush of lips across hers and the scent of shaving soap that clung to Mr. Brentwood's hands when he caressed her cheek.

Her abdomen tightened. She'd told Sir Randolph the truth. There was no use in thinking about Mr. Matson Brentwood. He was not the man for her to marry, but knowing that didn't keep her from daydreaming about him and wishing they'd had time to have that second kiss.

Six

To climb steep hills requires slow pace at first.

—William Shakespeare

MATSON COULDN'T BELIEVE HE WAS ACTUALLY sitting in Sir Randolph's drawing room, staring out the window and watching the late-afternoon sky turn grayer. It was ludicrous. He despised the man, yet here he sat. That he'd even set foot inside the Mayfair house was amazing. And he wouldn't have had it not been for Miss Hart.

She had intrigued him last night with her comment about his parents and Sir Randolph working together to send him and his brother to America. Because of all the gossip that had been spawned about the twins, he could see now that a visit was the civil thing to do. But Matson wanted to know what else Sophia knew. She tempted him in other ways, too, but considering whose house he was sitting in, he was trying to keep his thoughts away from those primal feelings. It was hellish enough that he found her attractive.

He'd already crossed and uncrossed his legs at

least a dozen times, and paced back and forth in front of the fireplace several minutes in the quarter of an hour he waited for Miss Hart or someone to make an appearance. He didn't know exactly what he would say if Sir Randolph came in rather than Miss Hart. He'd never actually had a conversation with the man. What would be the purpose? Matson couldn't very well ask him why he'd had an affair with his mother. That had an obvious answer he'd rather not hear.

Matson knew there was the possibility he wouldn't even be allowed to see Miss Hart because of who he was. He wanted only to ask her some questions. He was not foolish enough to get entangled with Sir Randolph's ward. And, had he known who she was, there was no way he would have been foolish enough to have coaxed a kiss from her.

Well…

Maybe he would have.

Probably.

He would have.

Damnation! She was just that enticing.

The decor of Sir Randolph's spacious drawing room surprised him. It was filled with dark wood furniture upholstered in embroidered silk fabrics of astoundingly vibrant colors and intricate patterns. The draperies covering the window were a bright shade of red. A statue of a gilt lion stood in one corner of the room, and a tiger in the other.

Life-size sculptures of Venus and Athena held up the marble mantel that graced the ornate fireplace. A gold-framed mirror, fashioned in the shape of a large pagoda, hung over it.

Matson chuckled to himself. Had he nothing better to do than look at the menagerie of items in Sir Randolph's home and pick them apart? Over the years, he'd done his share of waiting for young ladies when he called on them, but he'd never done it patiently. Today was no exception.

No, today was even harder.

At last he heard footsteps on the stairs, so he rose and looked toward the doorway.

Matson remembered the two older ladies who swept into the room. They were a slim, refined-looking pair, wearing high-waisted dresses cut similar in style, though the one he remembered as being called June wore a dull shade of gray, and the one named Mae wore a much more fetching shade of sky blue.

"Mr. Brentwood, I don't believe we've been formally introduced," Mae said.

Before he could comment, June said in a disapproving tone, "Sophia told us a few minutes ago that you were formally introduced by Lord Waldo last night during our absence."

He bowed slightly. "Yes, madam, that's true."

"Oh, we're not madams, Mr. Brentwood," Mae said, a faint blush creeping up her pale cheeks, "we're misses."

"Which is why proper introductions should always be made, Mr. Brentwood," June cut in quickly and sharply.

"Nonetheless, Mr. Brentwood," Mae answered, "sometimes it's simply not possible to handle everything as properly as it should be, is it? Of course we met on the street the other day but were not introduced. I am Miss Mae Shevington, and this is my sister, Miss June Shevington."

Shevington?

Was it possible Sophia Hart was the heiress to the highly successful Shevington Shipping? Of course, it made sense now. Sir Randolph's wealth came from his father's shipping business; he would have known Sophia's father well, and thus was asked to be her guardian. Matson hadn't made the connection because Sophia had a different last name.

Matson hid his surprise at this sudden revelation and bowed slightly again, hoping to in some small way win the ladies' approval. "It's my pleasure to meet you both, and I was hoping to see your niece, Miss Hart, as well."

"I'm afraid we can't allow that," June responded pointedly.

"You see, Mr. Bentwood," Mae added, "we aren't allowing her to accept calls today."

"Last night was the first party she's attended, and I'm sure you can understand that we can't possibly allow every gentleman she met to call on her."

"Oh, no, that would be far too many. There wouldn't be enough hours in the day. We must be very selective, per her father's instructions—"

"Before we decide who will be allowed to court her—"

"And who will not."

"With her beauty, intelligence, and wealth, we feel she will surely make a match with a viscount, an earl, or perhaps even—"

"A duke," Mae finished.

Matson almost chuckled out loud. It was amazing how the two ladies could follow each other's sentences flawlessly, as if only one of them were speaking. But at least he knew it was the sentinels keeping Sophia from seeing him, and not the young lady herself.

It was clear that Miss June Shevington was the more aggressive lady, and Miss Mae Shevington the more conciliatory of the two. He was very familiar with how the good-twin, bad-twin game worked. He and his brother had used it often and quite successfully.

He would have liked to say good riddance to the two ladies, and be done with Miss Hart once and for all, but his fighting spirit was too strong. He wasn't used to giving up so easily something he wanted. For all the blustering he'd done earlier in trying to convince himself otherwise, he wanted to see Sophia.

He intended to see her.

But why?

That puzzled him. She was Sir Randolph's ward, and he shouldn't want anything to do with a lady who was under the watchful eye of the man who fathered him—no matter how desirable she was.

"In any case, our niece is busy right now."

"Yes." Miss Mae Shevington's eyes lit up brightly.

"Lord Snellingly wants to call on her and read his poetry to her. We want her to have something to read to him, too, when that happens."

They were going to allow that pompous dandy, Lord Snellingly, to call on Sophia? The man had to be at least twenty-five years older than she was. And obviously, she hadn't heard the man's poetry. He wondered how encouraging the sentinels would be after they'd heard him recite a few lines of his verse.

"But of course we told him that she is not taking calls for a couple of more days. But she'll be happy to entertain him soon."

"Yes, she's in the back garden, working on her poetry right now."

"She's quite good with rhymes."

"But stronger in verse, Sister."

"I'm sure she'll write something lovely," Matson said.

"Though there is no way she could be as talented as Lord Snellingly," Mae said.

"I take it you haven't read his work," Matson said.

"No, but he told us he's quite good, so I'm sure it will be beautiful and inspiring."

Matson smiled. He would love to be around when Miss Hart heard a few lines of Lord Snellingly's poetry. Whatever she was writing, it had to be better than that man's efforts.

Matson stared at the two rigid spinster sisters and decided he wasn't going to let them get the best of him. He would win them over with a friendly chat. After all, he wasn't without a little charm when he chose to use it. He'd learned early in life that twins were rare. He and his brother were always a curiosity to people, and he and Iverson were always inquisitive when they happened to meet another set of twins. He'd bet these two ladies were curious too.

He relaxed his shoulders and his stance and asked, "Are you twins?"

"Why, yes, yes, we are," June said, obviously flattered he recognized the fact.

"That's just what I was going to say," Mae added, her lashes fluttering like a butterfly's wings in flight. "We are twins, though we were born on different days and different months."

Matson's brows drew together. "I don't believe I've ever heard of that happening before."

"Oh, yes," Mae said. "You see…"

Matson listened to their singsong telling of their birth, which ended with Mae saying, "Everyone always seems to be fascinated by us."

"I can understand that. I'm a twin, too."

They both looked surprised, and in unison said, "Truly?"

"Yes," he said, realizing there was no recognition in their faces of who he was. Could it be that these ladies didn't know of the Brentwood twins and their connection to Sir Randolph, when Miss Hart knew so much?

"I'm afraid our story is not nearly as appealing as yours," he continued. "My brother and I were born on the same day of the same month."

Mae asked, "Do you and your brother attract attention wherever you go?"

"Not as often as we used to. We don't look that much alike anymore. But you lovely ladies certainly do. I've grown this." Matson touched his chin. "And my brother's hair is longer than mine. But I can assure you we caused quite a stir when we first came to London."

"Oh, we did too. We always do, no matter where we go."

"Perhaps you'd like to stay for tea, Mr. Brentwood?" Mae asked suddenly.

Her sister quickly gave her a reproving look. "I'm sure he's quite busy, Sister."

That was the invitation he'd been looking for. Matson smiled. "No, no, I'm not busy at the moment. Thank you, I'd enjoy staying and hearing more about your lives as twins. I seldom meet other twins."

"See, Sister," Mae said and then gave her sister a satisfied smile.

Half an hour later, Matson walked out of the house with his hat and coat in hand. He'd thought surely when the ladies invited him to stay for tea, Miss Hart would eventually come bounding into the house and he'd see her, but that hadn't happened. Those two ladies certainly knew how to keep to their plan of not letting a gentleman see Sophia.

He stood on the top step of the stoop and looked at his carriage, and then looked from one side of the house to the other. The skies had turned gray, and the wind had kicked up considerably while he'd been inside.

The aunts had said Miss Hart was in the back garden, working on poetry. He hadn't heard any doors open or shut while he'd been in the drawing room. It stood to reason that Sophia was still in the back garden, and there was no doubt in his mind that he still wanted to see her.

Matson wondered how high and how thick the hedge was on either side of the house.

Only one way to find out.

Seven

In delay there lies no plenty; then come kiss
me, sweet and twenty.

—William Shakespeare

MATSON HESITATED, SHAKING HIS HEAD AT WHAT
he was pondering. Did he really want to go poking
around Sir Randolph's home? Just to get a glimpse
of Miss Hart?

"Yes," he whispered to himself.

Something about her kept drawing him. He was
smart enough to know it was more than her red
hair, her obvious beauty, and more than his desire
to learn what she knew about his past. And he
didn't need to go over in his mind again all the reasons
why Miss Hart was not a young lady he should
consider pursuing. Right now, they didn't matter.
He was going to do it anyway.

If he couldn't see her by fair means, he'd see
her by foul means. He looked both ways down
the narrow street with its rows of closely nestled
town homes, and didn't see any carriage or pedestrian
traffic nearby. He quickly walked to the right

side of the house and looked toward the back. The wide, high hedge wasn't yew, but a type of shrub with a bigger and fuller leaf. He casually walked to the other side and looked. A narrow path of less than three feet between the side of Sir Randolph's tall hedge and his neighbor's hedge formed a kind of tunnel effect. That was by far the better route to take to the back of the house in hopes of not being seen by anyone passing or by the servants.

Matson walked slowly down the narrow path, carefully peeking through areas of thinning leaves for sight of anyone in the garden. When he was almost at the road that led to the mews at the back of the property, he found a spot big enough for him to move some leaves and peep through the hedge. The garden was small, but the abundance of lavish flowers, shrubs, and trees seemed to be well tended. In the center of the garden was a large fountain in the shape of a cherub, with his head thrown back in laughter as he relieved himself into a vase. Water overflowed from the vase and into a birdbath. Near the back gate, a grouping of chairs and a table stood on a stone patio, but all the chairs were empty.

There was no sign of Miss Hart. No doubt the minute the twin guards shut the door behind him, they had called her inside. Those ladies were double trouble for him too. He scoffed a short, soft laugh. Perhaps he should call them Double and Trouble.

"Excuse me, sir, but are you looking for something?"

Matson froze at the sound of Sophia's voice behind him. He'd wanted to see her, but he hadn't wanted her to catch him peeping through the shrubbery.

He turned. She was walking down the footpath toward him. His stomach muscles tightened at the sight of her. She wore a pale melon-colored dress and matching bonnet. She had a dark brown shawl wrapped around her shoulders with the ends tied in a knot in front of her chest.

"Yes, Miss Hart, I am, but not something, some-one. I was looking for you."

Surprise brightened her eyes. "Oh, Mr. Brentwood, it's you."

She smiled, and suddenly he felt warm all over. He didn't understand it. Of all the young ladies in London, why was she the one who heated his blood like no other and made him feel desperate to touch her?

"Wouldn't the better place to look for me be at my front door, knocking and asking to see me?"

"Yes, it would, if your aunts were anyone other than the Misses Shevington. Your aunts refused to let me see you."

Sophia's lips twitched with suppressed mer-riment. "So you decided to spy on me through the hedge. That was very naughty of you, Mr. Brentwood."

"Did you just call me naughty?" He grinned. "I don't believe I've been called that since I left the nursery."

"The shoe fits, does it not?"

He placed his hand over his heart. "On my gentleman's honor—I will never own up to that."

Sophia laughed. "My aunts told me you had called, but I assumed you left."

"Then perhaps I should pat myself on the back because I managed to stay longer than your average gentleman caller."

"Yes, just how did you manage that?"

"Because I am also a twin, and your aunts adore talking about being twins."

"So they told you the story of how they got their names."

"In great detail and more than once," he said with a smile.

"That subject would definitely give them reason to allow you to stay. I believe I've already mentioned that they are a bit overzealous concerning their duties to me."

"A bit?" he said good-naturedly. "Surely you jest, Miss Hart."

She looked as if she was trying to stop another smile from spreading across her face, but her efforts went unrewarded. His comment had amused her, and it showed. That pleased him.

"All right, a lot, but perhaps you'll take comfort

knowing they have not singled you out. Lord Snellingly, Viscount Hargraves, Lord Bighampton, Mr. Parker Wilson, and others were all told that I won't be at home to visitors for a few more days."

"To be added in with those gentlemen is of little comfort. However, while I was having a delightful conversation with your aunts, Miss Mae Shevington let it slip that you were in the back garden, writing poetry, so I thought I would have a look and see if I could find you."

Sophia folded her hands together in front of her and lifted her head slightly. "Are you fond of verse, Mr. Brentwood, or did you decide you had to see me?"

Her teasing expression delighted him. He looked down at the sheet of vellum she held in her hand. "Very clever, Miss Hart. If your poems are as sharp as your wit, I'm sure I would enjoy them too."

Appreciation for his compliment sparkled in her eyes. She folded the paper once and then held it behind her back. "You will never know. I write only for myself, sir. A gust of wind swept this page away from me and up and over the back gate. I came out to chase it down. On my way back, I caught a glimpse of someone peering through the hedge."

Ignoring her comment about his peering, he said, "I think the lady doth protest too much. It must be very good poetry if you went to such lengths not to lose it."

The corners of her tempting mouth lifted again. "No, it's so bad I didn't want anyone to find it and read it."

Matson chuckled lightly. "I doubt that's true."

"I have to admit that I'm surprised to see you here. I had the feeling you were not very happy with me after our encounter last night."

He'd wondered if she would mention that. "I admit I was caught off guard when I discovered you were Sir Randolph's ward."

"I think we were both startled when we were introduced."

He nodded. "True. Yet your aunts showed no recognition of my name when I was talking to them earlier."

"My aunties are of the old, old school that ladies should not read newsprint."

"Not even the scandal sheets?"

"Especially so. Aunt June disapproves of such reading for ladies and only reluctantly allows me to read them because my father told her I could. When I first went to live with them, she would hide the newsprint and then come up with ridiculous things that might have happened to it, one time going so far as to say Lord Pinkwater's ghost was stealing it."

Matson chuckled. "A woman without curiosity about what others are doing and saying is very rare."

Her brows lifted, and her eyes widened. "Oh, I agree. I want to know about everything."

"Which brings me back to the reason I'm here," Matson said.

"Have you found the thief?" She took a hopeful step closer to him. "Did you recover my brooch?"

She seemed eager for good news, and Matson hated to say, "No."

"Oh," she whispered softly and looked away from him for a moment. "The constable's search hasn't yielded anything either."

"There's still hope it will be found," he offered.

"But less and less with each passing day."

"The brooch, it must have been your favorite."

She shook her head. "No." Her voice remained low as she continued, "And it's not even very expensive. It's just that it's all I had."

Matson could see in her eyes and hear in her voice she was still sad over the loss. "What do you mean?"

She brought her hands back in front of her and seemingly unconsciously folded the sheet of vellum again. "I lost everything of my mother's except that brooch in a house fire when I was seven." She blinked several times, breathed in deeply, and lifted her chin and shoulders a little higher.

"I'm sorry," he said, angry at himself all over again for allowing the boy to steal it in the first place. Now he knew why she'd been so frantic that day at Timsford's Square.

"Yes, so am I, but just as Sir Randolph reminded

me this morning, I have memories. I will always have those." Suddenly her forehead wrinkled. He could tell she was trying to decide if she should say more. He remained silent and gave her the time she needed.

"So, if you didn't have news about the lad, why did you want to see me?"

The change of subject let Matson know she didn't want to say more about her loss. But he made a vow to continue to look for the boy who stole that brooch, so he could return it to her.

"I wanted to finish the conversation we were having last night. You obviously know things about my past that I don't know, and I would like to hear more."

"I really don't know any more than I told you last night. I already admitted to being curious about conversations from time to time, so I'm certain I didn't hear the complete story. Your parents and Sir Randolph wanted to shield you and your brother from ever knowing that he was your father. They hoped, in sending you to America, you would make your life there in the new land and never return to discover the truth."

Matson had to admit to himself that he had been happier before he knew he was another man's son.

"And that's all you know?"

"Truly. Since I was a little girl, my father always said that I speak and act before I think about consequences. I'm afraid I've never outgrown such impulsive behavior. I was guilty of that last night. I spoke out of turn. I'm sure you are not happy about all the gossip that's been written about you, your brother, and Sir Randolph. I should have been more sensitive to your feelings and never brought it up."

"What has been said or written about us matters not a whit. What we don't like is how it reflects badly on our mother."

"I believe you. I shouldn't have mentioned the horrid story that poet wrote."

Their eyes met, held, and though he saw only softness, gentleness, and innocence in hers, he knew she was as dangerous to him as a sharpened blade. Sophia could never be the right lady for him, yet something about her beckoned him. His desire for her made him want to wrap her in his arms and hold her close. He wanted to kiss the light smattering of freckles sprinkled across the bridge of her nose.

"Why are you looking at me so intently?"

"Am I?" he asked, knowing full well that he was.

She nodded.

"Maybe that's because I'm wondering if you are thinking what I'm thinking right now."

"What are you thinking?"

A gust of wind caught a strand of her hair and blew it across her face. He caught it with the tips of his fingers and secured it behind her ear, caressing her delicate skin with the backs of his fingers as he lowered his hand. His mind was reminding him she was Sir Randolph's ward, telling him to leave, but his body was urging him to stay.

"That I want to kiss you," he said softly.

He watched her swallow. "I believe I'm thinking something very much like that, even though I know it's not the proper thing to have on my mind."

Matson didn't give a bloody hell about being proper. His problem was that she was Sir Randolph's ward. He didn't want to be attracted to her. But he was. He felt different inside when he looked at her, when he was near her. Whatever it was that caused those feelings, he seemed powerless to stop it. And the way she looked at him told him that whatever it was, she felt it too.

"I'm certain it's not proper too, but…"

He stepped closer and bent down and lightly kissed the bridge of her nose, then under one eye, and then over to the other side. He raised his head a little and looked into her eyes.

"Hmm," he said and then moistened his lips. "I wondered what your freckles tasted like."

She stared into his eyes and frowned. "Do they have a taste?"

He nodded once. "They taste like sugar. Soft, sweet, and they melt in my mouth."

"You are teasing me." She smiled cautiously. "I expected you to kiss my lips."

"Did you? And so I shall, but first…" He bent down and placed his nose on the soft skin just behind her ear and breathed in deeply. "Mmm. I knew you would smell as fresh as rainwater."

Matson slid his arms around her waist and pulled her up to him. He let his lips glide across to her mouth and slowly, softly, pressed them against hers.

"Yes," she whispered into his breath and melted willingly, easily into his arms.

Matson savored the taste of her. Her lips were warm, and the inside of her mouth as refreshing as a piece of summer fruit, making him want to devour her. His hand moved up and down her back, feeling her delicately rounded shoulders and straight spine. His hand slipped to her narrow waist and rested there for a moment before inching down the flare of her shapely hip. Her body was as slim, firm, and supple as he'd imagined it would be. The soft, feminine sounds she made heated his body and filled him with an eagerness to do the unthinkable…to lift her skirts and possess her.

"Oh, yes," he said huskily. "This is much more intoxicating than freckles."

She stretched her arms around his neck and pressed him closer. He moaned softly. He fitted his lower body tightly against hers by cupping her bottom with one hand while his other hand slid down her chest to capture her breast and cover it with his palm.

Sophia gasped and leaned into his palm. He heard a crinkling noise and knew her hand was tightening on the sheet of vellum she held. He liked what he was doing to her, and what she did to him.

Matson held her tighter and smiled to himself as his lips left hers and he kissed the warmth of her neck.

"Sophia," a high-pitched voice called.

They quickly broke apart.

Sophia raked the back of her hand across her lips as if she could erase what had just happened between them. "It's Aunt Mae. Did she see us?"

Matson looked through the shrub. "No. She's just coming down the steps. She couldn't have seen us."

"I have to make sure she doesn't. I must go."

Sophia spun and headed down the footpath.

Matson peeked back through the hedge, watched her enter the garden and greet her aunt by the fountain. He blew out a deep, sighing breath.

"Damnation," he whispered.

He was already trying to think of a reason to see her again.

───────

"Sophia, why were you outside the gate?"

"Looking for my poetry, Aunt Mae." She held up the sheet of vellum. "A gust of wind blew it away, and I had to run after it."

Her aunt took the paper from her and looked at it. "Thank goodness you found it, but it's wrinkled. What a shame. You'll have to copy it again."

"I shall be happy to do so. I'm just glad I saved it."

"This is very good, Sophia. Come inside and have a cup of tea while I read the rest of it."

Sophia gave another glance toward the hedge as she picked up her paper and pencils from the table and chair. She could have sworn she saw Mr. Brentwood watching her through the hedge as she followed her aunt into the house.

"You've been out a long time," Mae said. "Your cheeks are quite rosy, Sophia. You're not chilled, are you?"

"No, no, my woolen shawl has kept me quite warm."

"Good. I have to admit it gave me a start when I first went into the garden and you weren't there."

Sophia placed her writing materials on the center table in the drawing room and asked, "Would you have been shocked if I had told you I was meeting a handsome prince in secret?"

"No." Mae's eyes brightened. "I'd say that's the most romantic thing I've heard in years, but I wouldn't have believed you. Obviously, if your mind was on a handsome prince, you were getting ready to write romantic poetry."

"It's true that my mind is on a handsome

gentleman. But just as my poetry was swept away by the wind, I fear my dreams are being swept away too."

Sophia turned away from her aunt and touched the tips of her fingers to her lips. How could such a simple kiss breathe so much life into so many different feelings inside her? Feelings she hadn't known existed. Because it wasn't simple. The kiss he had given her in the corridor last night was simple. His kiss a few minutes ago was passionate.

Mr. Brentwood appealed to all her senses. She'd wanted him to kiss her. But it was foolish. She had to deny his charms and not give in to them again. He could never be the match for her. Fulfilling her oath to her father for her selfish and childish behavior and gaining redemption for ruining his life meant she must marry a title. And even if that vow were not weighing heavily on her shoulders, Mr. Matson Brentwood would not be the man for her. He was a very resourceful businessman. He would not welcome advice from his wife on how to manage a business.

"I know how you feel, Sophia, and I will not let your dreams fade as mine did so many years ago."

Sophia heard a strain of wistfulness in her aunt's voice. "Did you have a beau when you were younger?"

"Me? No," she whispered, sadness gathering in her eyes. "Not a beau, but June and I went to dances

the first year we were old enough. I had such a wonderful time dancing, talking, and smiling at all the
young gentlemen. But just before the Season was
over, June had declared that we didn't need dances,
beaus, or parties. No, we had each other. That was
all we needed, and that's the way it's been."

"Why did you stop going just because June did?"

"Oh, we always did everything together. We
still do."

"Why did she stop wanting to go?"

"I don't know. She never told me."

"And you never asked?"

"Oh, I did, but she made it quite clear I was not
to ask her any personal questions, so I never mentioned it again." Suddenly Mae's eyes brightened,
and she smiled. "I was so excited when your father
asked if we'd be your chaperones and help you find
the perfect gentleman to marry. I knew we could
go to parties again, see the glittering chandeliers
and watch the dances, hear the music, see all the
beautiful clothing and jewelry the ladies wear." She
stopped, laughed, and then said, "Oh, my, listen
to me! I sound like a young waiting for her first
Season. I don't know what's wrong with me."

"I know what's wrong."

"You do?"

"Yes. You want to be courted."

"Oh, yes, I do," she whispered in a breathy voice,
sounding as if she was in a trance. Suddenly, she

cleared her throat. "What am I saying? I mean, no, no, of course not. You allow me to fill my head with too many fanciful notions, Sophia."

"What's wrong with that?"

Mae looked flustered for a moment and then said, "Well, I don't want them. I have all I need to make me happy."

Sophia stepped closer to her aunt. "Are you being truthful with me?"

"Of course I am." Her eyes turned thoughtful again. She looked at Sophia and continued, "Mostly. Oh, Sophia, must you make me admit I do sometimes wonder what it would be like—to have married and had children? But you know the old saying that you can't put spilled milk back in the bottle. I was put on the shelf years ago, and there is no going back for me."

"I don't believe that, Auntie."

"Well, it's true," she said in a stronger voice and then gave a half chuckle. "I don't know what is putting all these silly ideas in my head. Perhaps it was being at the ball last night. I haven't been to one in so long. I certainly don't know what is making me say these outlandish things to you. I must be getting daft, or perhaps it was all the handsome gentlemen I saw. Maybe it was the lively music or the glass of delicious champagne I drank."

"Or possibly it's simply that an earl caused your breath to catch in your throat and a fluttering in your stomach."

Mae jerked around to face Sophia with surprise lighting her face. "Did you feel it too, when you looked at Lord Bighampton and Lord Snellingly?"

"No, Auntie," Sophia said, feeling her own wistfulness. But there was another gentleman who'd made her feel that way.

"Oh, oh, I didn't either," Aunt Mae said, turning her face away again.

Sophia knew her aunt was fibbing, again. "Auntie?"

Mae shook her head and laughed. "Yes, I admit that sometimes I yearn for the touch of a man. I have dreams even in my dotage. I imagine what it would be like for a gentleman to call on me, to hold my hand, to hold me. But that's all it is. A dream. I'm too old for anything else."

Sophia felt her aunt's passion deep in her soul. "Nonsense. You aren't forty yet, are you?"

"Thirty-eight. I'm like a dried flower on the shelf. No man is going to look at me. It's not realistic for me to dream about being courted, Sophia, but it is satisfying."

Sophia's heart ached for her aunt's plight. She had no idea why neither of her aunts had married. Even at their age, they were lovely in appearance and countenance. They were both intelligent and delightful to converse with. But whatever caused them not to marry when in their prime, it was obvious that Aunt Mae was having regrets now.

Without thinking it through, Sophia said, "If you would like to have a beau, I'll help you get one."

Startled, Mae looked at Sophia and laughed again. "What?"

"I'll help you get a beau," Sophia said, knowing she had no idea how she would go about doing something like this, but she wanted to make her aunt feel that all was not lost just because of her age.

Mae's eyes rounded in wonder. "You would do that for me, wouldn't you?"

"Of course," Sophia said earnestly. "I've never liked the accepted rule that a gentleman can wait as long as he likes to marry, but if a lady wants to take her time, she will be considered a weed on the shelf and not marriageable."

Her aunt seemed thoughtful for a moment and then said, "If I were interested, which I'm not, mind you—the idea is absolutely preposterous—but if I were, how would you go about helping me?"

"Well, it's simple," she said slowly, stalling while praying for an idea to pop into her mind. Now that she'd made her bold assertion, she had to come up with how to implement it. "Let's see, perhaps if there were a gentleman you were interested in, like Lord Bighampton."

"An earl!" Aunt Mae exclaimed. "Oh, my heavenly stars, Sophia! Lord Bighampton is such a splendid cut of a man. He would never be interested in me."

"You don't know that. Besides, I was using him only as an example. No matter the gentleman, if he wanted to call on me," Sophia said as an idea came to her, "I would agree, and then I could be late for our outing. I'd make him wait and ask you to keep him company until I was ready. And then I would have you join us for a ride in the park. That would work, wouldn't it? I could make sure he talked to you more than me. He could see what a truly lovely and charming person you are, and he would want to call on you."

"Oh, by all the saints in heaven, Sophia! It does sound doable."

Sophia blinked in surprise that her aunt actually liked her hastily thought of plan.

A worried expression settled on Mae's face. "But even if we could make it work, June would never approve."

"Why should she have to?" Sophia said. "She is your sister, not your mother and not your keeper. You can't worry about what she will think."

Aunt Mae laughed. "You know June can be very forceful, but thank you, dear one. Your ideas make me feel young again." She hesitated and then shook her head. "June is right. We don't need husbands in our lives. We have each other, and now you to look after."

"No, she isn't right." Sophia reached over and hugged her aunt. "Our plan is set, and I will not let you talk yourself out of it. Now, at the next party we attend, I want you to pick out three gentlemen you would like to call on you, and I will let them know that a call from them would be welcome."

"All right, I already have two in mind."

"Good. All we have to do is talk Aunt June into letting gentlemen call on me, so we can both get busy finding the gentlemen of our dreams."

"What is going on between you two?" June asked, walking into the drawing room. "You're laughing like schoolgirls pulling a prank on the governess."

"Oh, we are doing nothing of the sort," Mae said. "I was just complimenting Sophia on her poetry."

"So it's good?" June asked.

"Yes," Mae said with a smile. "It's very creative, and I think it's going to be very good."

Mae looked at Sophia, and she smiled.

Eight

A well-spent day brings happy sleep.

—Leonardo da Vinci

"IT'S SO LOVELY," SOPHIA SAID, LOOKING OUT THE coach window.

They had been queuing for almost half an hour along the lighted, tree-lined drive that led to Lord Tradesforke's large manor house at the end of the lane. According to Sir Randolph, Lord Tradesforke's party, always given on the eve of the opening of the Season, was his favorite to attend. The carriage ride from Mayfair to the earl's house took fifteen minutes, but it hadn't seemed that lengthy because Sir Randolph kept Sophia and her aunts entertained with stories about the crusty old man.

Much to the dismay of his family, the earl had spent most of his life sailing the seas and visiting other countries. He never took his rightful place in parliament, and he'd never bothered to marry, seemingly content to allow his brother's son to become heir to the title. Seeing all the different cultures in the world and bringing back pieces of them to display in his lavish homes were his only interests.

"Of all the houses I've been in, and that's been quite a few in my lifetime, Lord Tradesforke's house is the most impressive," Sir Randolph said. "I was pleased he agreed you and your chaperones could come with me tonight. He's a friendly gentleman, but he can be an old fig about whom he invites to his parties."

Sophia turned to Sir Randolph, who was sitting beside her in the carriage. Her aunts sat primly on the opposite side of the velvet-covered carriage cushions. "I'm delighted you arranged it for us. There are so many lights surrounding the house and shining in the windows that it almost looks alive."

Sir Randolph laughed. "I've always thought that too. With the houses so close together in Mayfair, it's not possible to entertain the way the earl does here. Wait until you get inside and see all of the artwork, statues, and oddities he's collected from his many tours to other countries."

"I can hardly wait, Sir Randolph. Tell us more."

"I don't think I understand the fascination of this gentleman," June said in a quarrelsome tone. "Just because the man has traveled the world, everyone wants to come to his parties and see his novelties?"

"That's not all there is, but perhaps you were sleeping through that part of my story," Sir Randolph said.

June huffed with indignation. "I have not been sleeping."

"Then I'll repeat myself just for you. One of the reasons everyone wants to come to the earl's first party is that he always gives a second one about midway through the Season. His rule is you can't come to the second if you didn't make the first."

"That seems high-handed to me," June said, pulling her wrap tighter around her neck. "It's a party, not an audience with the king."

"Oh, don't be so contrary, June," Mae said. "I'm with Sophia. I want to hear more."

Sir Randolph looked thoughtful for a moment. "I suppose you don't understand it because there is enjoyment for everyone in what he does, Miss Shevington, and perhaps you aren't too familiar with what that is."

June gasped. "That's not true, Sir Randolph. I know quite well how to enjoy myself."

"It doesn't show," he answered.

"Don't mind Aunt June, Sir Randolph," Sophia said, hoping to put an end to the friction developing between her chaperone and her guardian. "Continue with what you were saying."

He gave her a grateful smile. "He started this about five years ago. He does something different every year for the second party. The first year he had a masquerade ball, but what made it exceptional was that everyone had to wear a toga, and then when we arrived, we were all given the same mask to wear. No one could tell who anyone was. It was such a delight to be fooled. People still talk about that evening. One year he had transformed his ballroom into a carnival-like atmosphere, with men walking on ropes tightly stretched from one end of the ballroom to the other. There were jugglers, contortionists, and cages with live animals in the ballroom."

Her aunts gasped.

"Surely not," Sophia said.

"Oh, it's true. There were a tiger, a leopard, a lion, and a bear. I swear on my honor. About halfway through the evening, the lion roared, and half the women in attendance fainted, and the other half ran for the doors."

Sophia and Mae laughed, but June remained starchy.

"To this day no one knows where he got the animals or what he did with them after the party, but just ask anyone tonight who was there three years ago, and they will tell you it is true."

"That was very daring of him."

"What an exciting adventure that must have been," Mae said dreamily.

"I think it's outrageous, Sister," June said, "and you should too. I think it was shameful that the lion frightened all those ladies."

"Well, it wasn't, Miss Shevington," Sir Randolph

insisted. "Lord Tradesforke had no idea the lion would roar as if he was in a jungle somewhere. And besides, all the ladies came back the next year, so I guess they didn't mind being frightened."

"I wonder where he comes up with all these extraordinary ideas to enliven his parties," Sophia said.

"I suppose he gets them from his many travels around the world. Not every year has been so beyond the pale. One year he had a troupe of actors and actresses perform a play that was so amusing everyone laughed for hours afterward. Then there was the year he set up rings on the grounds and he had fencing and boxing matches for us to watch. Everyone waits to see what Lord Tradesforke will come up with next."

Sophia smiled at Sir Randolph. "I can hardly wait to see what he comes up with this year."

"That's the adventurous attitude I like."

Mae sighed, June made her familiar clucking sound, and Sophia looked out the window again.

When the carriage finally arrived at the house, they stepped down and entered the massive double doors. They left their wraps with servants standing in the vestibule and made their way down a long corridor into a large, opulent ballroom that was filled with chattering people and loud music.

Sophia had never been in a house so elaborately furnished with gilt chairs and settees upholstered in elegant fabrics that were striped with gold-colored thread. The ceiling of the enormous ball-room was painted in a pastel blue with heavenly beings and mortals mingling among colorful flowers. The walls were decorated in a grand style, with heavy emphasis on baroque woodwork, gilt framing, and silk padding. Two fancy sconces that held dozens of lit candles graced each wall. Tall, decorative French mirrors lined the walls, making the room look larger and overflowing with beautifully gowned ladies and impeccably dressed gentlemen. Sir Randolph had told her that other than vouchers for Almack's, Lord Tradesforke's party was the most coveted invitation among the *ton*. She could certainly understand why.

Before Sophia had time to catch her breath from the grandeur of the room, Lord Bighampton greeted her, her aunts, and Sir Randolph. For a moment she felt he had intruded on her evening, but she quickly remembered the reason for attending the Season was to find a husband—a titled one. She had much to do if she were going to find her aunt a beau and make a match for herself by the end of the Season.

Sophia watched the rotund earl and listened to him as he and Sir Randolph talked about the cool weather, the money scandal involving the Lord Mayor, and the ridiculously long line to get into Lord Tradesforke's home. Lord Bighampton had a title, but she couldn't find much else that sparked an interest in him. Perhaps she would be doing him an injustice if she discounted him so early in the Season.

"Would you like to walk with me to the champagne table, Miss Hart?" Lord Bighampton asked and then quickly added, "With Sir Randolph's permission, of course."

Sir Randolph nodded.

"Thank you, Lord Bighampton," Sophia said, knowing a few minutes alone with the earl would help her to learn more about his views concerning a woman's capabilities.

It amazed her that a man could completely trust the managing of a large estate with more than two dozen servants to his wife but thought her incapable of handling any other kind of business. Perhaps if Lord Bighampton was more forward thinking, she could overlook the fact that he was rotund, balding, and twice her age.

"This way," he said.

He ushered her toward the perimeter of the ballroom and away from the crowd chatter and music.

A young gentleman tried to stop the earl, but he waved the man away and gruffly said, "Not now," and kept walking.

Lord Bighampton was almost breathless by the time they made it to the champagne table set up at the back of the room. "So tell me, Miss Hart," he said, patting his forehead with his handkerchief, "what kinds of things make you happy, and what brings you the most joy?"

"It doesn't take much to make me happy, my lord. A sunny day will do that."

"In our climate, sunny days make almost everyone happy. Tell me, do you like to ride?"

"I've not had the opportunity to ride often, but I enjoyed the few times I was in a saddle."

"I have a stable of many fine, spirited horses as well as even-tempered mares at my estate in Kent."

He handed her a glass of champagne. "How often do you spend time at your summer estate?" she asked.

"As much as possible. Usually, I spend only spring in London. Of course, I wouldn't miss the Season. It's a good time to catch up with old friends and to see who's come of age, who has married, and who has given birth in the past year."

"But what about your business ventures?"

"My businesses?" he queried.

"Yes, I mean how do you manage your affairs, being far away from London so much of the time?"

"Oh, never worry about that, my dear. I have my solicitors and my managers to take care of everything for me. They send me reports on everything. Have no fear that I work too hard and have no occasions for recreation. I have plenty of time for house parties and fox hunting."

"I see," she said.

Sophia would not want to live most of her life in Kent, riding horses or planning menus for house parties. She wanted to be in London, where she could monitor Shevington's account books, shipments, and stay in touch with all their many suppliers in India.

She could see the differences between a gentleman like Lord Bighampton, who had not worked for his position in life but had had it handed to him, and a man like her father, who'd worked hard to build his company. Her father had never allowed others to manage his affairs or make important decisions until he was too ill to do it himself.

"My estate is quite large," Lord Bighampton continued. "If you would prefer, you can ride a carriage around the estate. I realize some ladies are frightened of horses. They are large animals."

"I am not afraid of horses, Lord Bighampton. I've just never had many occasions to be around them."

"Good evening, Lord Bighampton," Lord Snellingly said, bowing first to the earl, to whom he hardly gave a passing glance, and then to Sophia. "And how are you this fine evening, Miss Hart? No, no, don't answer me. I can see that you are enchanting every gentleman who is here this evening. And you are, quite simply, the most stunningly lovely young lady here. I was hoping you would delight us with your company tonight. I must say that looking at you makes my eyes dance with pleasure."

"Thank you," Sophia said, blushing at his effusive compliments.

"And good evening to you too, Lord Snellingly," Lord Bighampton said tightly.

Lord Snellingly sniffed into his lace-trimmed handkerchief. "I was in a dither earlier in the evening, but now that I've seen Miss Hart, I feel much better." He stepped between Sophia and the earl and said, "I wrote a short poem just for you." He reached into his coat pocket and pulled out a folded sheet of vellum.

"Now see here, Snellingly," Lord Bighampton said, pushing his way between the two of them. "I'm afraid we don't have the time for your poetry tonight."

"Nonsense, my lord," Lord Snellingly said, shaking the folds out of the paper. "It's four lines. What kind of foul and ill-bred beast wouldn't have time for four lines of poetry?"

He then turned to Sophia. "You want to hear what I have written, don't you, Miss Hart?"

"Yes, of course," she answered, not knowing whether Lord Snellingly couldn't tell that Lord Bighampton was seething, or if he simply didn't care.

"Very well then," the earl said testily. "But be quick about it."

Lord Snellingly bowed and then stepped closer to Sophia and looked solemn and intent as he read:

"Your eyes are the wooing color of an English hillside bathed in summer's sunny nectar. In the pool of their deep, dark green depths I see the shimmering glimmer of a million stars looking back at me, holding me captive, calling my heart to live, to laugh, and to love with vigor. In the labyrinth of my soul, I sense your heart and mine joyfully beating together as one in spirit and—"

"Give me that," Lord Bighampton interrupted, reaching for the paper, which Lord Snellingly jerked away just in time. "Now see here, Snellingly, that's enough."

Lord Snellingly looked as if he'd been slapped. "You interrupted the flow of the verse. I'll have to start over."

"The hel—heaven you will," Lord Bighampton said, quite agitated.

"Why did you interrupt me?"

"Perhaps because you read more than four lines."

"I did not. Look here." He shoved the vellum back toward the earl and tried to get him to look at it.

Lord Bighampton brushed the man's hand aside as if it were a worrisome fly. "I'm not looking at that. I take you at your word. We've not the time to listen to more. Find someone else to peddle your words upon. I must get Miss Hart back to Sir Randolph. Excuse us."

"Very well, if you must go with such haste, I'll walk with you."

Lord Bighampton was almost snarling at Lord Snellingly, but the poet seemed oblivious to the earl's ire. The two gentlemen continued to bicker as they walked back to Sir Randolph and her aunts. It didn't bother Sophia; it made her smile.

For the next two hours Sophia danced, stopping, it seemed, only long enough to change partners. She had graced the arms of Lord Snellingly and Lord Bighampton, the handsome Viscount Hargraves, and several other gentlemen, but the man who intrigued her most, Mr. Brentwood, was nowhere to be seen. She had also danced with two men who she thought might be perfect for her aunt Mae.

When she caught Mae without June hovering beside her, she said to her, "Do you remember meeting Mr. Parker Wilson and Mr. Alfred Boyd?"

"Yes, of course. They are both handsome gentlemen, don't you think?"

"And they seemed kind, too, when I danced with them. Would you like for me to let one of them know that a call would be welcomed, so you can spend some time with him?"

"Hmm. Do I have to choose between them?" Mae asked. "Can't we invite both?"

Surprised, Sophia smiled and said, "There's no reason at all that we can't. I'll talk with Aunt June, and we'll fit them into the schedule next week."

Mae clasped her hands together nervously. "Oh, must we do it that soon?"

"Yes. If we are going to do this, it's time to start. We can't just continue to talk about it."

Mae dropped her hands to her sides and said, "All right, let's do it."

"There you are, Miss Hart," Lord Snellingly said. "Are you ready for our dance?"

Another round of dancing left Sophia feeling ravenous, so rather than allowing Lord Snellingly to see her back to her aunts, she bid him farewell at the dance floor. She headed to the room where the buffet table had been set with gleaming silver trays filled with fish, lamb, fowl, and every vegetable and fruit she could imagine. Lighted, three-pronged silver candlesticks graced the table about every four or five feet.

There were a few people sitting around the perimeter of the room, but no one was serving from the table at the moment. This was the perfect time for her to indulge in a few bites with no one to watch her. Her aunts believed it perfectly fine for a lady to eat at a sit-down dinner party, where she would be served, but never from a buffet.

Sophia gazed at the feast fit for the prince himself, and her stomach rumbled. She picked up a small plate, fork, and a napkin. Her gaze flitted over the many trays of stuffed mushrooms, pickled beets, sugarcoated dates, and small vegetable tarts. She placed two mushrooms on her plate, and then picked up one with her fork and put it in her mouth. It was delicious, so she quickly ate the other one too. There were small slices of cheese topped with pieces of preserved apple, so she added those to her plate and quickly ate them, relishing every tasty bite.

Sophia was reaching for the spoon to help herself to a fruit tart when from behind her she heard, "Allow me?"

She froze. She had been caught eating, but it wasn't by her aunts or Sir Randolph. She turned to look into Mr. Brentwood's shining blue eyes.

Nine

Even if I knew that tomorrow the world would
go to pieces, I would still plant my apple tree.

—Martin Luther

SOPHIA'S BREATHING KICKED UP A NOTCH.

Several times throughout the evening she had
glanced toward the ballroom doorway, unobtru-
sively surveyed the crowd, and searched all the
faces on the dance floor, hoping for a glimpse of
Mr. Brentwood. She had almost given up hope that
he would attend the party.

He laid a plum tart on her plate. "I'm not surprised you're so hungry. You've been dancing since
I arrived."

Sophia tried to appear disinterested in him. She
slowly moved along the buffet table as if she were
more interested in the food than in him.

"Hmm. You were peeking at me through the
hedge, and now you've been watching me on
the dance floor. Is this becoming a habit, Mr.
Brentwood?"

He nodded. "It would seem that way, if not for

the fact that it's been three days since I last saw you. Have your aunts been keeping you in hiding?"

"I've been at parties every night this week but haven't stayed long at any of them."

"Maybe that's why we've been missing each other."

"That's not difficult to do, with so many different parties being given each evening. My aunts feel we must accept every invitation, if only for a few minutes, so we won't offend anyone." She stopped and looked into his eyes. "And perhaps after our last encounter, it is for the best that we haven't seen each other."

"Why is that, Sophia?"

She quickly glanced around. "You shouldn't call me that," she whispered.

"But that is your name. I've thought of you as Sophia since I heard your aunts calling your name when we first met."

"Still, you shouldn't. It's not proper."

"Neither is kissing," he answered.

"No, it's not, and you shouldn't tempt me to do things I shouldn't do."

The corners of his mouth lifted ever so slightly. "Did I tempt you to kiss me, Sophia?"

"You know you did." Sophia quickly looked around to see if anyone was close enough to have heard what he said, but no one was near. "I shouldn't have let that happen."

"But you wanted me to kiss you."

"Yes, but you should have been a gentleman and refused me."

He chuckled and then put a thin slice of apple in his mouth and ate it before saying, "I agree we shouldn't have kissed, but do you think you could have stopped it from happening?"

She hadn't expected him to agree with her. "Yes."

His eyebrows rose, but he didn't say anything.

"Maybe. All right, no," she admitted honestly. "No, not at the time."

He stepped closer to her. "But now you think you can keep me from kissing you again."

Sophia tried to back up, but the table stopped her. "You wouldn't dare try to kiss me here with all these people in the room, would you?"

"Probably not." He inched a little closer. "But I'm not promising."

"Even if you tried, it would do you no good. My sound reasoning has returned to me."

"That's not a challenge, is it, Sophia? Because if it is, I accept." He took the plate, fork, and napkin from her hands and placed them on the table behind her.

He was standing much too close to her. His nearness was doing strange things to her breathing, and she was certain he could hear her heart beating. She glanced at the tables where other people were sitting. Thankfully, no one seemed to be looking at them.

"No, no, of course it's not. I meant only that we shouldn't have kissed. I admit I wanted to know what it felt like, so I indulged myself. Now that I know what it's all about, I will have more restraint."

He chuckled softly again. "That still sounds like a challenge for me to prove to you that you will have no restraint."

Mr. Brentwood's eyes shone with amusement. He looked so handsome with his lips turned upward in a charming half grin. She had a great urge to wrap her arms around his neck and hug him. But she couldn't do that, and she couldn't encourage Mr. Brentwood. He wasn't a titled gentleman, and she couldn't settle for a man who wasn't.

"Tell me why you were dancing with Mr. Alfred Boyd. He must be thirty years older than you."

"Oh, for my aunt Mae." Sophia caught herself and stopped. "I mean, because my aunt Mae wanted me to, and I do like to please them when I can."

He looked at her curiously. "Are you sure that's what you meant to say?"

She had never been any good at fibbing, but she had to try. "Yes, why?"

"Because I don't believe you."

"It's the truth," she said as his eyes narrowed in disbelief. "All right, it's not the whole truth. My aunt Mae wants to be courted."

He grinned. "I think that is sweet, but why wasn't *she* dancing with Mr. Boyd?"

Sophia inhaled deeply and decided she might as well explain the entire story to him, so she did in great detail. "So you see I have no choice but to help Aunt Mae find a beau."

"I would be happy to discreetly let it be known that Miss Shevington would welcome a visit from an acceptable gentleman."

His words softly squeezed Sophia's heart. "That is very kind of you, but she is not ready for that. I would appreciate it if you would keep this between us for now. She's very worried Aunt June will find out and disapprove."

"You know I will keep silent, but if anything changes for your aunt and I can help, let me know."

"Thank you, I will, and speaking of my aunts, I must get back to them before they come looking for me."

"Good evening, Mr. Brentwood, Miss Hart."

Sophia turned and greeted Viscount Hargraves. She had met the young viscount the night of her first party, and she had danced with him two nights ago. He wasn't as tall, trim, or broad-shouldered as Mr. Brentwood, but he had a strong, sturdy look about him. His curly blond hair was overly long and seemed a bit unruly, but it didn't detract from his handsomeness. His smile was infectious and his manner pleasing. There was no reason why she shouldn't feel the same feelings and sensations that she felt when she looked at Mr. Brentwood, only she didn't. There was no spark of desire when she looked at Lord Hargraves.

"I was hoping you might honor me with a dance later in the evening," he said.

Sophia didn't know why, but her gaze darted to Mr. Brentwood's before she answered. He smiled at her and gave the slightest of nods. That irritated her. She would have given anything if she could take back having glanced at him. She certainly didn't need his approval or permission to agree to a dance with the viscount.

"Yes, of course, I'd be delighted, my lord. I have two other dances promised, and then I shall be free."

"Good. Perhaps you'd like me to escort you safely back to your aunts."

"That's not necessary, Lord Hargraves," Matson said. "Miss Hart had just asked me to walk her back to her aunts. She doesn't want them to worry about her, and they know she's safe with me." Matson did the briefest of bows. "Excuse us."

The viscount smiled affably. "Of course, Mr. Brentwood. I'll see you later in the evening, Miss Hart."

When they were out of the buffet room, Sophia turned to Matson and said, "I didn't ask you to walk me to my aunts."

"Didn't you?"

"You know I didn't."

He smiled charmingly. "But you did say you needed to get back to them."

"I think you didn't want me talking to Lord Hargraves."

"I didn't."

"So you admit you are jealous of the man?"

"I admit no such thing. I just happen to know that you are safer with me than you are with him. Besides, I want to say good evening to your aunts. We had quite the conversation the afternoon I had tea with them."

"I remember that you certainly charmed Aunt Mae."

"But not your aunt June?" he asked with a note of humor flowing in his tone.

"I've never seen anyone charm her. She is not as approachable as Aunt Mae."

"Does that bother you? That they look so much alike but are different?"

"Not in the least," she said as they entered the corridor. "Because they resemble each other, I think I'm glad they don't think, talk, or act the same. If they did, I'd never be able to tell them apart. Tell me, are you very much like your twin brother?"

"We're much like your aunts. We have the same face and build, but we have vastly different temperaments and different ways of doing things."

"I've not met him at any of the parties I've attended."

"He's been preoccupied the past couple of

weeks. The parody that recently came out upset him greatly."

"More than it upset you?"

"Not more. Just in a different way. Iverson seldom takes the time to think things through before he speaks or acts, and sometimes that puts him at odds with people."

She smiled at him. "I can certainly understand that."

Matson gave her a soft grin to let her know he knew she was referring to their kiss outside her gate, and answered, "I think we all can at times."

Sophia saw her aunts hurriedly making their way through the crowd toward her. They were charming in their own way, and she was very happy they had agreed to give up their lives to come to London to be her chaperones. At times she needed Aunt June's strict adherence to the rules of Society, and there were occasions she very much needed her aunt Mae's gentle spirit and wistful enthusiasm.

"Sophia, we found you just in time," Aunt June said. "Good evening, Mr. Brentwood."

"Miss Shevington," he said to June, and then turned to Mae and greeted her. "Miss Shevington. Both of you ladies look lovely tonight."

"Thank you, Mr. Brentwood," Mae said. "That's a nice way to make an old lady feel special."

"Come," June said impatiently, taking Sophia's

hand and pulling her forward. "Lord Tradesforke
has asked for everyone's attention. He said he had
an important announcement to make, and we don't
want to miss it."

"Did he say what it was about?" Sophia asked,
looking behind her to make sure Mr. Brentwood
was following them.

"No," Mae answered for her sister. "I wonder
what it could be."

"Shh," June whispered to them. "Listen, and we
shall find out soon enough."

Sophia knew when Mr. Brentwood moved to
stand beside her. She didn't have to look at him. She
felt the heat from his body and knew he was near.

"Your Graces, my lords and ladyships, sirs, ladies,
and gentlemen, may I have your attention please."

The hum of chatter died down, and the
room went quiet almost immediately. Everyone
looked across the ballroom to where the Earl of
Tradesforke stood on a small platform in front of
the musicians. It was the first time Sophia had seen
their host for the evening. He was a jolly-looking
tall and round man who had a tuft of gray hair and
a bushy gray beard that was long enough to rest on
his upper chest. Sophia never knew either of her
grandfathers, but this man reminded her of how a
grandfather should look.

"Thank you. Now, could I please have all of
the young ladies and gentlemen who are eligible

to make a match this Season step forward to the center of the room? And please, those of you who are already attached by the bonds of matrimony or betrothal, please step aside and let them make their way to the middle."

"Go, Sophia, go," June said, giving her a gentle push.

Sophia looked at Mr. Brentwood again, and he nodded to her.

"What about you?" she asked. "You are an eligible bachelor."

"But I am not looking to make a match this Season, and you are."

"Oh, it will be fun, Mr. Brentwood," Mae said. "Go on with her. Can't you see she doesn't want to go by herself? Be a gentleman and accompany her."

"If you insist, Miss Shevington, I'll stand by her. Come, Miss Hart."

Sophia and Mr. Brentwood stepped forward and into the crowd already gathering in the center of the room. She couldn't help but wish her aunt Mae could join in as well.

"I have no idea what this could be about," Sophia said to him.

"Neither do I, but from all that I've heard, this man is expected to do something outrageous."

"Thank you, my honored guests," Lord Tradesforke said. "I've been asked more than one hundred times this evening what my mid-Season party will be about this year, and because I'm tired of hearing the question, I've decided to put all of you out of your misery and tell you."

A loud roar of applause and shouts of agreement rang from the crowd.

The bearded earl laughed. "This year, I've decided to go back to the early years of old London and to the alfresco entertainment in the park. On the fourth Sunday in May, I will have a May Day Fair Day in Hyde Park. Along with all the food and drink you care to have, there will be games, cart and horse races, rowing on the Serpentine, and much more."

A murmur of discontent rose from the crowd. Sophia had to admit that such a day, while it would be an enormous amount of fun, didn't seem shockingly out of the ordinary. Certainly it didn't measure up to having caged tigers and lions in a ballroom.

"Ah, what's that I hear?" Lord Tradesforke laughed again. "You are wondering what is the *much more* and why I've asked the eligible young ladies and gentlemen to step forward—let me explain. In keeping with the Season and its purpose to help those looking to make a match, ladies, turn to your right."

Sophia turned and looked at Mr. Brentwood, and her arm brushed his. A prickle of desire rushed through her. He gave her a slightly amused look, and she wondered if he knew what she'd felt at their touch.

"Ladies," Lord Tradesforke continued, "if there is a gentleman standing next to you, he will be your partner the day of the fair. You will have the opportunity to compete against other couples in rowing, shooting and archery, wheelbarrow and cart racing, and too many other things to mention at this time. Now, ladies who see who your partner will be, quickly move aside so those who are left can find a partner when I give the word."

"What did he just say?" Mr. Brentwood asked.

"I think he said we would be partners for something he is planning called May Day Fair Day in the park."

"I thought he said that as well."

"What do you suppose it means?" she asked.

"I believe it means that if we choose to participate, I will be pushing you in a wheelbarrow, pulling you in a cart, and rowing you across the Serpentine, Miss Hart."

"If we so choose?" she needled as they stepped back to allow those who didn't have partners to move to the center. "Does that mean you aren't sure you are up to the tasks?"

Mr. Brentwood smiled at her as they turned away and started walking back toward her aunts. Sophia noticed that Sir Randolph was with them, and she saw that Mr. Brentwood noticed too. "I'm up to the task, Miss Hart. I was afraid you might not want to do it, for fear of getting your skirts dirty."

"Oh, I will participate, Mr. Brentwood, and I'll warn you right now that any race we participate in I intend to win. I don't like to lose."

"Neither do I, so I suggest you start practicing."

"Oh, Sophia," June said, rushing up to her along with Sir Randolph and Aunt Mae. "Who was standing next to you? Who will you be partnered with?"

"Mr. Brentwood," she said, and turned and saw that he was already walking away. She felt a pang of disappointment that he didn't stay by her side, and could only assume it was because Sir Randolph was with them.

June watched Mr. Brentwood melt into the crowd and said, "Oh, what a disappointment."

"I am not disappointed, Aunt June. Mr. Brentwood is a strong man, and we can win many of the races and games."

"But he's not titled." June turned to Sir Randolph and said anxiously, "Why didn't you do something?"

"About what?"

"About Sophia standing next to Mr. Brentwood. Now he will have to be her partner for the day."

He looked taken aback. "What would you have had me do, Miss Shevington? Read Lord Tradesforke's mind and know what he was going to say? I suppose you wanted me to place the man you wanted Sophia to partner with right beside her."

"Well, it would have been perfectly lovely if you could have accomplished that, of course."

"June," Mae said, "you are being too hard on Sir Randolph."

"He could have at the very least asked Lord Bighampton or that fine-looking Lord Hargraves to trade with Mr. Brentwood."

"I can do no such thing."

"But Mr. Brentwood is not titled."

"I'm aware of that, Miss Shevington, but she's not marrying him, she's just partnering with him for the day."

"But that's another thing. What if the sun is shining? She can't possibly spend all day outside. She'll get more freckles."

Sophia's hand flew to her cheek.

"More freckles will only add to her beauty," he answered. "Now, I suggest you leave Sophia alone so she can enjoy the rest of the party. Come with me."

"Where?" June asked.

"I'm going to get you a glass of champagne so you can calm your rattled nerves."

"What? I'll have you know my nerves are not rattled. I'm just trying to do what is best for Sophia."

Sir Randolph took hold of June's elbow and ushered her away while she was still complaining. Sophia looked at her aunt Mae, and they started laughing like tickled schoolgirls.

"June is very upset," Mae said after getting her

laughter under control. "You know we'll hear about this all the way home tonight."

"Not if Sir Randolph gets her to drink enough champagne to make her sleepy."

They laughed again.

Sophia said, "Now, while Sir Randolph has Aunt June occupied, let's you and I walk around and find the handsome Mr. Alfred Boyd and Mr. Parker Wilson and see if we can coerce them into asking to call on you."

Mae smiled. "You mean you."

"Yes, but for you."

Suddenly Sophia felt wonderful. She was going to spend an entire day in Mr. Brentwood's company. He may not be happy about it, because of her connection to Sir Randolph, but she was. She intended to enjoy every moment she could with Mr. Brentwood before she had to become another man's bride.

Ten

Though this be madness, yet there is a
method in't.

—William Shakespeare

MATSON STRODE THROUGH HIS FRONT DOOR, taking off his damp greatcoat. There had been a fine drizzle all afternoon, and he was glad finally to be out of it. He must have gotten in and out of his carriage more than half a dozen times.

What a hell of a day he had had. It was maddening to feel as if there was something he needed to do or something he needed to know about his brother. It was unusual for him to feel restless, uneasy for so long. Perhaps it was because if he wasn't thinking that his brother needed him, he was thinking about Sophia.

"Let me help you with that, sir," Buford said, hurrying down the corridor toward him.

"I have it," Matson said, pulling the sleeves off his arms.

Since returning to England, Matson was still trying to get used to having a valet. They weren't as common in Baltimore, but in London any man of means was expected to have a dresser, a cook, and a housekeeper to see to his every need. There were still times he questioned his move back to England. His life in America was much simpler.

"You had several callers while you were out today," Buford said, ignoring Matson's refusal to allow him to help shed the coat.

Matson stuffed the garment into Buford's arms and then did the same with his hat and gloves. "Callers as in more than one?" he questioned.

"Yes, sir."

"That's odd. I've been in London more than half a year, and I can count on one hand the number of visits I've had during that time, other than from my brothers."

Buford laid the outerwear aside and picked up a small silver tray from a side table. "I'm aware of that, sir. But today you had two earls, a viscount, and four gentlemen of lesser nobility knock on your door."

The unease Matson had felt all day grew. He'd awakened with a restless feeling. Usually when he felt that way he'd find that something out of the ordinary was going on with Iverson. When he hadn't been able to shake the feeling by midday, he went looking for his brother but hadn't found him at home. Matson then went to the usual clubs he frequented and back to Iverson's home again, where he left word that he was looking for him. Matson wouldn't rest easy until he'd heard back from his brother.

"Did any of the gentlemen mention why they wanted to see me?"

"No, sir, only that they would call again at another time."

"What about my brother? Did he stop by?"

"I've not seen him today, sir. But Sir Randolph Gibson stopped by to see you. He appeared quite anxious to speak with you as soon as possible and asked if he could wait for you. If it's not convenient for you to see him at this time, I can ask him to make an appointment and come at a later time."

Matson frowned. "He's here?"

"Yes, sir. I lit a fire in the drawing room. I opened a fresh bottle of port and offered it to him. I laid out the afternoon news sheets for him to peruse while he waited."

Matson's breath kicked up a notch. "Get rid of him."

Matson put his booted foot on the bottom stair, and Sophia crossed his mind. A pang of something he didn't recognize stabbed through his chest. This man was the reason why he couldn't pursue Sophia.

"Buford, wait. I'll see him."

"Yes, sir. Can I do anything else for you?"

"No, that will be all."

Matson walked into the drawing room and saw

Sir Randolph standing in front of the fire. A look of relief washed down the man's face. Obviously there had been some fear that he might have been thrown out of the house when Matson came home, and that thought gave Matson a little perverse pleasure.

"Thank you for seeing me, Mr. Brentwood."

"It was difficult not to, since you were already in my house." Matson walked farther into the room. He didn't bother to ask Sir Randolph to take a seat or offer him a drink, as the efficient valet had done.

"Then perhaps it was my lucky day you were out when I arrived."

"I won't argue with that. What do you want?"

"I've never been one to meddle in anyone's business."

Sir Randolph paused just long enough for Matson to say, "It wouldn't be wise to start with mine."

The dapper old man chuckled softly. "I must. The thief who stole Sophia's brooch and now Lord Tradesforke's shenanigans with this May Day Fair Day event have brought you and my ward together."

"I had no control over either of those things."

"Oh, I'm aware of that, but still I must take action."

Matson frowned. "What, or maybe I should say why?"

"Sophia's future was settled a long time ago."

"You're mistaken if you think I've made claims on the young lady."

"I'm not mistaken, and I feel I must make you aware that she will marry a title."

The hair on the back of Matson's neck prickled. For some reason that comment from the man rankled more than his previous remarks. "You seem so certain on that."

"I am. Her attributes are spotless, and her inheritance is legendary, since she is not only her father's heir, but she will be mine too."

"That is of no interest to me."

"But these things must be said. She is the daughter I never had. I will guide her in her choices while she is on the mart, but she made a vow to her father on his deathbed that she would marry a title. I have known Sophia all her life. She won't go back on her word."

Matson didn't have to be told that. She might be adventurous and want her first kiss from a stranger, but she wasn't flighty. "Why are you telling me this?"

"I don't want there to be any misunderstandings between you and me."

Matson chortled. "Misunderstandings between us? Considering your affair with my mother, that's quite laughable, don't you think?"

"I meant concerning Sophia." The old man shielded his eyes with his lashes for a moment. "I've never talked about your mother with anyone."

"Is that supposed to make me feel better about your affair with her?"

"No, but perhaps I owe you an explanation."

Matson stiffened. He wanted to tell the old man he didn't owe him a damn thing, and he didn't want to hear anything he had to say, but Matson couldn't get the words out.

"There was no long affair between us. No pining or unrequited love. It was a night when opportunity presented itself, and it just happened. There was nothing we could do to stop it. Your mother was a beautiful and gracious lady. That is all I have ever said about her and all I will ever say. I'll take anyone to task who argues differently."

"Do you really think I want to hear about you and my mother?"

"You do for this reason: I won't have you seeking revenge on Sophia for something I'm guilty of."

Matson finally understood why Sir Randolph had come to see him. But if Sir Randolph thought he was going to put his mind entirely to rest, he had another thought coming. Why shouldn't he needle the man just a little?

"You know what they say about that, don't you, Sir Randolph?"

"What's that?"

"There are two things a man will wait forever for—love and revenge."

The old man's eyes narrowed and darkened. "Those words trouble me, Mr. Brentwood."

"Do they?"

"I will protect Sophia at all cost and however is necessary."

Matson didn't doubt that. "I will put your fears to rest for now. I have no desire to have designs on *anyone* connected to you, and that includes Miss Hart. If it is fate that has brought us together, I will rely on fate to separate us. Furthermore, Sir Randolph, I'm outraged you think I'd stoop so low as to take revenge on an innocent young lady for your wrongdoings. If I wanted revenge, I'd go straight to you."

Sir Randolph nodded once. "I'm a man of my word, Mr. Brentwood. I'll take you at *your* word." He then walked past Matson and out of the room.

Matson walked over to the glowing fire. His stomach felt as if it was in knots. He held out his hands and felt the warmth and huffed out a deep, sighing breath. What he'd told Sir Randolph was true. God help him, he didn't want to have any desire for Sophia Hart, but he did. And as much as he hated to admit it, he respected Sir Randolph for wanting to guard her.

Matson rolled his shoulders and massaged the back of his neck. He turned from the fire and untied his neckcloth, dropping it and his collar onto the settee. It didn't matter what he'd said to Sir Randolph, he didn't know what he was going to do about Miss Hart. So quickly, she had charmed him to the point he didn't want to dance with any other ladies. He went to parties just in hopes of seeing her, having a conversation with her. He delighted in teasing and frustrating her. He loved to provoke her with a question and then watch her fidget. She was so tempting when she was trying to explain something that was unexplainable, like kissing.

But he couldn't forget the fact that she was Sir Randolph's ward. Matson had had a delightful time with her last night at Lord Tradesforke's party, until he saw Sir Randolph standing with her aunts. The man would always be a part of her life, and Matson sure as hell didn't want that man in *his* life.

It didn't surprise him that Sophia wanted to be the bride of a titled man—as if a title made a gentleman a better man. All it did was make her seem weak and shallow, but on the surface or deep inside, she didn't appear that way to Matson.

What was he going to do about this May Day Fair Day that Lord Tradesforke had concocted? Matson was having a hard enough time staying away from her as it was. In truth, the last thing he needed was to be her partner for a day. He didn't need anything to make him more attracted to her than he already was. Was it in his best interests to stay as far away from her as possible, or could he continue to flirt with her and not lose his heart?

Matson's gaze swept across the drawing room of the leased town house. There was very little furniture in the room and nothing that he owned.

He thought back to Sir Randolph's and Lord Tradesforke's residences. Their homes were filled with things that represented their lives, where they'd been, what had caught their attention, and what intrigued them enough to want to see it every day.

Matson was almost thirty. Perhaps it was time he started looking for a house to buy and start filling it with things that gave him pleasure. He'd returned to England to make his birthplace his home, and more than six months later, he'd done nothing to make that happen.

He turned back to face the warmth of the fire and to stare into the dancing, crackling flames.

"Don't tell me I've caught you daydreaming."

Matson looked up to see Iverson standing in the doorway. A feeling of relief washed down him.

"Where have you been? I called at your home twice and looked in at all the clubs and couldn't find you."

Iverson walked into the room. "You sound disturbed. What's wrong?"

"With me?" Matson countered. "Nothing, but I had this odd feeling when I woke this morning that you needed me, and it's been with me all day. I haven't been able to shake it."

Iverson chuckled. "Don't tell me that after all these years you're finally giving in to that old myth that twins know when the other is in trouble."

Matson ignored his comment and said, "So something *is* wrong."

"Plenty was wrong this morning, which was probably why you were feeling as you did. But not anymore."

Matson didn't trust his brother's words. Something wasn't right with him.

"What happened?"

"I won't give details, but I will say it's been a long time since I've had to jump out of a bedroom window."

Matson muttered a laugh. "So did she throw you out, or did you almost get caught?"

"A little of both, as I recall, and I was damned lucky not to hurt my ankle. All is well now."

"I'm not so sure it is, if you jumped from the window of the young lady I'm thinking about."

"No, everything is fine now."

"All right. Good. I'm glad to know that. Let's go over to White's for a game of billiards."

"And have you shake me down for a few shillings? No, dear Brother, I know how good you've gotten. I think I'll keep my blunt."

"Fine, we'll play cards, and you can win a few coins from me."

"That's a tempting offer, but I can't do it this afternoon. I'm here for another reason."

Matson remained standing in front of the fireplace and watched Iverson walk over to the sideboard and pour a splash of port into two glasses. His brother might indicate nothing was wrong, but Matson knew better. Something was up with him.

"Good or bad?" Matson asked.

"I'll let you decide that for yourself after I tell you."

"Then share it."

Iverson handed Matson a glass. "I wanted you to be the first—no, that would be second—person to hear that I'm getting married next week. I want you to be there."

Matson wasn't certain he heard Iverson correctly. "I think you'd better say that again and slower this time."

Iverson laughed. "There's no need. You heard me correctly. I'm getting married. I just came from applying for the special license."

"Miss Crisp?"

"You know there is no other."

This worried Matson. There was bad blood between Iverson and her father. "So you did get caught in her bedroom?"

"No. No one saw me leave, and no one will ever know I spent the night with her."

"But you still feel obligated to marry her?"

Iverson's face tightened quickly. "I am not marrying her out of obligation."

"I knew you were smitten with her, but marriage? Are you sure?"

"Damn sure. I'm marrying her because I love her, not because I feel I have to make her my wife."

Matson winced. "What about her father? You know how you feel about the man."

"I've already talked to him, and he agreed to the marriage."

"You found the man? You never told me."

"He finally came home today while I was with Catalina—well, never mind that. That's a detail best left unsaid. Her father heard I'd been looking for him, so actually he found me."

"How did that go?"

"Better than I'd thought. I still don't like the man. I probably will never like him. But we managed to have somewhat of a friendly talk about his writings, and we see eye to eye on that now."

"Are you sure it was friendly?"

"Close enough. After we settled that, I asked for his daughter's hand, and he agreed. I will send a letter to Brent as soon as I get home, in hopes he and Gabrielle can make it in time for the wedding. Catalina and I are well suited for each other. We are sure of our feelings. There's no reason for us to wait to be together."

"In that case, congratulations." Matson held up his glass and said, "Here's to wedded bliss."

———

Matson had spent many hours at White's, drinking rather more than usual. He'd played so many games of billiards, his back was aching from bending over the table.

After Iverson had left his house, Matson had decided to skip all the scheduled parties for the evening. He simply wasn't up to gliding young ladies around a dance floor or listening to them chatter. And he was forcing himself not to think about Sophia. He'd come to the club to drink and play billiards, and that's what he'd done, and done well. His ears were buzzing, his eyes felt dry, and his pockets were heavy with coins.

It had been years since he'd drunk so much in one evening, and he wasn't exactly sure why he had tonight. It couldn't be that he was troubled by his twin getting married. He was happy for Iverson. Matson had known from the first time Iverson had mentioned Catalina Crisp to him that his brother felt differently about her.

Perhaps Matson was still restless because he didn't want to be attracted to Sophia. And the only reason he regretted not attending any of the parties tonight was because he'd miss the chance of seeing her.

Damn fate for making her Sir Randolph's ward. How had a man he'd never heard of until a few months ago become such a frustrating part of his life?

Matson had heard a few things about the elderly

and well-respected man, but not much. He looked to be near fifty, but Matson had heard he was much older. That was probably why he was still so popular among young and older ladies, including widows, spinsters, and innocents.

He had no family that Matson knew about, which must be the reason Sophia would be his heir. Matson had heard that a duke, a marquis, and an earl watched out for the dandy and had saved him from losing a large portion of his fortune on risky business ventures more than once. Matson didn't know the three gentlemen or why they were always so eager to come to Sir Randolph's rescue, but considering the old man's past, Matson would bet anyone that a lady was behind the reason.

"Mr. Brentwood."

At the sound of his name, Matson blinked his dry eyes and turned to look behind him. The robust Earl of Bighampton stood before him.

"Good evening, my lord," Matson said with the slightest of bows. Bowing to a titled gentleman was one of the rituals he had not missed when he was in America.

"Might I have a word with you? I have a table over in the corner where it's a little quieter."

Matson looked down at the short, round man and nodded. He picked up his brandy snifter and followed the earl to his table. Matson waited until after Lord Bighampton was seated before taking the chair opposite him and placing his drink on the table in front of him.

"I didn't see you at any of the parties this evening, Mr. Brentwood."

"I wasn't at any," Matson said. "What can I do for you?"

Lord Bighampton laughed. "I like a gentleman who gets right to the point. I understand you are the one who was standing beside Miss Hart when Lord Tradesforke announced his ridiculous plans for his May Day Fair Day event at Hyde Park later this year."

Matson nodded.

"What I want is simple. I want to be her partner. I want you to change with me, and you partner with the lovely and worthy Miss Matilda Craftsman. Can we consider it done?"

Matson blinked. His first thought was *yes, sure, you bet.* Miss Craftsman was a lovely young lady. He'd chatted with her from time to time, and he'd danced with her at least twice. He didn't remember that she tried to impress him with her many accomplishments, like some of the girls. But Matson hesitated and took a moment to think before blurting out his agreement. He didn't have anything against the earl, and he'd just been thinking it would be better for him if he didn't have to spend so much time with Miss Hart.

But unbidden, the memory of kissing Miss Hart invaded his mind and stirred him. Her lips had been soft, sweet, and eager. She'd felt warm and exciting in his arms. Matson realized it wasn't that he didn't want to be her partner. What he wanted was for her not to be Sir Randolph's ward. But that was a fact he couldn't change.

"Mr. Brentwood, did you hear me?" Bighampton said, the jowls under his chin moving with each word. "Are you in agreement with my proposal?"

Matson straightened in his chair and looked at Lord Bighampton's ruddy cheeks, large girth, and the age lines circling his eyes. The man was an earl, but he was also twice Miss Hart's age. He wouldn't make a very good partner for her. Matson doubted the man could row half the length of the Serpentine. And he was probably as cranky as a boar rooting around for his supper when he didn't get his way. But did fathers, guardians, or young ladies care about those things if a man was titled?

Matson didn't know the answer, but he knew he didn't want this man being her partner for the May Day Fair Day event and possibly stealing a kiss from her too.

Matson rose. "No, we don't have a deal."

With some effort, the earl rose too. "I should have known you'd want an incentive. I'll give you money for the swap. Just name your price."

Matson looked down at the portly man. "I said no, my lord. My partner is not for sale at any price."

Leaving his unfinished drink on the table, Matson walked out of the club.

Eleven

There are charms made for only distant
admiration.

—Samuel Johnson

"Sophia," Mae said, rushing into Sophia's
bedchamber excitedly. "He's here. You must
come quickly."

Laying her quill aside, Sophia rose from the
chair at her small desk and looked at her aunt's
flushed face. She was positively glowing. "No,
Auntie, I'm supposed to wait here for a few minutes and give you a little time to converse with
Lord Snellingly. We did the same with Mr. Parker
Wilson yesterday, remember?"

"Yes, I know that was the plan, but Lord
Snellingly is an earl."

"He is still a man."

"June said I must come get you immediately, and
for you not to keep his lordship waiting."

Sophia smiled. "That's because June doesn't
know what we are doing. Tell her I will be down
shortly, and you go and keep the earl company."

She frowned. "But June's doing that."

"June is not trying to learn how to converse with a gentleman so she can have a beau, and you are. Go into the drawing room and take charge. Ask Aunt June to go and check on the refreshments. While she is out, engage Lord Snellingly by asking him what the weather is like outside, what is his favorite card game, and if you fail to get enthusiastic comments from him on those subjects, you can always ask him about poetry. I've realized he never tires of talking about it."

The worried expression stayed on her face. "I'll try, but Mr. Parker Wilson seemed very distracted yesterday when I tried to talk to him while we waited for you."

"Did you tell him the story about you and Aunt June being born in two different months?"

Her eyes widened. "Yes. How did you know?"

"Because you have told it too many times, Auntie." Sophia was trying to be kind. "I do think everyone in London has heard it now and you don't need to tell it again."

"But it always fascinates people to hear it."

Sophia smiled sweetly. "It's such an extraordinary thing to have happened, it does fascinate them the first time they hear it. But try to talk about the kinds of things that interest a man: cards, horses, and politics. Once you get started, you will think of many things to ask."

"Oh, Sophia, how? I am too old for this."

"Nonsense. You must buck up."

"But you can't find a match of your own if you are trying to help me find a beau."

"We've already been over this, Auntie. That is what makes this perfect. I'm looking anyway, so I can look for you too. Now, go talk to Lord Snellingly for me. And tell Aunt June I will be down shortly, before she comes up here looking for both of us."

"How does my hair look?" Mae asked anxiously. "Are my cheeks rosy? Should I change dresses again?"

"No, but..."

"But what?"

"Let's do this."

Sophia hurried over to the small secretary in the corner of her room and opened a drawer. She took out a pair of paper shears and hurried over to Mae. Sophia grabbed hold of the wide band of lace at the neckline of Mae's dress and started cutting it out.

"What are you doing?"

"I'm showing a little of your bosom."

Mae grabbed hold of Sophia's hands. "You can't do that. I'm a spinster. It wouldn't look right."

"You are a woman, Aunt Mae, and it's time you showed all the gentlemen you are a woman. Now turn me loose. There is nothing wrong with showing a little cleavage, even at your age or at this hour of the day."

Mae let go of Sophia's hands and watched as she trimmed the lace from the neckline, revealing the firm swell of Mae's breasts. Sophia couldn't help but smile because Mae was looking at her chest as if she'd never seen it before.

Mae's eyes widened as she looked up at Sophia. "Do you think Lord Snellingly will notice?"

"Of course he will." *And probably June, too!* Sophia thought. "Watch him. When you first walk back into the room, I know his gaze will fall on your bosom."

"Oh," Mae breathed softly and pressed her open hand over her breasts.

"Don't try to hide them, Auntie."

Slowly she removed her hand, and a look of confidence spread across her face. She asked, "Can you help me with all my other dresses?"

Sophia's heart melted. "Of course, but perhaps we shouldn't take the lace and trim off all of them or Aunt June will be wondering what we are doing."

"You're right. Now tell me, do I need to do anything else?" Mae asked.

Sophia folded her arms across her chest and walked all the way around her aunt, while pretending to look her up and down. She stopped and said, "I can find only one thing wrong."

Mae's eyes widened. "What?"

"You haven't put on your smile."

Mae laughed, kissed Sophia's cheek, and rushed from the room.

After her aunt disappeared, Sophia walked over to the window and looked out at the garden. Every time she saw it she was reminded of the afternoon she spent a few moments in Mr. Brentwood's arms. She'd never experienced anything like those eager feelings of wanting more and more.

She didn't look forward to this process of looking for a husband. It might be more enjoyable if she were free to pick any gentleman she wanted, be he titled, knighted, or just a handsome, intriguing, and engaging man like Mr. Brentwood. She closed her eyes and leaned her forehead against the cool windowpane. If only she could go back and change the past, change what she'd done the night her father had come home excited about the new love in his life. But going back in time wasn't an option. And she had to stand by her word. She couldn't allow these new and wonderful feelings Mr. Brentwood created in her to make her lose sight of the fact that she owed her father.

She owed him for saving her from the fire. She owed him for keeping him from the woman he loved. Her mind drifted back to his frail body lying in bed, gasping for every breath he took. His words still whispered through her mind.

"You must do this for me, Sophia. My money could not buy me a title, but it will buy one for you. With your beauty and inheritance you'll have your preference of the eligible peers. I won't be here to help you, so

promise me now you will marry a titled man and fulfill my dying wish. If you promise me, I know you will do it. Promise me now so I can die at peace, knowing I did my best for you."

That was all he'd ever asked of her. How could she forswear what she had pledged to him that day? She couldn't. She must deny the feelings growing inside her for Mr. Brentwood and live up to that vow.

It wouldn't be easy. Mr. Brentwood was immensely charming. She remembered every touch, every breath, every detail of Mr. Brentwood's kiss. She liked the way he smiled at her and the way he said her name.

"What in Heaven's name are you doing at the window?"

Sophia spun from the window and faced her irritated aunt June. "I was just checking to see if there was a mist. I thought perhaps Lord Snellingly and I could take a walk in the park."

"You will not be doing anything with him if you continue to make him wait. Earls expect young ladies to be timely when they are called on."

"All right." She walked over to her mirror and moistened her lips as she pinched her cheeks.

"Is this your poetry?" June asked, picking up several sheets of foolscap from her desk.

"Yes, but it's really not very good."

"It doesn't matter, my dear. No one would expect

you to write as cleverly as Lord Snellingly. Take it, and let's go."

Sophia took the poetry her aunts had insisted she write and walked out of the room. Much to June's consternation, Sophia took her time walking down the stairs. She stopped at the mirror in the vestibule to look at her hair and face one more time. Finally, she raked the palms of her hands down her dress and took a deep breath before entering the drawing room.

She was pleasantly surprised to see her aunt Mae sitting on the settee with rapt attention while Lord Snellingly stood in front of the fireplace and read to her from sheets of paper he held in his hands. At least this was going better than it had with Mr. Parker Wilson yesterday. That man hadn't tried to hide his displeasure that he'd been left to entertain the chaperone for far too long.

Lord Snellingly stopped reading, and Mae rose when she and June walked in.

Sophia curtsied. "Please excuse my tardiness, my lord."

"It's perfectly all right," he said. He took hold of her fingers lightly and planted a ghost of a kiss to the back of her hand. He couldn't bend his neck very well because his collar and neckcloth were so high. "It gave me time to read some of my latest poetry to Miss Shevington." He held up several sheets of verse.

"That's very kind of you, my lord. Reading poetry is one of her favorite pastimes, isn't that right, Aunt Mae?"

"Oh, yes," she said dreamily. "I read it every afternoon, and at bedtime too."

Sophia glanced at June and saw the surprised look on her face and knew she needed to do something before June caught on to what they were doing. Mae wasn't good at hiding the fact that she was infatuated with Lord Snellingly.

"I brought some of my musings to share with you too."

"Splendid, Miss Hart. A woman who can write inspiring poetry is rare, but I would love to hear your effort."

"Do sit down, Lord Snellingly," June said.

"After you, ladies," the earl said.

Mae started to sit back on the settee, but June whispered, "Heavens have mercy, Mae, the way you are acting you would think the earl was calling on you. Would you please check on the tea for our guest?"

"Oh, yes, yes, I should do that."

"If you don't mind, Auntie," Sophia said, "it's so beautiful out, I thought we might enjoy a walk in the park. Would you be agreeable to that, Lord Snellingly?"

"That sounds like it would be a pleasant outing."

"Aunt Mae, you'll join us, won't you?" Sophia asked.

"Of course."

Sophia turned to June. "And you, Aunt June? You'll come as well?"

June held up her hand and took a step back. "No, dearest," she said tightly. "One chaperone is enough for a walk in the park. Since Mae is so fond of poetry"—she stopped and rolled her eyes around to her sister—"I think she should go. I'll stay here this time."

"Thank you, Auntie."

Little more than an hour later, Sophia was almost in a state of nervous exhaustion. They had strolled the paths in Hyde Park and were on their way out. She didn't know if she would make the fifteen-minute walk back to her house without losing her sanity and suggesting to Lord Snellingly exactly where he could stuff his poetry, and hers too.

She had tried and failed to converse with the earl on a number of subjects that had been talked about in the newsprints, Lord Truefitt's Society column, and the latest accounts—that she hardly understood—about a new revolutionary steam engine. No matter the subject she brought up, he quickly reduced it back to poetry. Sophia was ready to either be done with the man or start pulling her hair out.

Since the earl's verse wasn't having the same effect on Mae as it was on her, Sophia slowly increased her pace until she was walking a little ahead of them. They hadn't seemed to notice.

She heard the thunderous sound of a horse's hooves on hard-packed ground and looked up. She saw a large roan heading their way. Suddenly her heart raced. It was Mr. Brentwood on the magnificent steed. He looked powerful sitting atop the horse, riding with the ease of a man well seasoned to a saddle.

Sophia couldn't take her eyes off him. She hadn't seen him since Lord Tradesforke's party, which had been only four days ago yet it felt like years had passed. She knew the moment he saw her. She smiled and waved to him.

He slowed the horse and let it canter over to where she had stopped to watch him. Mae and Lord Snellingly caught up to her as Mr. Brentwood reined in his horse beside her. The large animal snorted and neighed and lifted his front hooves off the ground in a show of strength before Mr. Brentwood jumped down. He kept a short rein on his horse and swiped his hat off his head. As was custom, he bowed and greeted Lord Snellingly first, and then he spoke to Mae, and then Sophia.

"It's a lovely afternoon to be enjoying the park," he said.

"My, yes," Lord Snellingly said. "We've been reading poetry, enjoying the walk, and talking about everything under the sun, have we not?"

Did the earl actually think they had talked about anything other than poetry? "That's a fine horse you are riding, Mr. Brentwood," Sophia said.

His gaze lighted on her face and held there. "Thank you, Miss Hart. I try to exercise him every day."

"Always here in the park?" she asked.

He nodded. "Yes, and about this time every afternoon. He likes to be on a schedule."

That was good to know. "I don't know much about horses, but I've heard it's good for them to be ridden every day."

"That is why he is so healthy and always eager for a run when I saddle him every afternoon."

She turned to the horse and ran her hand down the wide, flat bridge of his nose. His hair was coarse. Heat radiated from the roan to her hand. "What is his name?"

"Dash."

"Was he given the name because he is fast?" She patted the animal's firm neck, and he jerked his head as if telling her he loved the attention.

"And because he likes to run."

"He's a beautiful horse. Have you had him long?"

"I brought him over from Baltimore with me."

As if knowing he was being talked about, Dash snorted and jerked on the short rein Mr. Brentwood held.

"I can tell he still has a lot of spirit in him," she

said, wanting to think of a reason to prolong the conversation with Mr. Brentwood.

"You know, Mr. Brentwood," Lord Snellingly said, "horses are magnificent animals and feature prominently in many works of poetry."

"I didn't know that."

"Oh, my, yes. I've written some myself. And I've thought about traveling to America for a visit, but I've heard that they are still somewhat uncivilized over there. Do you think I could find poetic inspiration in such a place?"

"I think someone like you could find inspiration no matter where you are."

The earl smiled and sniffed into his handkerchief. "Yes, I think you are right. How long is the voyage? I do have a fear of the seasickness that grips some poor souls. Are the seas unbearably rough?"

"It's best you not plan a trip, if that's the case, Lord Snellingly," Matson said. "The waters can be calm as a stagnant pond for days and then turn violent within an hour."

"That's what I've heard from others. That settles that."

Dash jerked his head, and snorted again. He sidestepped restlessly. "I think he's ready for a gallop down Rotten Row," Matson said. "It was good to see you again, Miss Hart, Miss Shevington, Lord Snellingly."

Sophia watched Mr. Brentwood swing into the saddle, tip his hat to them, and gallop away.

She watched him until he was out of sight. When she turned back to Mae and Lord Snellingly, who had resumed their chatter, she realized she hadn't felt as lonely as she did right now since her mother died, and that was thirteen years ago.

Twelve

Not the cry, but the flight of the wild duck leads
the flock to fly and follow.

—Chinese Proverb

MATSON WATCHED DUST PARTICLES SWARMING
in the late-afternoon sunshine that filtered
through the windowpanes. The drawing room was
quiet except for the one man talking. Everyone
else listened.

Iverson and his lovely bride, Catalina, had
already said their vows to each other, but the vicar
obviously had more to say. Matson's older brother,
Brent, stood next to him, and Brent's charming wife, Gabrielle, was on the other side of him.
Wedding ceremonies always went on too long, as
far as Matson was concerned, and his brother's was
no exception.

Something touched his leg, and Matson looked
down. Gabrielle's dog, Prissy, had gotten bored
with the solemn ceremony, too. The fawn-colored
mastiff was still a puppy, though you wouldn't know
it by her size. She nudged his leg again, hoping he

would take pity on her and take her out to the back garden for a romp. He lowered his arm and patted the dog's big head, letting her know he was a friend and would play with her later. Right now, he must do his brotherly duty.

Matson never could have imagined when he came to London last autumn that both his brothers would be married within the year. But looking at them now with their wives, he knew they were happy. He was glad for them. That's what brothers, even twin brothers, did—they grew up and married.

After the last ceremonial word was said and Matson had offered his congratulations and best wishes to Iverson and Catalina, he grabbed Prissy by the neck and led her toward the back door. He supposed the only wedding he would enjoy would be his own, and he certainly didn't plan on that happening any time soon. He couldn't see himself enjoying more than an evening or two with any of the uninspiring young ladies he'd met so far. But as soon as that thought entered his mind, so did the lovely Miss Hart. He wouldn't put her in that uninspiring group. She was far too direct and lively for that long list.

He had to put her in the category where he'd put Mrs. Delaney all those years ago: the unattainable list. Sophia didn't have a husband in her life; she had Sir Randolph. And that made her just as unacceptable as a married woman. But it didn't keep him from overlooking that fact whenever she was near. When he'd seen her in the park yesterday, his heart pounded so hard in his chest that it ached for an hour after he left her.

As soon as the door was open, the large dog barked once and scampered down the steps. She immediately loped toward the bushes to scratch and sniff and see what she could find. Matson looked around the well-tended grounds and finally found a small limb he could throw for Prissy to retrieve.

Matson chuckled to himself and tried to remember the last time he'd had a dog. It had to have been before he went to America. Dogs could be good friends. He would get a dog when he found a house of his own.

"So Prissy suckered you into bringing her outside?"

Matson turned around to see Brent coming down the steps. It was good to see his older brother again. He'd been at his estate in Brentwood since before Christmas.

"It was Prissy who saved *me*. I was afraid the vicar might start talking again, and I wanted to get out while I could."

Brent laughed. "Weddings are so bloody boring, but there's no other way to get a wife, so what are we to do?"

Matson grinned. "Pay the vicar to make it short?"

"I wish I had thought of that."

Prissy brought the stick to Brent, and he took it and threw it toward the back gate again. The dog barked and went charging after it. "Would you please remember to do that when you get married?"

"That's a promise, Brother."

"Speaking of weddings, have you found a diamond among the bevy of gels that are offered on the marriage mart?"

Matson shrugged casually. "I can't say I'm looking too hard, but there's always hope one will be found when you least expect it, right?"

"Iverson told me about Sir Randolph's ward. Have you seen her?"

"Yes," Matson answered, trying to keep his interest casual.

"You've talked to her?"

"Yes."

"Danced with her?"

Matson knew where this conversation was leading, and he wasn't going to be dragged into it. "Yes, and don't go any further with your questions, Brent. You've asked quite enough."

Brent grinned. "You've answered only enough to make me curious."

"I've answered all you need to know."

"According to Iverson, it appears her arrival in London did one thing you predicted."

Matson frowned. "What was that?"

"It took you and Iverson off the scandal sheets and out of the gossip columns and promptly installed her."

"They're writing about her?"

Brent nodded. "So I'm told. I don't know about you, but Iverson is quite happy she came to Town and took that honor away from the two of you."

Matson remembered the soft taste of Sophia on his lips and the warm feel of her in his arms. Yes, he was happy she came to Town too. He remembered her face in laughter and her trying her best to convince him she would not let him kiss her again. Soon he must show her she was wrong.

"What the devil are my two favorite brothers doing out here in the garden without me?" Iverson said from behind them.

"We didn't want to take you away from your bride of ten minutes," Brent said. "You should be with her."

"I will. I told her I wanted to check on you two and give her and Gabrielle some time to get to know each other. Besides, after that long ceremony, I needed a little fresh air too. I thought the vicar would never shut up."

The three brothers laughed. Prissy came running up to Brent. He rubbed the dog's head and took the stick out of her mouth and threw it. The mastiff went loping after it.

"Tell me," Brent said, "how is the business going? Do you have everything set up yet?"

"Our ships came in about two weeks ago," Matson said, "but we haven't started unloading them yet because we've been trying to find Gabrielle's father."

"Why do you need the duke?"

"That's right, you don't know," Iverson said. "Not long ago we discovered that Sir Randolph owns the space we're leasing at the docks. The last thing we want is to be connected to him. The farther we keep our distance from the old chap, the happier we will be."

"We certainly don't want him thinking we need him for anything," Matson added. "We've been holding off in hopes we could get the duke to recant his edict and allow us to lease space from him or someone else, so we don't have to move our equipment twice. We've been to see his manager and his solicitor, but we can't get either man to talk to us without a letter from the duke giving them permission. And we can't find him."

"You don't by any chance know where the man is, do you?" Iverson asked.

"Not exactly," Brent said. "Why didn't you make me aware before now that you found out you were leasing from Sir Randolph?"

"We only found out a few days before our ships came in. By that time, we'd already sent a letter by courier to His Grace's home. He wasn't there, nor was he at any of the places our man was told he would be."

Brent rubbed his chin, and a thoughtful expression settled on his face. "I'm sorry to say he's not likely to be found any time soon."

Matson didn't like the sound of that. "What do you mean?" he asked.

"The duke received word that his brother was traveling somewhere along the northern coast of Scotland and had an accident. Apparently it was quite serious, and the duke's gone to be with him."

"You don't know where in Scotland?"

"No. The letter Gabrielle received was vague concerning the exact whereabouts of the accident or how it happened. I'm sorry, Brothers. I'll speak to her, and I know she'll do her best to find out for you and let you know."

"That would be good of her," Iverson said.

Sometimes Matson felt as if fate was against their moving back to England. Not only had they had the scandalous story of their parentage to deal with, it had been impossible to get their business started. More and more he was beginning to doubt the move back to England was the right thing to do. Not that Iverson would ever agree with him, especially since he had met the lovely Catalina and made her his bride.

Matson looked at his brother. "As much as I am loathing the prospect of it, Iverson, I think we should go ahead and prepare to unload our ships into Sir Randolph's space."

"I agree. We have no more time to wait for the duke to reverse his dictates concerning us. We have ships to build, and we need to get started on them. I don't think we should waste any more time."

Brent clapped both his brothers on the back. "Enough business talk for today. I should have never brought up the subject. This is a wedding celebration. Let's get Iverson back inside to the lovely Catalina so we can have a glass of wine and toast the bride and groom."

———— I ————

Matson shrugged out of his coat and handed it to the attendant at the front door of White's. He'd cursed the Season all the way to White's. There were just too many damned parties each year. After Iverson's wedding dinner, Matson had made an appearance at three different parties and couldn't find Sophia at any of them. He'd chatted with Miss Craftsman at one party and danced with Miss Slant and another young lady before he said his goodbyes and quit the gathering. It was quite frustrating that he couldn't find Sophia. If he was going to see her, he had to know what events she would be attending each evening.

The place to go when he was in a foul mood was to White's. He didn't immediately see anyone he wanted to talk to or have a drink with. He heard balls smacking together and decided he'd much rather watch a game of billiards, so he headed in that direction to check out who was in the gaming rooms.

All three billiard tables were in use, so he sat on one of the side chairs that lined the perimeter of the room and ordered a glass of port to enjoy while he watched the players. It was good that games were in progress. Matson was too wound up after the wedding and his search for Sophia to play well, and Matson didn't like to lose.

The gentlemen at two of the tables were passable players and having a good time making their shots. The gentlemen at the third table were very good, and it looked as if a serious wager was going on between the two. Matson recognized one of the men as Viscount Hargraves. Matson had seen him talking and dancing with Sophia on more than one occasion. He didn't know the other gentleman, but would have to be on his best game to win if he were playing either man. They were both excellent.

The viscount looked to be Matson's age, and he supposed most ladies would consider him a handsome man. Matson didn't know Lord Hargraves well. Having spent the winter at his country estate, the viscount had come to town only a couple of weeks ago. Being a young, titled bachelor made him one of the most eligible gentlemen in London. It was no wonder Sophia was giving him due consideration, especially when the other eligible peers were Lord Snellingly and Lord Bighampton. Matson couldn't see that she had much of a choice, if what Sir Randolph had said about her marrying a title was true.

Matson's stomach tightened at the thought of her being the wife of either man.

"Good evening, Mr. Brentwood."

Matson looked around to see Lord Waldo standing beside him, holding a snifter of brandy.

"Lord Waldo," he said, wondering if the man expected him to invite him to sit beside him. The Duke of Rockcliffe's youngest brother wasn't a bad fellow. He simply had a talent for always saying the wrong thing. He'd actually had the nerve to ask Iverson why he looked so much like Sir Randolph Gibson. Everyone was thinking it, even gossiping about it, but he'd been the only one crass enough to ask. He hadn't liked Iverson's answer.

"Are you waiting for a game?" Lord Waldo asked.

"Just watching tonight."

Lord Waldo continued to stand quietly beside Matson, watching the players. After a couple of minutes, Matson said, "Would you like to sit down, Lord Waldo?"

His brows lifted in surprise. "Me?" He smiled. "Thank you, Mr. Brentwood, I would."

Lord Waldo made himself comfortable in the opposite chair, and they talked about the three games in progress. Matson didn't really pay attention to his prattle until he caught the words "his pockets are always light."

"Whom did you say?" Matson asked.

"Lord Hargraves. I suppose it's not widely known yet, and I really shouldn't be talking about it. My brother is always telling me I talk too much and I should watch what I say." He took a sip of his brandy.

Lord Waldo's brother was right, but this wasn't the time for Lord Waldo to be judicious with his words. Matson wanted to hear more about the viscount and his money problems.

"Does he have high gambling debts?" Matson asked, trying not to sound too interested.

"From what I've heard, he wins a lot but loses more. Some say he hasn't paid all his debts from the winter house parties."

That wasn't acceptable gambling principles. "What about his income from entailed property?"

"His estates are not as large as one would think, given the title. Whatever acts of valor his forefather did for the King to earn the title and lands must have been slight. His holdings are considered some of the smallest of all entailed properties. From what I hear, as soon as the profits come in, they go out."

Matson watched as the man the viscount was playing handed him a small velvet bag, clearly filled with more than a few coins. They shook hands, and another gentleman picked up a cue stick and joined them. Obviously he'd been waiting to play the winner.

Half an hour later, Matson's glass was empty, and he'd gotten all the useful information he could from Lord Waldo about the viscount, Lord Snellingly, Lord Bighampton, Mr. Parker Wilson, and a few other gentlemen Matson had seen with Sophia. Most of them had called on her, so he could only assume she had some interest in each of them. It didn't add up that if Sir Randolph was going to insist she marry a title, that she accept the attentions of men like Mr. Parker Wilson, who was merely a poor relation of the Duke of Norfolk. She had to be seeing them for her aunt's benefit.

Matson was about to say good night to Lord Waldo, when suddenly a black velvet bag landed with a thud on the center of the small table that stood between Lord Waldo and Matson. He glanced up and saw Lord Hargraves smiling down at him. He had a feeling he knew what the purse meant, but Matson wasn't interested in playing the viscount. He pushed the bag toward Lord Waldo.

Matson rose and said, "This must be yours. Lord Hargraves doesn't owe me anything."

"It's not mine," Lord Waldo said and stood up too, never touching the bag. "I never wager. I'm not good at billiards or card games."

"It's yours, Mr. Brentwood, if you can beat me. I hear you are a natural with a cue in your hand."

"I've been known to hold a stick from time to time, but it's late. I was just saying my good-byes."

Lord Hargraves remained affable and said, "You don't understand. This is a challenge. Gentlemen, come gather round." He motioned with his hand for the other men in the room to come nearer. Several of them walked closer to see what was going on. "I'm challenging Mr. Brentwood to a game. He'll get that bag of coins if he wins, and if I win, I will get his partner for Lord Tradesforke's May Day Fair Day event."

Matson's eyes narrowed, and his skin prickled in defense. What kind of flimflam was this man trying to pull over him? "I don't accept your challenge," Matson said. "I don't need your winnings."

Matson turned to walk away.

"Mr. Brentwood."

Matson started not to look back to see what the man wanted, but did. The viscount's gloves struck him across the face so quickly he didn't have time to react. The offense was so unexpected Matson blinked. Gasps sounded from the onlookers, and suddenly the room went deadly quiet. Anger like he'd never felt before rose up in him. His right hand balled into a tight fist. His eyes and mouth tightened.

"Now you have to accept," Lord Hargraves said

with a smile. "Or you can choose to be considered a coward by all these gentlemen."

Matson didn't mind playing the man, but he sure as hell didn't like being forced to do it by the popinjay's challenge. Matson was a good player, and he was fairly certain he could beat the viscount. He just didn't like what was at stake if he didn't.

Matson studied the man. His eyes were bloodshot, and there was sweat on his forehead. He looked tired. He'd already played three games that Matson knew about, and maybe more. But Matson had had a few drinks too.

"Must we stand here the rest of the night to hear your answer?" Lord Hargraves asked in a loud voice.

Matson wanted to answer by smashing his face in, but decided the gentlemanly thing to do was just beat him at the game. There was no way in hell he was going to let this man walk away with Miss Hart as his May Day Fair Day partner.

Matson picked up the bag of coins, threw them to Lord Waldo, and said, "Hold this for me." He turned to Lord Hargraves and said, "Rack your balls, and let's see what they're made of—my thoughts are they are made of chalk."

"Cotton!" a man yelled.

"Brass!" another man yelled.

Hargraves laughed, and so the game began. Word of the challenge stormed through White's, and soon the room was overflowing with curious men placing their bets. Twice Matson had asked men to step back and give him room to bend and make his shots. His concentration was on the green baize.

In the end, Lord Hargraves's playing wasn't even a difficult match for Matson. The game was over quickly when Matson shot the last ball into the side pocket. A roar of victory went up from some in the crowd, while groans of misery were heard from others as they paid their bets.

Matson laid his cue stick on the rail of the table and walked over to get the bag of coins from Lord Waldo. He then walked over to a sullen and red-faced Lord Hargraves and said, "If you ever challenge me again, it had better be with a sword or a pistol, and you should be prepared to die."

Matson turned and waded through the crowd, receiving cheers and claps on the back as he left the club.

The heavy bag of coins in his pocket suddenly felt very light.

Thirteen

If it were not for the company of fools, a witty
man would often be greatly at a loss.

—François de La Rochefoucauld

SOPHIA WALKED INTO THE BREAKFAST ROOM
where her aunts and Sir Randolph were having their
meal. "Good morning, everyone," she said, feeling chipper. Sir Randolph was just the person she
wanted to see. "I trust all of you slept well."

While she helped herself to scrambled eggs and
small chunks of boiled ham, she heard mumbles of
agreement that their night had been pleasant. Sir
Randolph sat at the head of the table, looking at his
newsprint. Mae sat to his right and June to his left.
Sophia took the chair opposite Sir Randolph at the
end of the table.

"I know you've been very busy, Sir Randolph,
but have you had the time to talk with anyone at
Bow Street about what we discussed last week?"

"What's this about Bow Street?" June asked.

He lowered the newsprint. "Nothing that need concern you, Miss Shevington," Sir Randolph answered.

"I beg your pardon, sir. If it concerns Sophia, it concerns me."

"I only wanted someone to help the authorities look for the boy who stole my mother's brooch, since you will not allow me to go search for him."

"Certainly not. How will you ever get Lord Snellingly or Lord Bighampton to ask for your hand if they hear you have been off chasing thieves?"

Sophia's sunny disposition evaporated. Sir Randolph and her aunts didn't understand how important the return of the brooch was.

"All right, Sophia, you've sufficiently reprimanded me," Sir Randolph said.

"But I didn't mean to sound like I was doing that."

"I know. That was my poor attempt at humor. Why don't I take you to the area of Timsford's Square later today and let you have a look around? We'll stop by and get the constable to send someone with us. If you spot the lad, he can give chase."

"That won't work," June said quickly. "Lord Hargraves is coming at two."

"We'll be back by then, Miss Shevington."

Sophia felt lighter. "Thank you, Sir Randolph. I would very much appreciate your doing that for me."

"It's settled then. We'll go at noon."

Sophia hated pushing her luck. Getting to go back to the square was what she'd hoped for, but she had to ask, "What did you do about the letter concerning the lease and Mr. Peabody?"

"What letter?" June asked.

"Miss Shevington, this does not concern you as her chaperone or her aunt. I never got around to sending Mr. Peabody a letter or drafting one about the lease. We'll visit Timsford's Square today, and then send the letters tomorrow. How does that sound?"

"Like a plan." Sophia smiled at Sir Randolph, but she couldn't help but wonder how he could be so uninterested in her mother's brooch or how her inheritance was managed. How could such a wonderful man, who loved her, care so little about the things that were important to her?

Sophia turned to June. "It looks like there might be sunshine this afternoon, Aunt June," Sophia said. "I think it will be the kind of day that makes one want to take a walk in the park."

The only response Sophia received was a quiet "Mmm."

"I think that's a splendid idea," Mae said. "You know we love to take walks, but we've been so busy getting you ready for the Season, we've gotten out of the habit. It's time to start back."

"Thank you, Aunt Mae."

Sophia remembered that Mr. Brentwood said he exercised his horse every afternoon at the same time. She had missed seeing him at the parties the past couple of nights and was hoping to see him again in the park. She knew it was foolish to spend so much time thinking about him, but she couldn't stop the way he made her feel when he was near. And she couldn't seem to stop longing to see him again.

"That's a large stack of note cards before you."

"Indeed it is," June said, finally looking up at Sophia. "Each day, more and more invitations come in for balls, parties, card games, and some ladies simply want you to come for tea. And I'm happy to report that you have received your first voucher for Almack's as well."

Sophia spread plum preserves on a piece of toasted bread. "See, you had no reason to worry about me being shunned. Sir Randolph saved the day once again."

Ignoring Sophia's compliment giving Sir Randolph his due credit, June said, "We're all simply delighted, Sophia, but I don't know how we can keep up. With all these invitations, we simply can't keep trying to attend every ball, every dinner party, and every event."

Sophia was missing Mr. Brentwood as it was. If they stopped going to all the parties, she might not ever see him again.

"Oh, but I really shouldn't miss any. I have an idea, Aunt June. Why don't you and Aunt Mae take turns going with me? I truly don't need both of you every night. That way you would be going out only every other night."

"Oh, I don't know if we can do that, Sophia. What do you think, Sir Randolph?"

"That is your call, Miss Shevington, and you shouldn't have to ask my opinion. I might have mentioned before that you are her chaperone."

"Well, I've never been—"

Sir Randolph interrupted her. "Furthermore, I will say that most young ladies have only one chaperone and manage quite well to make good matches."

"I think it's a splendid idea," Mae said. "Sophia needs to be out every evening, and most afternoons too, but we don't. I will be happy to go out only every other evening, if that suits you."

"Problem solved," Sir Randolph said.

"It's settled then," June said tightly. "That's what we'll do. Oh, here's a card with your name on it, Sophia. There's nothing on the outside to indicate whom it's from."

"Thank you," Sophia said, laying down her fork. Her gaze immediately went to the bottom of the short note to see whom it was from. Expectancy flooded her chest when she read Mr. Brentwood's name at the bottom. She quickly scanned the paper.

He wanted to see her!

"Don't keep us in suspense," June said. "Whom is it from and what does it say?"

Sophia tried to keep the excitement out of her voice as she read aloud:

Miss Hart,

Would you do me the honor of meeting me at the eastern bank of the Serpentine at half past three this afternoon so we might practice rowing for Lord Tradesforke's May Day Fair Day event?

Sincerely,
Mr. Matson Brentwood.

June huffed. "That man is unbelievable. Imagine him asking you to meet him for such a ridiculous reason, when you hardly have time to fulfill all your social engagements as it is."

Fearful her aunt was going to deny his request, Sophia looked up from the note. "I don't think it's ridiculous."

"I don't either," Mae agreed. "I think it's a very good thing for them to do if they want to win the race, don't you, Sir Randolph?"

Sir Randolph lowered his news sheets and seemed to ponder the question. "I see nothing wrong with it, but I have no idea if it will help them win anything."

"Everything is wrong with it," June announced. "First and foremost, he's not titled and can't even be considered as a possible match for her."

Sophia felt a pang of regret at the truth of her aunt's words. Mr. Brentwood stirred her senses and awakened things inside her that none of the other gentlemen she'd met had even touched.

"I felt the same way about Mr. Parker Wilson," June continued. "Why should we allow her to waste time on someone she will never marry? I don't see the wisdom in letting gentlemen who are not qualified to marry her call on her. She must be more selective."

Sophia, Mae, and Sir Randolph remained silent.

"In fact, Sir Randolph," June said testily, "you should have already done something about this travesty and tried to find her a different partner. It would have been very easy that night while we were still at Lord Tradesforke's house, but I don't see a reason why it can't still be done."

"We've already discussed that, Miss Shevington, and you know I can't do that, nor would I if I could. I'll leave it completely up to Sophia as to whom she wants to spend time with."

"I think you are merely shirking your responsibility. She's been in Society only three weeks, and she needs guidance from you."

"Aunt June, I have some say in this," Sophia said. "I do not want to change partners."

Sir Randolph laid down the sheet of newsprint. "And you are being a tiresome shrew for no good reason, Miss Shevington."

"Ah!" June gasped.

"She's not planning on marrying the man," Sir

Randolph added. "If I had any fear of that, I would step in. This is a harmless outing in a rowboat. Mr. Brentwood has handled it perfectly well by asking that she meet him. You can watch them from the shore and make sure everything is proper."

"Why does anyone need to practice rowing, anyway?" June said, pulling all the cards together and stacking them in a neat pile. "It can't be that difficult. This is just a ruse so he can spend time with her."

"Of course it is," Sir Randolph said. "Almost every eligible man in London wants to spend time with Sophia. I see nothing wrong with that. I'm satisfied that she is committed to keeping her oath to her father. That doesn't mean she is not capable of making her own decisions about whom she sees until she settles on whom she shall marry."

"Which brings me back to the fact that Viscount Hargraves is coming to call on her at two o'clock," June added. "We certainly don't want to hurry his visit, so I don't see how we can possibly make a half-past-three appointment."

"The viscount doesn't need to stay more than an hour. He needs to know that Sophia is sought after by a variety of gentlemen and at times he might have to stand in line to be with her. Being busy can only enhance her possibilities of making the right match."

"Oh, that is a good point, Sir Randolph," Mae

injected. "And I think if she and Mr. Brentwood win, it will make her even more attractive to the titled gentlemen."

June sighed heavily. "I don't understand why I don't get even a thimbleful of help from my own dear sister. Sophia has beauty, intelligence, fortitude, and a fortune. How much more attractive can she be, Mae?"

"Miss Shevington," Sir Randolph said, "you are right. She doesn't need anything else to bolster her attributes, but you need to remember that you are her chaperone, not her jailer."

June gasped again.

"Thank you, Sir Randolph," Sophia said quickly, hoping to stop the antagonizing banter between her aunt and her guardian before it worsened. She didn't know why Aunt June was constantly taking Sir Randolph to task over something. "I'm quite delighted to spend the afternoon rowing on the Serpentine. I'll pick out something warm to wear."

"Which will probably be difficult to do," June said, making no effort to hide the fact that she was miffed. "It looks quite blustery out today. Why couldn't the man have waited and picked a more pleasant-looking day?"

"And if you'll excuse me, I must be going." Sir Randolph rose.

"Me too," Sophia said, leaving her breakfast

half-eaten. "I'll go upstairs now and write a note to Mr. Brentwood, telling him that he can expect us to be there. I'll then get my bonnet and wrap and be ready to go to Timsford's Square as soon as you are, Sir Randolph."

Ignoring her sister's complaining, Mae said to Sophia, "I should like to come with you and help pick out what to wear this afternoon, if you don't mind."

Sophia smiled. "I'd love the help, and from you too, Aunt June, if you'd care to join us."

June lifted her chin defiantly. "Of course I'll come. If you are going to this trumped-up outing, I want to make sure you are properly dressed."

Fourteen

There is no instinct like that of the heart.

—Lord Byron

MATSON STOOD ON THE BANK OF THE Serpentine, watching the carriage pathway that led down to the man-made lake that was fed by the River Westbourne. A brisk wind carrying a late-afternoon chill whistled past his ears, but the waters of the lake had remained relatively calm. The solid wall of gray sky threatened rain, though so far not a single raindrop had fallen.

He hadn't paid any attention to the weather outside when he'd penned the hastily written note to Sophia that morning. Coming on the heels of his win off Lord Hargraves, the only thing that had been on Matson's mind was that he wanted to see Sophia. This ruse was the best he could come up with to get her alone for a few minutes.

He'd been elated when he'd received her response saying that she would come. It was never easy getting past Double and Trouble.

He didn't carry a pocket watch, but he guessed

Sophia was already about ten minutes late. Her aunts may have decided they wouldn't chance the rain. He could hardly blame them. The dreary weather and chilling wind had already driven most of the people away from the park. A few hearty ones sat on blankets, enjoying their picnics, and there were at least three rowboats still on the water.

Not far from the shore, Matson's footman had spread a blanket and placed a basket in the middle of it. His cook had filled it with bread, cheese, and preserved apricots. Matson had added a tankard of hot chocolate with a little sherry added to it, as well as a flask of spiced tea. On either side of the basket he'd placed two low-back chairs. He wanted to make sure the Misses Shevington were comfortable and happy while he enjoyed Sophia's company.

The minutes ticked by. Matson looked down the lonely-looking pathway again. He was fast losing hope of Sophia arriving when, much to his relief, he saw a landau making its way down the stretch of lane toward the bank. He strode over to the carriage and greeted them as it stopped. He helped the Misses Shevington down first, and then reached for Sophia. Even through her gloves and his, he felt her warmth. Just touching her made him feel good inside.

"Oh, my, it's dreadfully windy out here."

"You shall be fine for an hour, Aunt June," Sophia said. "You have on a heavy cloak with a hood, and you have your umbrella."

"Of course we will be fine," Mae said. "Go enjoy yourself, Sophia, and don't worry about us."

"Miss Shevington," Matson said, looking at June, "I brought chairs for you and extra blankets and refreshments to help keep you warm while you wait." He pointed to the blanket he'd spread out for them.

"You did all that for us?" Mae asked.

"The day hasn't turned out as sunny as I had hoped. I wanted to make sure you would be as comfortable as possible."

"Thank you," June said in a more conciliatory tone. "That was very thoughtful of you, Mr. Brentwood. All right, go, off with you. Sir Randolph's footman will help you get Sophia in the boat."

"I'd like to do it alone, Miss Shevington, if you don't mind," Matson said. "No one will be allowed to help us on May Day Fair Day, so we need to do it on our own today as well."

"All right, he can help us get settled," June said. "Now, the sooner you get started, the sooner you can get back and we can be on our way home."

"Yes, Miss Shevington," Matson said.

Matson and Sophia walked down to the water's edge, where the rowboat sat half-in and half-out of the water.

"You look very fetching today, Miss Hart."

"Thank you, Mr. Brentwood."

He studied her for a moment, looking her up and down. "But…"

"But what?"

"But I'd like to make some suggestions on how you should dress for the May Day Fair Day."

Sophia's arched brows lifted. She looked down at the skirt of her muslin dress. Most of it was covered by her heavy black cloak, but the ruffled flounces with neatly tied bows on the hem showed where her cloak parted.

She looked back at him. "All right, I'm listening," she said.

"First, since it's still a couple of weeks away, we will hope for better weather than we have today so we won't have to wear our cloaks. Your dress should be as plain as possible, with no bows, ribbons, lace, or ruffles of any kind that might get caught on something. That would cost us time to stop and free it. Your dress needs to have a fuller skirt and be at least two inches shorter than the one you are wearing today, so when you're walking or running you won't have to worry about tripping over it."

She smiled at him. "Understood, and I'll take care of it." She started to turn toward the boat.

"Wait. There's more. No slip-on shoes like the ones you have on today. They could easily fall off if you are running and cause you to turn your ankle or worse. You need to wear low-heeled, lace-up boots. Probably something similar to what most housemaids wear."

THE ROGUE STEALS A BRIDE   207

Sophia smiled at him again. "All your suggestions sound reasonable, Mr. Brentwood. You are full of information today, aren't you?"

This wasn't his first *fair day*.

He shrugged. "That is what a practice run is for. And I don't want you to get hurt. Just consider them helpful ideas. And, I should add, I intend to be the winner of the rowboat race or any other races I compete in during the event."

"I like to win as well, Mr. Brentwood. Now, help me get in the boat."

"One other thing."

Her brow lifted. "So there's more?"

He humored her with a slight grin. "I'm thinking that most of the ladies will not want to help their partners row. We can go much faster if you do, but of course it's up to you."

"I want to row. I'm strong."

"Good. That's what I thought, so I brought an oar for you and an extra should either of us lose one." He paused. "I'm sure if it's a bright, sunny day, your aunts will want you to wear a bonnet with a much wider brim than you are wearing today, but don't go so wide it will impair your vision."

She gave him a knowing smile. "You are stuffed full of helpful hints today, Mr. Brentwood. Have you done this sort of thing before?"

"I might have done something similar when I lived in America and won one or two rowboat races." He smiled guiltily for a moment and then continued, "Lord Tradesforke might be calling this event the kind of alfresco entertainment people enjoyed in London's parks many years ago, but we had something similar many summer Sundays in Baltimore. I've raced a few boats."

"Did you usually win, Mr. Brentwood?"

He grinned. "Quite often. Now, the boat will be just like it is today. You will step in and immediately step over the first seat and go to the second, sit down, and pick up your oar. As soon as I see you seated, I'll push the boat as far out into water as I can and then jump in. You place your oar in the water on your right side. That's where we'll start."

"Simple enough."

"I will help you get in today, because of your cloak and your shoes." She lifted her hand to him.

And because I'm aching to touch you.

Matson took her warm, gloved hand in his and helped her board the boat. "Leather gloves will protect your hands better," he said, but was glad she had on cotton gloves today.

She did exactly as he told her: stepped over the first bench seat, sat on the one at the back of the boat, and then picked up her oar.

He pushed the boat away from the shore, jumped into the boat, settled himself on the first seat, and looked back at her. "Follow my lead as I move my oar from right to left."

Matson was surprised they had no trouble rowing away from the shore, and once they got underway, he glanced at her, smiled, and said, "That was very good, Miss Hart. You learn fast."

"This is not the first time I have been in a row-boat, Mr. Brentwood."

"What?" His brows drew together. "Then why did you let me ramble on with instructions?"

She laughed softly. "Because I knew it would make you feel good to think you were teaching me something."

"Then perhaps my idea of practice wasn't even necessary for us," he said, setting a course for the center of the lake.

"I think this was an excellent idea. I enjoy being on the water. Besides, this will help me build up my muscles. Though I'm sure I'll be quite sore from this tomorrow."

He laughed. "I'm quite sure of that too. Now, let's see how fast we can row, Miss Hart."

They had been rowing up and down the Serpentine for the better part of half an hour, stopping occasionally for a rest and a bit of conversation, when Matson noticed that the wind had kicked up considerably and the air felt heavy. The water that had been so tranquil when they started was now choppy, causing the boat to rock up and down. They should go in soon. He stopped a good distance from shore and the watchful eyes of her aunts. Matson pulled his oar out of the water and laid it in the bottom of the boat. He swung his feet around on the seat and faced Sophia.

She looked delectable. Wispy strands of hair had escaped the confines of her bonnet. They curled and blew attractively around her face. Her cheeks and nose had a ruddy glow, and her lips were invitingly pink. Matson had a desperate urge to untie the bow of her cape and remove it from her shoulders. He wanted to look at her. He didn't want to imagine the swell of her breasts beneath her dress; he wanted to see it. He wanted to peel off her bonnet and take the pins from her hair. He wanted to see it flowing down her shoulders.

Matson swallowed hard and wondered if she knew just how attracted he was to her. It wasn't just her luscious red hair or her lovely face. He was attracted to everything about her.

"You are beautiful, Sophia."

"I don't see how that can be. I feel quite windblown." She laughed lightly. "Rowing is hard work, Mr. Brentwood, but I do feel quite invigorated."

Suddenly his chest constricted. Matson wasn't fooling himself. She was Sir Randolph's ward. She planned to marry a title. Those were two very good reasons why he needed to keep his hands off her. Spending time with her like this would have to be enough.

"Is there a reason you are looking so intently at me, Mr. Brentwood?"

Matson cleared his throat. "I was thinking you look chilled. We should head to shore."

"No, not yet, please," she said, placing her oar in the boat at her feet. "My nose is cold from the wind. Otherwise I am fine. I'm having such a wonderful time, I don't want to go yet. Can't we sit here for a few more minutes?"

Oh, yes.

"All right," he said, easily giving in to her. "A little longer." He withdrew a flask from his pocket and pulled the stopper out. "This is brandy and will make you feel warm inside. Have you ever had it?"

She wrinkled her forehead. "Of course," she said, taking the silver container from him. "My father allowed me to taste it a long time ago."

Matson chuckled. "Are you sure about that? Did he give you your first taste, or did you take it upon yourself to sneak a sip when he wasn't looking?"

"I believe you have gotten to know me too well in the short time we've known each other. I did have a sip once without his permission."

"I thought as much."

"My reason for doing so was natural curiosity as to what it was that gave Papa, Sir Randolph, and his other gentlemen friends such pleasure that they had to withdraw into the book room after dinner to drink it." She laughed softly, and Matson could see a faraway look settle in her eyes. "You know, I never told my father I had tasted his brandy."

"I don't think you had to. He probably knew."

She quirked her head slightly to the side and asked, "Do you really think so?"

He nodded. "He knew you were an inquisitive child and eager to learn. And I bet you got more adventurous as you got older, didn't you?"

She looked down at the flask in her hand. "Yes. He would not have been upset if I'd told him." She inhaled a deep breath and then took a drink from the flask. "Whew! Oh, my. That burns all the way down, doesn't it?"

Matson laughed. "Especially when you take a big swallow as you just did. Fine brandy is to be sipped like this." He took the flask from her and took a small drink, letting the liquor sting his tongue before sliding down his throat.

"All right," she said. "Let me see if I can do this right." She took the flask and sipped. "Mmm. Much better." She sipped again.

"Perhaps that is enough, Sophia. I don't want the Misses Shevington thinking I plied you with brandy and then had my way with you."

"Aunt June will probably assume that anyway. Look, she's standing on the shore, waving to us." Miss Hart waved back and then took another small drink of the brandy.

Matson twisted around and saw Sophia's aunts

on the shore. Something wasn't right. They weren't just waving. "It looks like they are motioning for us to come in," he said.

"I suppose they think we have stayed beyond our allotted time."

"And we have," Matson said, knowing he didn't want the afternoon to end, but if he was to have any hope that Double and Trouble would let them come out again, he needed to get her to shore. He reached for the flask and popped the cork back into it. "We should head back, or they might not let us practice again."

"We certainly don't want that," Sophia said.

He looked at the shore again and realized that Miss June Shevington was frantic to the point of jumping up and down. She was definitely trying to get their attention. He turned and looked behind him at the opposite shore. It wasn't there. A thick wall of misty fog had completely covered everything in its way and was moving rapidly over the Long Water section of the Serpentine and straight toward them. They were about to be engulfed by the fog.

Matson dropped the flask onto the floor of the boat and said, "Put your oar in the water and row. We have to hurry." He swung his feet over the seat. He picked up his oar and said, "Row fast, Sophia, or the fog is going to overtake us."

He started slicing the oar through the water as

hard and fast as he could, but within moments of starting, the eerie fog had caught them and silently washed over them, covering them with a heavy gray mist. Matson lost sight of the shore and the Misses Shevington within seconds.

He stopped rowing and pulled his oar out of the water and told Sophia to pull hers out as well.

He should have been more diligent. He knew the wind had kicked up, but he'd never seen fog roll in so fast. He turned and looked all around him. There was no marker, no light of any kind to guide them safely to the shore. He tried to remember where the other boats were in connection to them, and he didn't even remember how long ago it was that he saw them. He thought they were still on the water but wasn't sure. He hadn't paid much attention to their position. Had they all gone in? Could he risk continuing to row when his visibility was diminished to the point he couldn't see a blasted thing?

"Damnation!" he whispered under his breath.

"Where did you go, Mr. Brentwood? I can't see you."

"I'm still here, Miss Hart. I have not jumped in the water and left you." Matson looked back toward Sophia. He couldn't see her either.

Matson laid the oar on the bottom of the boat. It was foolhardy to keep rowing when he had no idea which direction he was going.

"We have to stop and drift until the fog lifts or until someone on shore lights a lantern to show which way to go. I didn't mean to strand you out here in the middle of the Serpentine. No wonder Miss Shevington was so frantic. She must have seen the fog sweeping across the water. I'm sure your aunts are not happy about this."

He wasn't happy either. "They are probably swimming their way toward us right now," he said. "Once at the harbor in Baltimore I saw the fog this thick, but I don't remember that it came in so fast."

There was silence.

"Are you all right, Sophia?"

He heard nothing but the wind whipping around his ears and water sloshing against the boat. She hadn't spoken since she said she couldn't see him.

Matson's skin prickled. "Sophia."

He turned around in the seat but saw nothing but gray at the other end of the boat. "Sophia," he said again, his chest tightening in alarm. "I really need you to answer me right now."

Fifteen

What will not woman, gentle woman dare;
when strong affection stirs her spirit up.

—Robert Southey

"SOPHIA." MATSON SAID HER NAME LOUDER AND
with more urgency than before.

He heard movement, and the boat started rocking, dipping precariously from side to side. "Sophia,
what are you doing? Don't stand up."

"I can't see you. Where are you?" she asked softly.

Thank God she'd finally answered him. For
a moment he'd feared she might have somehow
slipped soundlessly into the water. Suddenly the
boat tilted dangerously again.

"No, Sophia, don't move. You're not standing up,
are you? Sit down. You'll tip us over."

Matson knew if she fell into the water wearing
that heavy cloak it would drag her to the bottom of
the river.

"Do you smell smoke? I can't find you."

Smoke?

"No. Stay where you are." Matson didn't even

smell fish or the sea. He certainly didn't smell smoke. He quickly swung his feet over his seat and said, "I'll come to you."

Matson dropped to his knees and cautiously crawled to the other end of the boat. It dipped and swayed as water sloshed up against the sides. The fog was so thick he could barely make out her black cloak as he touched her knee. She threw her arms around his neck, knocking his hat off his head. She buried her face securely in his chest and held him in a tight, frightened grip.

"I'm so glad you found me," she whispered. "I was lost and couldn't see you. Hold me. I can smell the smoke, and I can't breathe."

His arms slid beneath her cloak and round her waist, pulling her tightly against him. She was trembling, her chest heaving dramatically as if she were truly choking and having trouble breathing. Why had she mentioned smoke again?

He quickly untied the bow at her throat and shoved the bonnet off her head. Next he unfastened her cape and shoved it away from her neck. He placed his fingers under her chin and tried to force her to lift her head so she could get air, but she refused.

"I smell smoke," she whispered again.

Matson sniffed in deeply. There wasn't even a faint hint of smoke in the air. Anger at himself rose up in him. He shouldn't have put her in a position of being so frightened, but he had been more interested in Sophia than he was in the weather.

"There's no smoke, Sophia, just fog."

She shook her head. "No, you're wrong. I can't see it, but I can smell it. I couldn't find you."

Matson stroked her back and shoulders, comforting her, reassuring her with the only words he knew to say. "I'm here with you, Sophia," he whispered. "You're not alone. I won't let go of you. There is no smoke on the Serpentine. Just fog. Listen. You can hear the water lapping against the boat. You can feel the rocking, right?"

He heard her hiccup and felt the tremor leave her body.

"But I smelled it. It was choking me. I couldn't breathe."

She tried to bury her face further into his waistcoat. Matson assumed the fog must have prompted a memory from her past. An ache sprouted in his chest.

"But it's gone now." He continued to slowly rub his hands up and down her back, wanting to calm her and chase away the last of her fears. "The smoke is gone, and you're safe. Move down here on the bottom with me," he coaxed. "It will make the boat steadier, and I can hold you closer."

Matson helped her scoot off the bench seat and make herself comfortable beside him on the floor. She never took her arms from around him or lifted her face from his chest. He immediately felt her soothing warmth against him. He felt better knowing that she was in his arms and right beside him. Matson leaned against the corner of the boat made by the junction of its side and the seat. He kept one arm around her waist and slid his other arm around her shoulders.

"Are you cold?" he asked, trying to wrap the ends of his cloak around her too.

"No. I don't know what happened. All of a sudden it smelled just like it had the night I couldn't find Papa."

Matson went still. Sophia had told him that she lost all her mother's things in a fire. Was she in the house when it caught on fire?

"When was that?" he asked cautiously.

"Years ago, but sometimes it seems like it was yesterday."

"Do you want to talk about it?"

"I woke up coughing. I knew something was wrong, so I grabbed my doll and opened my door. Smoke rushed at me the way the fog covered me just now. I couldn't see down the corridor. I couldn't see the door to Papa's room. I called to him, and he didn't answer at first."

A shiver stole over Matson, and he kissed the top of her head. "How old were you?"

"Seven." She rubbed her cheek across his chest. "I started down the hallway, trying to find him. I tried to scream for Papa, but the smoke was choking me. I couldn't breathe. I remember hearing Papa calling my name over and over, but he couldn't find me either."

"How did you get out?" Matson asked.

"I must have fallen to the floor, because I remember he scooped me up in his arms. He buried my face in his nightshirt and held it there. He told me not to look up and that I couldn't breathe until we were out of the house. He was coughing and stumbling. He fell twice as we went down the stairs, but somehow he held on to me, and we finally made it out of the house."

She paused and sighed heavily. "Papa kept me safe from breathing in the smoke, but he had to breathe it in to get us out of the house. His lungs were never the same after that. If I hadn't left my room, he wouldn't have had to spend time searching for me. He seldom had a day where he could draw a deep breath after that."

"Is that the fire where you lost all of your mother's things?"

Sophia nodded. "There was nothing left of the house or anything in it. My mother had died six months earlier. For years after the fire, I had this recurring nightmare where I'd see my mother's dress catch on fire. The flames would eat their way up her dress until she was completely consumed by the fire and the smoke. There would be nothing of her left. Not even any ashes. It was as if she'd never been standing there."

Matson felt as if something squeezed his chest. "That must have been a horrible dream for such a little girl, Sophia. I'm sorry." He bent his head and kissed her cheek several times.

"I hadn't had the dream in a long time, years maybe, until I lost the brooch. Now—"

"Shh," he said and kissed her forehead and cheek again, willing her to feel his comforting embrace. "Don't think about it ever again. You are safe from the fire, safe from the smoke, safe from the nightmare. I don't want you to have that dream tonight or tomorrow night or ever again. Raise your head and look at me." She resisted again. "Come on, Sophia. I want you to see that this is gray fog. It might look like gray smoke, but it's not."

She slowly raised her head. "But I can't see you."

Matson cupped her cheeks in his hands, but in the dense vapor he couldn't make out her features either. "You can feel me, right? You are safe with me."

Sophia nestled closer to him, burying her nose against the bare skin of his neck. Emotions Matson didn't want to recognize stirred within him. He felt her warm breath against his damp skin. He knew he couldn't take the pain of her past away from her, but he would give it one hell of a try to help her bear it.

"How did you manage to save the one brooch?"

"That morning before the fire, Papa let me look

through Mama's jewelry to pick out something for my doll to wear. I liked the flower brooch, so I pinned it to her dress. Somehow I made it out of the house with my doll still in my hands, saving the brooch."

"Why did you have it in your reticule that day on the street?"

"The center stone was missing. I couldn't find it. My aunts and I were taking the brooch to a jeweler to have it replaced. I still can't believe it's gone."

Matson was silent for a few moments. His eagerness to find that boy thief and recover her brooch grew. He held Sophia close, enjoying the feel of her in his arms. He smiled to himself. At first he thought she was safer the closer she was to him, but the way his body was reacting to her, he wasn't so sure that was true.

"Better?" he asked.

"Much better," she said and raised her head again. "I'm sorry. I'm not usually such a weak ninny, but the fog came in so quickly, I felt as if I were in that smoky corridor again, searching for my father."

"Sophia," he murmured softly, "that doesn't make you weak. It makes you human. And you certainly don't have to apologize to me for memories you can't control." He touched her cheek. "Don't think about that night again. You're safe with me."

Suddenly she reached up and kissed him on the

cheek, allowing her lips to linger on his skin for a moment before letting them glide to the corner of his mouth, where she kissed him again. The brush of her lips against his was warm, enticing, and instantly arousing.

The only sounds he heard were his own heavy breathing and the water lapping at the sides of the boat. Matson knew it was going to be damn near impossible for him to stay a gentleman.

"You are entering dangerous territory, Sophia. Are you sure you want to go there?"

"I am sure I want to kiss you, Matson."

"Did you just call me Matson?" he asked cheerfully, hoping to tamp down his growing desire as easily as he'd denied the loving emotions swelling and swirling in his chest.

"When I think about you, I always think of you by your Christian name."

He smiled. "So you are admitting that I cross your mind from time to time."

"More often than you should," she said softly.

"Me too, Sophia," he murmured huskily. "I think of you much too often."

She turned more toward him and kissed the side of his mouth again. His body reacted strongly to her touch.

"How much of the brandy did you drink?" Matson asked.

"Not much, why?"

"I think that could be what is inspiring your kisses."

"I didn't know that drinking brandy makes a person want to kiss."

Matson chuckled but thought about what she'd said. "It's not that it makes anyone want to kiss," he explained, "but if you drink too much, it can certainly cause you to lose your inhibitions so you would be more willing to kiss."

He heard her feeling around on the floor of the boat. "Here is the flask. Take it and see for yourself that I have not had enough brandy to make me tipsy."

Matson felt in the gray mist and took hold of the flask. She was right. "It's still full."

She rested her arm on his chest and leaned over him. "Then drink some brandy, Matson, because I want you to be willing to kiss me."

"Do not try to tease me, Sophia. I don't need brandy to encourage me to kiss you. All I have to do is think about you, look at you, or touch you, and I want to kiss you."

"Then don't make me wait any longer."

Matson had known he was attracted to her the moment he saw her, and that hadn't changed, no matter how desperately he'd wanted it to when he found out who she was. She tempted him as no other lady ever had, and right now he was powerless to do anything other than her bidding.

Matson dropped the flask to the floor of the boat. An urging from deep inside prompted him to hastily remove his gloves and let them fall to the floor of the boat too. He then swung his cape off his shoulders and made a pillow for Sophia's head against the edge of the seat. He'd tried to deny his attraction to her. He had tried to deny her, but every once in a while a man had to go with his instinct, and his was telling him that here on the water, under the cover of thick fog, was the perfect time to kiss Sophia with all the abandon he'd long desired.

He bent his head as he placed his hands on each side of her face, and captured her lips with his. He sought her sweet mouth with his and moaned with pleasure. He kissed her softly and lingeringly at first, taking his time to run his tongue along the seam of her lips, before easing it into her mouth to taste her fully. His hand skimmed down her neck, glided across the top of her shoulder, and drifted down her arm.

She leaned into his chest. Through his waistcoat, he felt her soft breasts pressing against him. He let his lips drift away from her mouth to the soft skin of her neck just under her jawbone, lingering there for a few moments before skimming down to the hollow of her throat. He felt the erratic beat of her pulse against his lips.

He lifted his head and tried to look into her eyes, but it was too gray and misty to peer into their green depths. He managed to make out that she smiled at him. She reached out her hand and cupped the side of his face. Pleasure washed over him.

Her touch was gentle, comforting. "Did my beard scratch your skin?" he asked.

"No," she whispered. "There's so little of it I hardly notice it's there. I just want to touch you."

Keeping on with his slow manner, he took her hand in his and gently, finger by finger, pulled off her gloves. He then pressed his nose into her palm. He breathed in deeply, filling himself with her essence. He planted a kiss in the center of her hand before gently sliding his fingers through hers and linking their hands.

Their lips met, and Matson kissed her again and again, trying to get his fill, hoping his body would tell him "enough" so he could set her from him. But all the endless kisses made him want was more and more. And the way her lips clung to his let him know that she felt exactly what he was feeling.

He plundered her mouth with growing passion and sweet freedom. Each kiss melted into the next, and all he could think was how good, how right, how desirable she was in his arms. He gently laid an open hand on her chest between her breasts, wondering if he should go further.

"Don't be afraid to touch me," she whispered.

The tone of her voice warmed him like flames from an open fire. Heat rose from deep within him.

He no longer felt the breezy wind whipping at his hair or the cold spray from the water on the back of his neck.

"I'm not afraid of touching you," he answered. "I'm afraid only of hurting you."

"I am not worried that you will hurt me. I want your touch, Matson. I want us to be together like this."

The heel of his palm rested on the crest of her breast, and his fingertips played in the hollow of her throat. He slowly moved his hand over one breast and then the other, taking his time to feel her firm yet soft shape beneath the layers of clothing, wishing he could find her nipple. He loved the feel of her breasts in his hand, even though they were hidden by the firm stays and crisp fabric of her dress.

She lay quietly, allowing him to intimately caress her, seeming to know that he was building tension and passion in both of them.

"I want to feel your skin," she whispered.

He chuckled softly. "Oh, believe me, Sophia, I would love for you to. I would love to feel your skin against mine, but that isn't possible."

"Why?"

"This is not the place or the time for such intimacy between us."

"How long do you think the fog will last?" she asked.

"I have no way of knowing."

"Then we must hurry." She started unbuttoning his waistcoat.

"You are treading on dangerous ground once again, Sophia."

"But it is ground I must cover while I have the opportunity."

She pulled the front of his shirt out of his trousers and slipped her hands beneath his shirt, skimming his bare skin. He gasped from the pleasure of her touch. A tremor of arousal slammed through Matson. His skin pebbled deliciously at her caress. His lips fastened over hers again in a provocative onslaught of desire to make her his. He pulled her closer, urging her to fit her softness more fully against the curve of his body.

Matson desperately wanted to feel her smooth skin. She tempted him with her gentle touch, but he knew the folly of trying to undress her. They were under the cover of fog for now, but it could leave as quickly as it had come in. He'd have to make do with the clothing on.

Sophia leaned into their kiss, keeping her hands on his bare skin, causing torrents of desire to shoot through his manhood like fire. He deepened the kiss, and she responded, matching him desire for desire and passion for passion. Her heat drew him, covered him like a warm blanket. Her hands roved over the contours of his bare back. Her touch soothed and yet tortured him, making him want to beg for more. He wanted her to slip her hands past his waist, and suddenly, as if reading his mind, she did.

He kissed her lips tenderly and enjoyed the unrestrained freedom with which she touched him. Matson threw his head back as his muscles contracted in sweet pain.

Matson skimmed his hand down the plane of her hip, and when he brought his hand back up, her dress came with it. He caressed the warm, bare skin of her shapely outer thigh and slowly let his hand slip between her legs. He had no control, because she was so willing and so eager to have him touch her. With a sure, steady hand, he found her most womanly part beneath her undergarments. His lips came down on hers with hard, demanding pressure. Their tongues met. Their breaths mingled. Through her fervent touch and soft feminine sounds, she let him know that she wanted him to bury himself deeply within her, and he was eager to do so.

But the gentleman side of his mind forced him to say between kisses, "Sophia, it's not too late to stop."

"I know. I am aware of what we are doing and what I am asking of you."

He shook his head. "You do not have to ask this. I am eager and ready."

"I've found in my life that sometimes things are worth the risk, Matson."

"And being here with me like this is one of them?" he asked.

"Yes. Please, don't stop touching me, don't stop kissing me. I know there is something more. My body is telling me that we are not finished and there are more wonderful sensations to come."

No further confirmation was needed. Sophia wanted this union between them as much as he did, and she was receptive to whatever he had in mind. That thought sent his imagination into action and aroused him all the more. He hadn't planned this, but how could it be wrong when they both wanted this mating of their bodies?

"How can I deny you?" he whispered.

"As a gentleman, you can't deny a lady her desire for you, can you?"

"No, not this time."

His masculine feelings had never felt so alive, so in command. He had never been so caught up by raw desire for a woman that he was willing to take her on the cold, damp floor of a small rowboat in the middle of the Serpentine, but God help him, right now he was.

Matson desperately wanted to take his time and undress her. He wanted to gaze at her beautiful body and touch her bare, softly rounded breasts. He wanted to pull her nipples into his mouth and savor the taste of her on his lips and tongue, but he knew the folly in that route.

With desires at a fevered pitch, they crushed, clung, and grabbed at clothing, pushing it up, moving it aside, and pulling it down. Matson felt so frantic to possess her that his soul hungered for her.

His tongue plundered the depths of her mouth, and his fingers softly caressed her most womanly part. He felt her body tremble with urgency, and he ached with need. Her lips were soft, damp, and delicious. He found satisfaction in each soft, pleasure-filled sound she made as he touched her. He allowed her hands to go lower and close around his hardness, feel its thickness and weight. He gulped in a ragged breath. Her featherlight caress teased him and offered no mercy to his burning need. A spiraling heat of desire swirled and seared deep in his loins.

"You should be wooed," he whispered against her lips.

"I have no patience with wooing. I want you to show me what my body is yearning for, because no other man has come close to making me feel the way you do."

"Oh, Sophia, that's exactly what I wanted to hear you say."

She arched her hips toward him, and he surrounded her back with his arms and cradled her head in his hands.

"You know," Matson said, "there can be no commitments between us."

"That is the way it has to be."

He rolled on top of her and whispered, "You mustn't cry out if it hurts at first. Sound carries on the water, and I have no idea how close we are to shore."

"I will not make a whisper, Matson."

He then covered her mouth with his and quickly— forcibly— joined his body to hers. She stiffened, and he swallowed the soft grunts and moans she made. He knew it was the easiest and quickest way, but he hated like hell hurting her. After her maidenhead was broken, he took his time and rocked back and forth, kissing her cheeks, her lips, and her eyes. He let his throbbing shaft rest inside her while the initial pain subsided, but he could not contain a low groan of pleasure. It rushed past his lips, and he sucked in a hard, ragged breath.

Slowly he moved a hand between them and found her most intimate part and tenderly caressed her. He needed to build up her passion once again. He wanted to make damn sure she enjoyed their union as much as he did. He found her lips with his and lovingly kissed her as he slowly began to move inside her.

"Sophia," he whispered against her lips, "you are so beautiful, so womanly, and so desirable. I swear to you I have never desired a woman the way I have ached for you. I wanted you beneath me like this the moment I saw you."

"Then why did you take so long?" she asked between choppy, desire-filled breaths.

He chuckled into her mouth. "It is difficult to get you alone."

"My aunts."

"I've named them Double and Trouble."

She tried to laugh at his admission, but her breathing was too erratic. "I don't know what you are doing to me, but I think I'm going to explode."

"Go ahead," he whispered. "That is the joy of what we are doing."

She moaned in pleasure and trembled beneath his touch. Matson smiled against her lips. Her breaths were uneven, but he gently demanded that she participate in what they were doing.

"Help me, Sophia, join me and move with me."

Her arms completely circled his back as she kissed his lips, cheeks, and neck, and back up to his lips once more. He moved slowly, pushing in and out with long, easy strokes.

He moved inside her, and her lower body quickened in response, her hips lifting to meet him with a desperate eagerness, as if to take more of him into her.

Their kisses moved from gentle to passionate to frantic. When she gasped and dug her fingers into his back, he knew he had satisfied her. He couldn't leave his seed inside her, no matter how much he wanted to. He knew where that could lead, and he was not willing to go down that road. He strained to hold himself in check for a few more strokes and then, with willpower that came from an inner strength, he withdrew from her and rolled away as he found his own release.

Matson winced at the pain of the quick withdrawal. He gasped and groaned as his body pulsed rapidly and then started to calm. He lay with his back to her, knowing he wasn't satisfied. He still wanted her. Their coming together had been too fast, too strong, and over too quickly. He needed more of her. He wanted to stretch her on a bed and spend the whole damn night loving her, looking at her, touching her.

He turned back to her. Perhaps there was time for a few more kisses, a few more touches.

He looked down at her and realized he could almost make out her face. Time was short.

Matson sat up in the boat and said, "The fog is lifting. Let me help you straighten your clothing."

"No, I've got mine. You take care of yours."

He stuffed his shirt back into his trousers and rebuttoned his waistcoat while he watched her smooth down her skirts. Her back was to him, so he touched her shoulder. "Are you all right, Sophia?"

She looked up at him and gave him a sweet smile. "I am fine," she said.

"I think we should talk about what just happened between us."

"Why should we? Are you sorry about what we did?"

"No, never," he said, surprised by her response.

"And neither am I. I knew perfectly well what I was doing, so I don't think words about it are necessary. Look," she said, pointing over his shoulder, "there is the blur of a light."

The gray was dissipating quickly. "Finally," he said, forcing his fingers back into his gloves, "a beacon to show us the way to shore."

She touched his arm. "Thank you for chasing all the smoke away."

He expected her to be nervous or shy, but she wasn't. He looked closely at her features, wanting to make sure there were no hidden regrets behind her smile.

He smiled. "It was my pleasure, Miss Hart, but I fear your lips look ravished, and there's a healthy blush to your cheeks."

"No doubt the wind caused it. It's been blustery out here on the water for an hour."

"Do you think Double and Trouble will buy that?"

She smiled again. "I will immediately fall into Aunt June's arms. I'll tell her I'm wet, cold, and near frozen to death, and ask her to please rush me home. She'll not suspect a thing."

"Sophia—" He stopped.

"Don't, Matson. As far as I am concerned, nothing has changed between us."

She picked up her gloves and started putting them on.

"That's not true," he objected. "A lot just changed between us. Something just changed for you. You are no longer a virgin."

She looked up at him with imploring eyes. "I am well aware of that. I knew that when I encouraged you, and I don't regret it. What has not changed is that I am committed to marry a titled man, and I will."

Matson's temper rose. "Then why did you let me touch you?"

"Because I wanted to."

"Is Sir Randolph forcing you to marry a title?"

"No," she whispered and started putting on her other glove. "It was a vow I made to my father while he was dying, and I will keep that vow. That is why I said nothing has changed. It will be as if nothing happened between us. Please."

Matson could argue further or be a gentleman and accept things the way she wanted it. "All right," he finally said. "Nothing has changed between us. That is the way we both want it."

"Yes," she said and picked up her bonnet and placed it back on her head.

Matson helped her fasten her wrap around her shoulders, and then threw on his cloak before moving to his seat at the front of the boat. He picked up his oar and started rowing, feeling very empty inside.

A few minutes later they reached the shore. The footmen were there to help pull in the boat.

"Sophia, we were so worried about you," June said, grabbing her and hugging her as soon as she stepped out.

"Are you all right?" Mae asked, patting her on the back. "You look near frozen to death."

"Yes, I am cold," she said, "but otherwise I'm perfectly fine, Aunties." She glanced at Matson and gave him a shy smile. "Mr. Brentwood took excellent care of me."

"Didn't you hear us calling out to you?" June asked, giving Matson a disapproving look.

"Not in time to make it to shore," Sophia said quickly, not giving Matson time to answer. "It was quite scary at one time, Aunt June. The fog was so thick, I couldn't see my hand in front of my face. I wanted to get close to Mr. Brentwood, but he insisted I stay where I was for fear any movement could cause the boat to tip over and land both of us in the water."

"Oh, my, he was right," Mae said in alarm. "How frightful that would have been."

"It is my fault we were caught in the fog, Miss Shevington. I should have been paying more attention to the skies."

"Indeed you should have," June said.

"But thank you, Mr. Brentwood," Mae said kindly, "for keeping our Sophia safe. I shudder to think what would have happened if Sophia had fallen in the water."

"She was very brave." He smiled at her. "I think what she needs is to get home and have something warm to eat and drink."

"And then I shall be fine," Sophia said.

"Absolutely," June said. "Come, dearest."

Sophia stopped her aunt and looked back at Matson. "Thank you for teaching me how to row, Mr. Brentwood. Perhaps we can do it again before May Day Fair Day?"

Matson's breath leaped in surprise. "I would like that, Miss Hart."

"No, no," June said. "I'm afraid that won't happen. Sophia does not have the time to spend another afternoon on the Serpentine. Her schedule is simply too full."

"Perhaps you can practice for the wheelbarrow race next time," Mae said. "Mr. Brentwood can come to our house for that. You can practice in the back garden, where it is much safer."

"Mr. Brentwood?" Sophia asked.

"I'd be pleased to do that, Miss Hart."

"Good."

Matson helped the ladies into the carriage, said his good-byes, and shut the door. He stood and watched the landau until it was out of sight. The fog had almost completely faded away. Nothing changed except that Miss Hart was no longer a virgin, and while she seemed all right with that when she left, he wondered if she'd still feel that way in the morning. It couldn't be made right.

He suddenly thought about his mother and Sir Randolph. What was it the old man had said to him? *It was something that just happened. We were not in love, and there had been no long, unrequited desire between us. The time and the place were right, and we couldn't stop what was happening between us. That's all there was to it. There was no long affair, no other times, just that one chance meeting that resulted in twins.*

Matson finally knew what the old man meant.

Sixteen

Zeal is fit only for wise men but is found
mostly in fools.

—Ancient Proverb

SOPHIA SAT ON THE WIDE-STRIPED BROCADE
settee in Sir Randolph's house, sipping tea and listening to Lord Bighampton talk about his horses,
his lands, and his latest attempt to see the ill king. It
was easy for her to smile, nod, and show concern in
all the right places. Thankfully, it was quite unnecessary for her to say a word. Lord Bighampton was
happy to do all the talking.

Occasionally, Sophia would look over at her
aunt Mae, who was seated in a straight-back chair
near the fireplace, seemingly enthralled with every
word the earl spoke. They had not had much luck
in getting a gentleman interested in her by inviting
them to call on Sophia. Mae needed to let gentlemen know she was open to being called on, but
Sophia didn't know how she was going to talk her
into doing that when she was determined that June
not know of her desire to be courted.

Because Lord Bighampton required her to say little, Sophia found it easy to let her thoughts drift to a gentleman who was far more intriguing than the earl. Every time Matson Brentwood crossed her mind, her breasts tightened and her lower abdomen quivered. Her chest ached from her heart pounding against the back of it, because she wanted to see him and be with him again. She'd lain awake the past few nights, thinking about their afternoon in the boat. The air was heavy with a damp chill, but she had never felt so warm in her life.

In her wakefulness, she had wondered if she would have been so bold and encouraged him to touch her in such intimate ways if the encompassing fog hadn't forced her to relive the horror of the night her house burned down.

Yes, she had concluded. She had needed to be wanted, to be touched by a gentle hand, and to be reassured that even when life was unfair and took away something loved, it would give something special back to you at another time.

That afternoon she was reminded of how much she'd already lost: her mother and all her belongings, her father, and the right to marry whomever she chose. Sophia couldn't bear the thought of losing the opportunity to have Matson show her how a man desires a woman. That was something she had control of, and she wasn't sorry about her decision. She knew it meant she would not be an innocent for her husband, and in a way, perhaps that was a betrayal of the man, whoever he might be, but she would never be sorry she had that time with Matson.

She hadn't seen Matson at any of the parties she'd been to since the afternoon in the boat. She hadn't seen him at the park either. He'd told her he rode his horse every afternoon at the same time, but he hadn't been there yesterday when she walked in the park with her aunts after a most uninspiring visit with Mr. Alfred Boyd. The man had been so boring, not even her aunt Mae was interested in him.

"What about you, Miss Hart? Were you surprised by Lord Tradesforke's choosing couples for his May Day Fair Day event?"

Sophia cleared her throat and set her cup down on the tray. "I'm still so new to London, I think everything surprises me, my lord. I was just thinking I should send for hot tea. Would you like that?"

"Splendid idea," he said. "Lord Snellingly told me that you like to have poetry read to you. Perhaps you could ask Miss Shevington to speak to your cook about the tea, and if she doesn't mind, perhaps she could look for a book on poetry for me. I would love to read to you." He turned to Mae. "Would you do that for us, Miss Shevington?"

Mae jumped up. "Oh, yes, of course, your lordship. I'd be happy to."

Lord Bighampton rose too. "Thank you, Miss Shevington, so kind of you to be so willing."

"Oh, no," she said, beaming. "Not at all. I know exactly where the poetry books are in Sir Randolph's book room. Did you have a favorite poet? I'm sure Sir Randolph will have it. His collection of books is quite extensive."

"Any of them will do. I'll leave it to you to choose."

"I'll take care of it right now," she said eagerly, already halfway to the door. "And I'll see to the tea too."

"Take your time," he called to her as she walked out of the drawing room.

Lord Bighampton surprised Sophia by sitting down very close to her on the settee. He picked up her hand from her lap and kissed it.

She smiled nervously as she pulled her hand away. "Now what were you saying about Lord Tradesforke?"

"Nothing of any consequence, Miss Hart," he said, and without warning, grabbed her upper arms, jerked her to him, and planted his lips on hers.

Sophia was so stunned at first all she could do was shudder while his lips pressed harder and harder on hers. When she realized what was happening, she tried to pull away from the earl. His big, puffy hands tightened on her arms, alarming her. She flattened her hands on his chest and pushed as hard as she could, but he didn't budge. She twisted her face away from his, but all that did was allow him to kiss her cheek, over her jaw, and down her neck.

She squirmed, and with the palms of her hands tried to shove his full cheeks away from her face as she exclaimed, "What are you doing, my lord?"

"I'm kissing you, my dear," the earl huffed breathlessly. "I know you are an innocent, but surely you know what a kiss is."

Sophia jerked down hard with her arms and broke his hold on her. Wrenching her body to the side, she jumped up and rushed to the other side of the settee, putting it between them.

"How dare you, Lord Bighampton!" she admonished. "You should be ashamed of yourself for forcing a kiss on me."

He rose from the sofa. "Then come willingly into my arms and favor me with another stirring kiss."

Stirring kiss?

"I will not. You are not behaving like a gentleman, my lord."

Lord Bighampton quickly rounded the corner of the settee toward her. Sophia moved at a fast walk in order to keep the small sofa between them.

"I know ladies like to be chased, Miss Hart, but there is no time for that today. Miss Shevington will return soon."

Not soon enough!

"I do not want to be chased," she managed to huff out while she sped around the settee.

"I've already made my intentions clear to Sir Randolph, my sweet cherry blossom, and soon you will be mine."

Sophia gasped. She rounded the corner of the settee again as the earl continued to pursue her. "I know nothing about your intentions. I have not agreed to marry you or anyone else."

"You don't have to," he said, reaching out and grabbing hold of a ribbon on the waistline of her dress.

For a moment Sophia's forward momentum was stopped, and she was yanked backward, but fearing she might be caught in his gripping arms again, she used all her strength to hurl away from him. The ribbon ripped from the fabric of her dress, but she safely darted away from him again.

"Your guardian and I will take care of everything. It's merely a matter of formality, and we will be betrothed. Now, stop scampering away from me and stand still and let me kiss you again before Miss Shevington returns."

"I will not allow you to kiss me again," she said firmly, knowing that if he continued she would have to embarrass him and seek the aid of her aunts to control him.

Winded, Lord Bighampton stopped and held on to the back of the sofa. Sweat beaded his forehead and upper lip. "Stop this nonsense immediately, Miss Hart. I am quite out of breath. You might think it is amusing to lead me on a merry chase, but I do not. Now come let me kiss you."

"Lord Bighampton, was there something you needed from my niece?"

Sophia let out a sigh of relief. She was never so thankful to hear her aunt June's cold, judgmental voice.

The earl spun and cleared his throat loudly. He pulled on the hem of his coat and the cuffs of his shirtsleeves before saying, "No, Miss Shevington. I was just telling Miss Hart that it's time I must be going."

"Very well," June said. "I'll be happy to show you out."

"Thank you," he said and tried to pull the lapels of his coat together, but his large girth made that impossible. "Do say hello to Sir Randolph for me, Miss Hart. Tell him I'll look forward to talking to him soon."

Sophia refused to answer, and for once her aunt didn't remind her of her manners.

The earl lifted his chin unusually high and strode out of the drawing room with her aunt on his heels. Sophia wrapped her arms around herself, suddenly chilled. She couldn't believe she'd actually considered the possibility of making a match with that odious man. She would have to see Sir Randolph as soon as he came in and make sure he knew that she had no designs on Lord

Bighampton and he could not be considered an acceptable match for her.

Sophia walked over to the window, brushed the sheer panel aside, and looked out at the hazy afternoon. Lord Bighampton was stomping toward his carriage. That meant she would soon have to make a choice between Lord Hargraves and Lord Snellingly. Neither man excited her senses.

A wave of sadness washed over her. She was caught in a trap of her own doing. The man she wanted was forbidden to her by her vow to her father. She couldn't break that vow, and she had grave doubts any man would measure up to Matson. She feared the truth was that she had not only given her body to him, but her heart as well.

Mae walked in, carrying a book. "Where's Lord Bighampton?"

Sophia turned away from the window. "Aunt June is seeing him out."

"But I have a book of poetry by John Donne for him to read. I have hot tea coming."

"Mae, where have you been?" June asked sharply as she walked into the drawing room.

Startled by her sister's accusing tone, Mae stuttered for a moment before saying, "I was getting Lord Bighampton a book to read to Sophia, and I asked Cook to bring hot tea."

"You left Sophia alone with Lord Bighampton, and he was not being a gentleman."

"No," Mae said, looking from Sophia to June. "What are you saying?"

"When I walked in, he was chasing her around the furniture, trying to kiss her!"

Mae looked stricken. "He wouldn't."

"He did," June said. "I saw him. Thankfully, Sophia had the good sense to run from him."

"Did he hurt you, Sophia?" Mae asked.

Sophia laughed lightly. "Of course not, Aunt Mae. I'm perfectly fine. I am not in the least injured by his behavior. Aunt June is making far too much of this. But I do think I will mark him off my list as a possible match."

"You don't think you're being hasty, do you?" Mae asked. "He is so handsome and titled. I don't think you can hold it against a gentleman for wanting to kiss you. That's what men do."

"That's quite enough about kissing," June said.

"I agree," Sophia said. "Now, I know we don't have another gentleman scheduled to call on me this afternoon, so would one of you mind walking with me in the park? It's such a lovely day, and I feel the need to be outside for a little while."

"Of course, dear," her aunts said in unison.

"Good," Sophia said. "I'll go change my dress and get my bonnet and wrap."

Matson sat atop his horse and surveyed St. James's Park again. The blue sky and warm afternoon had brought many people out to enjoy a stroll or refreshments. He quickly scanned the faces of the people he could see, hoping to catch a glimpse of Sophia. He'd ridden all over the damn park twice, looking for her. He'd told her he rode Dash every afternoon about the same time. Surely she knew he wanted to see her.

Another oath of frustration whispered past his lips. Except that he hadn't ridden Dash yesterday or the day before because he'd spent the entire day at Timsford's Park, looking for that wretched little thief who had outsmarted him. Matson was determined to recover that brooch for Sophia. He wouldn't rest until he did. He knew if he could find that brooch for her, the nightmares would leave her again.

Much to his dismay, he'd also missed seeing her at the parties he'd attended the past two nights. There were more than a half dozen parties each evening during the Season. He'd had no luck at trying to guess which one she would attend or at what time she would be there. Given how her aunts hovered over her, he would have thought they would be taking her to the larger parties, but if they had, Matson had missed her.

But this morning Matson woke knowing he couldn't go another day without seeing Sophia.

Even if it meant going to Sir Randolph's house again and facing the wrath of Double and Trouble.

He half chuckled to himself. Had he really told Sophia he'd nicknamed her aunts? That wasn't his finest hour, but neither was making love to her in a small boat. But there was no way either of them could have stopped what was happening between them that afternoon on the Serpentine. They had both wanted it. He had no regrets, but what about Sophia?

Did she?

His stomach knotted, and he felt like a fist had lodged in his chest. Was that the reason he hadn't seen her? Maybe she was remorseful. He wanted to see her and find out.

Matson started to knee his horse and make another pass through the park when he saw three women walking about one hundred yards away. His breath caught and held in his lungs. The ladies were Sophia and her aunts. They looked just as he'd seen them that first day on the street: the aunts walking on either side of her, guarding her as the ribbons on their parasols fluttered with each step they took.

He squeezed Dash's flanks and headed the animal toward Sophia, but while about fifty yards away, he saw Sir Henry Braxton stop and talk to them. Matson halted Dash. No doubt the man was another possible beau for Miss Mae Shevington. He would wait until Sir Henry left before he approached them. He could enjoy looking at Sophia when she didn't even know he was around.

Matson knew he was thunderstruck the first time he saw her, and that hadn't changed. When she was around, he was sensitive to every move and every sound she made. Right now he ached to touch her.

She was the most intriguing woman he'd ever met. Something about the way she looked at him with those sparkling green eyes, smiled at him with those gorgeous lips, and took him to task over little matters as well as important things kept him coming back to her when he should run as far away from her as possible. Sir Randolph had made it very clear he would be a part of her life. She was his heir, and Matson wanted no part of that man.

Finally he saw Sophia and her aunts bid Sir Henry farewell, so Matson kneed his horse again. When he was near, Sophia must have heard his horse, because she looked in his direction. She stopped and smiled. Matson halted Dash, jumped down, and walked the horse the rest of the way to them. He tried to look each of them in the eyes when he greeted them, but it was hard to do when he had eyes only for Sophia.

"You ladies look lovely on this warm afternoon," he said.

"Thank you, Mr. Brentwood," Mae said. "We enjoy a walk in the park no matter the weather, don't we, June?"

"We do, but days like this make it especially nice," June added.

He looked at Sophia. "How have you been, Miss Hart? I know you were chilled after our boating. I trust you had no lingering consequence from our being stranded on the Serpentine."

"None whatsoever, Mr. Brentwood. My health is excellent. What about yours?"

"Couldn't be better," he said but was thinking how amazing it was that just being near her lifted his spirits. "I haven't seen you at any of the parties, so I was worried that maybe you had suffered a chill."

"No. I've been at parties every night since our boating."

"So have I. I suppose we just managed to attend different parties."

"It seems that way. I'll be attending parties at Lady Windham's and Mr. and Mrs. Gilbert's."

"Don't forget the Talbots, Sophia," Mae added. "We'll be going to their house first."

"That's right, Auntie," Sophia said, turning to Mae. "There are so many to choose from each evening that it's easy to mix up the names. Did you say we would go to Lady Windham's house last?"

Matson smiled to himself. Now he knew at which parties he could find her and when.

"Oh, my, yes. Her soirée will be the bigger affair, so we'll naturally want to stay longer there."

Sophia's gaze hadn't left his face since he arrived.

He loved the way she was looking at him. He knew that, like him, she was thinking of kisses, caresses, and sweet sighs.

Matson swallowed hard. "You had mentioned that perhaps we could practice for the wheelbarrow race," Matson said. "Is there any chance you will be free an afternoon this week?"

"I'm afraid not, Mr. Brentwood," June piped into the conversation with her usual commanding tone. "Sophia's schedule is completely filled. Since she is new to the *ton*, everyone is requesting time with her. I'm sure you can understand that."

More than she knew.

"We really should be going, Mr. Brentwood," June continued. "Do excuse us."

"Of course," he said, unable to think of anything that might delay them longer. At least he now knew Sophia was all right and which parties to attend this evening in order to see her. "Good afternoon, Miss Shevington, Miss Shevington, Miss Hart."

Matson watched the three ladies turn and walk away. Suddenly he heard a screech and a gasp and saw Miss June Shevington fall to the ground, clutching her ankle. Matson let go of the reins of Dash and rushed over to June.

"Auntie, what happened?"

"June, are you all right?" Mae asked.

"No, I'm not all right." She grimaced. "I must have stepped in a hole and twisted my ankle."

"Let me have a look," Mae said. She went to pull up the hem of June's skirt, but June jerked it back down.

"Please, Mae. You can't pull up my skirt. Mr. Brentwood is right there."

"Oh, hush up," Mae said, "and let me look. Mr. Brentwood doesn't care a fig about seeing your old ankle."

Matson rose. "Nevertheless, I don't want to cause Miss Shevington more anguish. You and Miss Hart look at her ankle and tell me how I may be of help."

Matson turned his back and walked a couple of steps away from the ladies. He couldn't help but wonder what, as he stood and listened to them chattering, had turned Miss June Shevington against men. That woman needed a man to give her a big hug and kiss and take the starch out of her ruffles.

Within a couple of minutes, Matson heard footsteps come up beside him and he turned to face Sophia. "How is she?"

"I don't think it's broken, but she must have given it a good twist. There's no way she can walk home."

"I'll ride to my house and get my carriage to take her home."

"That is what she wanted, but I told her that was foolish. It will take too much time. I said she should let you put her on your horse and walk her home. Is that not the more sensible thing to do?"

Matson smiled. "Yes, and I'm willing to do it, but

I'm not sure Miss Shevington will allow it. I don't think she wants me touching her."

"She doesn't want any man touching her."

His eyes narrowed. "Can you and your aunt lift her onto the horse?"

"Maybe." She smiled mischievously. "But I've insisted to her that we can't. If she wants to get home quickly, she will have to allow you to help her onto the horse. She saw the value in that and agreed you could assist her."

He chuckled. "Then let's get her on the horse and home before she changes her mind."

Matson walked the horse close to June. He told Mae to hold the reins short and tight while he gently helped June to stand.

"Now, Miss Shevington, I will need to take hold of your waist, and on the count of three, I need you to jump up, and I will lift you onto the saddle."

"I understand, Mr. Brentwood. Get to it quickly, and let's get this done."

With little effort, Miss Shevington was cautiously and comfortably settled onto the saddle. Matson led Dash, and Sophia fell in step beside him. Mae walked beside her sister.

"I've missed seeing you, Sophia," Matson admitted.

She quickly glanced back at her aunts. "Shh. You mustn't call me Sophia when they are close enough to overhear."

Matson shrugged. He wouldn't mind shaking up her aunts a little, but he supposed doing it when June's ankle was hurt wasn't the best time to send her into a fit of outrage.

"We are talking very low, and the sound of the horse's hooves is between us. It might help if you walked just a little closer to me."

She looked at him and smiled. "You are a devil at times."

"Does that smile mean you like it when I am a rogue?"

"I'm not sure," she answered demurely. "You know, I've been to the park the previous two days but I haven't seen you."

"I didn't come. I was—busy," he said, realizing at the last second that he didn't want to mention the brooch when it would cause her unnecessary anguish. He never wanted to see her frightened and trembling again, remembering the fire that almost cost her and her father their lives.

"So you don't exercise your horse daily as you said."

Matson grinned. She did like to test him, and he liked that she did.

"I suppose I should I have said I exercise him daily when I don't have more important things to do."

"Oh, yes, I'm sure you have many more important things to do."

"Did you need me for something?"

"No. I was just worried about you and wanted to make sure you were all right."

He chuckled lightly. "Tell me, how is your quest to find Miss Shevington a beau coming along?"

Sophia frowned. "Not well. I can't seem to get any of the gentlemen to pay her any attention."

"I believe I suggested as much would happen."

"Don't remind me you were right."

Matson laughed again.

"If you two would stop laughing and pick up the pace," June called, "we might get home before dark."

"Of course, Auntie," Sophia said before turning to smile at Matson.

Matson's heart tumbled. "Save me a dance at Lady Windham's house tonight, if you can fit me in between all your many suitors and your aunts."

"I can always make room for one more," she said and then laughed, but quickly put her hand over her mouth so her aunt wouldn't hear.

Matson picked up their pace.

Seventeen

That which ordinary men are fit for, I am qualified in; and the best of me is diligence.

—William Shakespeare

IT WAS ALREADY MIDAFTERNOON OF MARKET DAY
in Timsford's Square, and Matson had made several
trips around the area where he'd last seen the boy.
As he had for several weeks now, Matson took his
time and carefully looked at all the youngsters he
passed. He was banking on the hope that by now
the boy would have regained his courage and come
back to the place where he'd been so successful.

Near one end of the square there was a milliner's
shop that had four steps leading up to the door.
The landing was quite large and the perfect place
to watch the square for a while undetected. Matson
leaned against a post, settling in for another long
afternoon of watching people. He didn't mind the
solitude so much because it gave him time to think
about Sophia.

He'd checked in with his manager, and things
seemed to be going well in getting the ships

unloaded and the warehouses stocked. One of his ships would be heading back to America within the month. He and Iverson had decided to keep a business open there to take care of their customers and take orders for new ships, but all the building would be done in England. It would require that either he or Iverson travel back to Baltimore once or twice a year to check on the progress, but they'd agreed it was the right thing to do for the clients who'd helped them build their successful business.

Though he spent some time thinking about Brentwood's Sea Coast Ship Building, it wasn't long before Sophia crowded his mind again. He'd noticed last night at Lady Windham's that she hadn't danced with Lord Bighampton, though he'd seen the earl talking to her and Sir Randolph more than once.

She'd danced with a host of gentlemen, including Lord Waldo's brother, the Duke of Rockcliffe, who'd just returned to London from his winter absence. Matson had made a note to watch the man when he was with Sophia. He'd heard that the duke was notorious for cheating at cards and expected that gentlemen should forgive him because he was a duke. Matson didn't care if he was a duke, the king, or the devil himself; if you couldn't trust a man to play a fair hand, you couldn't trust him with anything else in life, especially a young lady.

Matson had equal disdain for Lord Hargraves,

and when she'd danced with him last night, Matson had to grit his teeth. Thankfully they were dancing a fast quadrille and not the more intimate waltz. Sophia had saved the last dance of the evening for him, and it had been a quadrille, too, but he didn't mind because he'd loved seeing the smile on her face as they had danced.

Afternoon sunshine grew dim and dusk lay on the sky, when suddenly Matson stiffened. All of his senses went on alert. He spied the lad wearing the same clothes and same innocent expression on his face. Matson's diligence had been rewarded; now he had to be careful. He'd be damned if he'd let the little bugger get away a second time.

The lad casually walked around the square, appearing disinterested in all the possible booty before him, but Matson knew better. The boy was studying the people behind all the tables and carts, trying to decide who would be the easiest prey.

Matson took off his hat, gloves, and coat and laid them on one of the steps. If he had to give chase, he didn't want the extra clothing to hamper him. Now that he had the lad in his sights again, he didn't intend to let him get away from him. The lovely Miss Hart wanted her mother's brooch back, and Matson intended to get it for her.

After stopping to pay for a sheet of newsprint, Matson held it up to his face, just below his eyes, and started toward the boy. He moved as fast as he could without causing suspicion. Matson had already discovered the little bugger was fast when he ran. But luck was with Matson when the boy halted before a table spread with sweet cakes, fruit tarts, and sugared biscuits.

As inconspicuously as possible, Matson let the paper drop to a table he passed and then eased up beside the lad and closed his hand around the back of the boy's neck with a firm hold. The lad froze at first, but slowly he turned his head and looked up at Matson. His dark brown eyes told his story. He couldn't believe he'd gotten caught.

"What's your name?"

He blinked slowly again and sniffed before saying, "'Enery."

"Do you have a last name?"

He shook his head.

"What's your papa's name?"

The lad shrugged.

"Mama?"

He shrugged again.

"It doesn't look as if you have much to say, Henry, but we're going to change that. Let's you and I go have a talk."

Holding tightly to the boy, Matson ushered him away from the square and back onto the boardwalk. Most gypsies and street thieves would be squirming and fighting to get away. Henry obediently followed him, as if their meeting were friendly. However,

Matson had mistaken Henry's mild manner before and he wouldn't make that error twice.

He steered Henry over to the steps where he'd left his hat and coat and sat him down on the bottom step, hemming him in with his body. "I'm not letting you go until I get back what you took from me and the lady."

Henry raked his forearm across his dirty nose and then spread his dirty hands palms up for Matson to see. "I don't 'ave anything of yers or anyone else."

Matson smiled derisively. "Let's try this again, shall we? Now we can do it the polite way or the difficult way. It makes no difference to me, but I assure you it will make a difference to you."

"Whatcha mean, mister?"

The little imp was good, but Matson was not going to be fooled by his innocent face again.

"You know very well what I mean. And take my word for it, you won't like the hard way. Now, I want the dagger and the purse back. No doubt you've already turned them over to your parents, so take me to where they are."

The boy kept his innocent gaze fixed on Matson's face and once again shrugged his small, thin shoulders as if he didn't have a care in the world. "I dunno know what yer talking about."

"Then you'd better start praying your memory returns to you quickly, or you'll be spending the night on the cold floor of a dark dungeon without a bite to fill your empty stomach or any hope of being returned to your parents. But if you return what you stole, I'll give you a few coins to buy bread and a tart if you like, and you can go about your merry way."

"I 'ave no help for ye," he said again, his smudged face remaining passively innocent.

Matson had had enough. He reached down and picked up his hat and popped it on his head. He stuffed his gloves in his coat pocket and threw his coat over his arm.

Scowling his displeasure at the boy's indifference to the possibility of a harsh punishment, he said, "Very well, let's go. I'm taking you straight to the constable and telling him to throw you into the deepest dungeon he has and not let you out until you're ready to talk."

He took a firm grip on the lad's upper arm and lifted him off the step and started walking him down the boardwalk.

"Wait, wait," Henry said, straining and pushing against Matson's firm hold.

Henry squirmed, kicked, and hit him, but Matson disregarded his ineffective struggles and kept walking. He had to let the rascal know he meant business or he'd continue to thwart him. "Wait, mister. Wait! Ye can't throw me in a dungeon."

"I can and I will."

"No, please don't do that," he begged, dragging his feet and trying to halt Matson's long strides.

When Matson heard real fear in the boy's voice, he stopped and looked down at him. "Do you have something to say to me?" he asked sternly.

A tear rolled out the corner of one of the lad's eyes and ran down his cheek, cleaning a streak of his smudged skin as it went. Matson's heart lurched. He didn't like what he was doing, but what choice did he have? Obviously the urchin had no one else to teach him a lesson. If he didn't stop stealing now, he would find himself in prison or floating in the Thames.

"I've 'eard it said that a gentleman always keeps 'is word once 'e's spoken. Is that true?"

"It is."

Henry's bottom lip trembled, and another tear slid down his cheek. His eyes riveted on Matson, he asked, "And ye're a gentleman, are ye not?"

"I am."

"If I give ye back yer knife and yer purse, will ye promise to give me the money ye spoke about?"

"You have my word."

The boy nodded once and said, "I'll take ye to where yer things are."

Matson pulled his handkerchief out of his coat pocket and gave it to the lad. "Clean your face, and we'll go."

A couple of hours later, Matson found himself sitting in Sir Randolph's drawing room, waiting to see Sophia. His heart drummed hard and steady in his chest. He couldn't wait to give her the brooch and end her pain of loss. If the nightmares of seeing her mother's dress go up in flames had started again when she lost the brooch, then surely they would stop when it was returned.

He took the brooch out of his coat pocket and unfolded the handkerchief it was wrapped in. It was fashioned in the shape of a flower with a gold stem. The five petals of the flower were covered in diamonds. The larger center stone was missing. He wondered if that had been a diamond, or perhaps one of the colored gemstones. Maybe it had been an emerald the same exact color of exotic green of Sophia's eyes.

If he knew what type of stone had been there, he could have found a jeweler and had it replaced before returning it to her. No, he wouldn't have. He wanted to get it to her as soon as possible, and deciding on a stone and having it set into the brooch would have taken time Matson didn't want to waste. It was already early evening. Perhaps he'd suggest to her that she have the jeweler come to her with his tools and replace it right here in the house, so there would be no chance of losing it again.

He wished they could be alone when he gave it to her, but he knew there was no chance Double and Trouble would let her out of their sight. And it wouldn't be right for him to prolong her agony any longer than necessary by keeping it until he found a time they could be alone.

Matson heard the shuffling of feet and muted voices, so he folded the handkerchief and put it back in his pocket and rose from the settee. The Misses Shevington walked in, with Mae helping June to walk.

He strode toward them and said, "Miss Shevington, may I help?"

"No, no, Mr. Brentwood. My ankle is much better. I am just taking care with it so as not to do more harm."

"She says she's better, but I'm not so sure," Mae said.

"You worry too much, Sister. I'm fine. I just need an extra hand to steady me. Sit down, Mr. Brentwood."

Matson waited until the ladies were seated on the settee before he took one of the side chairs. "I'm glad to hear you're better, Miss Shevington."

"So am I," June said. "I don't like being dependent on anyone to help me get around. So tell me, what can we do for you, Mr. Brentwood?"

"I'd like to see Miss Hart."

"I'm afraid she's indisposed," June said, completely uninterested in his request.

Mae smiled at him. "She's resting before she has

to get dressed for the parties this evening. It's quite taxing on one's constitution to be out every night and so late."

"I'm sure it is, but I won't take too much of her time, if you'll be so kind as to get her for me."

"Perhaps you can see her at one of the parties this evening," June said. "We really can't disturb her now."

Matson knew there would be little chance of getting Sophia alone tonight long enough to give her the brooch. And he wasn't about to give it to her in front of a hundred people.

"You don't understand. I have something to give to Miss Hart."

Both their gazes fell to the handkerchief he pulled from his pocket.

"We couldn't possibly allow you to do that, Mr. Brentwood," June said, leaning back as if she were afraid he was pulling a mouse out of his pocket.

"Yes," Mae said, looking down at the folded handkerchief with surprised eyes. "Perhaps if you'd brought flowers or sweets from that nice little shop down the street, we could have allowed you to give it to her, but that…"

Even before he'd heard their words and saw their disdainful expressions at his undignified offering, he knew they were not going to let him see Sophia. They had no idea what was wrapped in his handkerchief, and they had no desire to find out.

He wanted to say good riddance, shove the brooch in their hands, and be done with Sophia, her aunts, and Sir Randolph once and for all, but his fighting spirit was too strong. He wasn't used to giving up something he wanted so easily, and he didn't want to tell them it was the brooch.

He had found the brooch, and he would give it to her.

Matson just didn't know when or how right now. He slipped the brooch back into his pocket and rose. "I understand, ladies. Don't trouble yourselves to get up. I'll see myself out."

"Oh, but we must," Mae said.

"No, Miss Shevington," Matson said before June had the opportunity to do much more than part her lips. "I insist you stay here with Miss Shevington." When Matson made it to the doorway of the drawing room, he turned back and said, "Excuse me, Miss Shevington, but what kind of stone was in the brooch that Sophia had stolen from her?"

"It was a pearl," Mae and June said at the same time and then looked at each other and smiled.

"Not a very expensive one," June added, "which was why her father had allowed her to put it on her doll. Why do you ask?"

"Just wondering," he answered with a smile. "Good evening, ladies."

Matson placed his hat on his head as he stepped outside. He huffed out a short laugh. He had to hand it to those two ladies. When they set their minds to something, they didn't give an inch.

Much like Sophia.

Now that he thought about it, he was glad they hadn't let him see Sophia. He'd rather be alone with her when he gave it to her. But getting her alone was the problem. Double and Trouble seldom let her out of their sight.

Matson stepped off the stoop and headed down the walkway. He had to think of a way to get Sophia alone. In the meantime, he'd take the brooch to a jeweler and have the pearl replaced.

Eighteen

Lord! I wonder what fool it was that first
invented kissing.

—Jonathan Swift

Sophia had hardly been able to sleep at
all, and she'd been filled with expectancy since
she rose and dressed for the day. Though she'd
tried to tamp it down, she couldn't dispel the feeling of excitement that filled her. Matson wanted
to see her again, and that elated her. She should
instead be thinking about the differences between
Lord Hargraves and Lord Snellingly, and there
were plenty.

Lord Hargraves was younger and more appealing to her senses. He never mentioned poetry, but
she worried that he might not give her the freedom she wanted to continue her involvement in
her father's company. The Season would be over
soon. She knew Sir Randolph would be asking her
to make a decision, but all she could do was think
about Matson. He was the only man who set her
heart to racing every time she thought about him.

He was the only man she wanted to touch her in such an intimate way as he had on the boat.

When he'd seen her at the party last night, he'd asked her if Sir Randolph and her aunts were early risers. He'd smiled when she told him no, and that they seldom came downstairs before noon. He then asked her to meet him in the narrow passageway beside her house at nine o'clock. Sophia had said yes without hesitating.

She went about her usual morning routine without raising any suspicions with the servants, telling her maid that the morning was so lovely she wanted to sit in the garden undisturbed, have her tea, and work on poetry. She dressed in a simple morning dress of robin's egg–blue with sheer long sleeves and a scooped neckline. As was her custom for morning, she pulled the sides of her hair up and away from her face and secured it with a hand-painted comb, leaving the rest to drape down her back.

When she'd finished dressing, it was still half an hour before Matson's appointed time, but Sophia couldn't wait any longer to get outside. There was something about meeting him in secret that made her feel a little bit wicked.

She took one final look at herself, picked up her pencil and foolscap, and headed down the stairs. Mrs. Anderson insisted on helping her get settled in the garden with her tea, the morning newsprint, and her paper and pencil. As soon as the door closed behind the housekeeper, a pebble hit on the stone patio near Sophia's feet. She looked up at the hedge and saw the leaves rustling.

Her heart raced. She rose and walked over to the hedge and pretended interest in looking at the shrub.

"You're late," he said.

Sophia couldn't see Matson through the thick wall of leaves, but said, "I am not, and you know it. I am early, and so are you."

"Does that mean you were eager to see me?"

"Only if it means your haste in getting here was that you were impatient to see me."

"I admit I couldn't wait. I've been here an hour already. Is it clear for you to come outside the gate?"

An hour!

Sophia inhaled deeply. "As clear as it will ever be. I'll be right out."

The gate squeaked when Sophia opened it, but she quickly shut it behind her and walked the few feet down to the pathway between Sir Randolph's hedge and his neighbors', and entered it. She had walked about one-fourth of the way down when Matson stepped out in front of her.

Sophia's heart tumbled at the sight of him. Her stomach quivered deliciously, and teasing warmth tingled across her breasts. Matson was divinely handsome in buff-colored riding breeches, golden-brown waistcoat, and black coat. The shiny knee boots he wore added to his tall, rakish good looks. All she could think was that she hoped he had wanted to meet her so he could wrap her in his strong arms once again and kiss her.

His eyes seemed to devour her for a moment before he said, "Turn around. I've never seen your hair down, and I want to."

Sophia turned her back to him. She felt his open palm start at the top of her head and slowly run down the length of her hair. He lifted its long weight in his hands, and she felt him gently crush it in his fists as his fingers caressed it. Sophia had never had anyone touch her hair with such reverence. She couldn't see him, but she knew he buried his face in a handful of her hair and inhaled deeply. It pleased her that such a simple thing gave him such pleasure.

"Your hair is as gorgeous as rays from the sun, and smells like rainwater."

Sophia laughed. "Rainwater has no smell."

"Oh, but it has," he said. "I knew your hair would be soft and warm in my hands."

"That is because there is so much of it." She faced him, feeling the strands of her hair glide through his fingers as she turned. "I've always wished I had hair as black and shiny as a raven's feathers."

A touch of devilment twinkled in his eyes. "Hair that color wouldn't look good with your freckles."

She smiled. "Well, since I'm wishing, I'll go ahead and wish I didn't have the freckles."

He skimmed a finger across her nose and underneath her eye. "I'm glad you do. I like them. I like kissing them."

His words made her heart soar. "Do you really?"

He nodded.

They were quiet for a moment. Sophia heard a morning dove cooing and the sounds in the distance of carriage wheels rolling over hard-packed ground. Still, all she could think was that if he didn't kiss her soon, she'd have to kiss him.

"Did you want to come see me so we could talk about the May Day Fair Day on Saturday?"

"No. I have something for you, and I didn't want anyone else to be present when I gave it to you."

Sophia couldn't imagine what he had for her, but she was certain that if her aunt June found out about it, she'd force her to return it. She watched him reach into his coat pocket and pull out a handkerchief. He picked up her hand.

"Open wide," he said.

She did so, and he laid the handkerchief in her palm and carefully unfolded it.

Before the last fold was removed, Sophia gasped a shaky "No." Tears clouded her eyes so quickly she didn't have time to blink them away. "My mother's brooch," she whispered without looking up. "You found it. You found the boy."

"Yes."

She looked up at Matson. Warm early-morning sunshine slanted through the tall shrubs and glanced off his face. He was smiling gently. She quickly glanced back down at the brooch again to make sure it was there, that this wasn't a dream or a trick. She laid her other hand over the precious treasure to protect it. Her tears would not be dammed and spilled onto her cheeks.

She sniffed, and more tears of happiness and gratitude followed. She cupped the brooch to her chest directly over her pounding heart. From a clogged throat, she said, "I can't believe I have it back."

She tried to blink away the tears, but all she succeeded in doing was causing more to rush down her cheeks. Quickly, she wiped them away with the back of her trembling hand, but more followed.

"I don't know what to say except thank you. I am—"

Sophia stopped talking when Matson reached up and wiped her wet cheeks with his thumbs, and then dried the rest of the tears from her skin. His touch was tender and sensual. The masculine scent of shaving soap that clung to his hands pleased her senses.

"No more needs to be said, Sophia. Tears of happiness are good," he said softly. "There's no need to erase them all."

"You can't know how I feel right now," she said earnestly.

He smiled. "I have a fairly good idea."

"No, I think I had given up hope of ever seeing it again."

"That's understandable. It's been weeks since it was stolen."

"Sir Randolph took me to the square a couple of times, but he had no patience to wait and watch for the boy." She pressed the brooch tighter to her breast. "Where did you find it? How? Did the boy still have it, or did you find it somewhere else?"

"He still had it. There will be plenty of time for me to tell you all the details later. None of that is important right now." He took her hand and tried to open it, but she kept her fingers closed tight. "May I?" he asked softly.

At first she didn't want to open her hand. She had the brooch and she didn't want to let go, but somehow she knew he didn't want to take it from her. She slowly released her grip and her fingers unfolded. He took the brooch out of the handkerchief and started fastening it to the neckline of her dress. "Did you see I had the pearl replaced?"

"No," she said, embarrassed that she hadn't noticed it. She looked down at his strong, capable hands as he slipped the pin into the fabric and notched it into the catch. "My eyes were so full of tears, all I could see was that it was my brooch. Thank you, Matson. I don't think I would have ever had it replaced if you hadn't done that. How did you know what was in it? I don't remember telling you."

"You didn't. I asked your aunts."

"When?"

"A couple of days ago. I came over immediately to give it to you after I found it, but Double and Trouble wouldn't let me see you."

Sophia sucked in a shocked breath. "They knew you had my mother's brooch and wouldn't let you give it to me?"

"No, in fairness to them, they didn't know what was wrapped in my handkerchief. Don't be mad at them for the short delay. I realized that I would rather be alone with you when I gave it to you. How does it look?"

She looked down at the flower, and a peaceful feeling slowly seeped through her. "Like the most beautiful thing I've ever seen." Her eyes teared up again, but thankfully, this time she checked them. "I'm so happy to have it that I feel I should offer you a reward. I would have paid anything to get it back."

As soon as she said the words, she knew she had spoken without thinking again, and she wanted to bite her tongue. A gentleman would never take a reward from a lady. And the last thing she wanted to do was insult Matson when he'd just given her her heart's desire.

He stepped a little closer to her, and in a soft voice said, "If you offer a reward, I will accept."

Startled that he'd agreed, she quickly said, "Oh, then please name your price. How much would you like?"

He moved closer to her. He looked so intently into her eyes she couldn't have turned away from his penetrating gaze if she'd wanted to.

"I'll take as much as you can give, Sophia."

Sophia tried to remember how many coins she had in her possession. "I don't have much money here in the house, but I can get more later today."

His lips inched closer to hers. "Sophia, surely you know I'm not talking about money."

A warm, shivery awareness eased through her. Matson was too near, his words too provocative. She swallowed hard. "You're not?"

"You know I'm not." His gaze never left hers, but his hand slipped over to her ear, and his fingers caressed her earlobe. "I'm talking about kisses as a reward. How many kisses do you think that brooch is worth?"

"Many kisses," she answered without hesitating.

Sophia's body, mind, and all her senses were so aware of how close Matson was to her that she trembled. He wanted to kiss her again, and that elated her.

"I was thinking the same thing." He took the empty handkerchief from her hand and stuffed it in his coat pocket. "And do you know what else I was thinking?"

She shook her head, wondering what could be more enticing than kisses.

Matson followed the curve of her lips with his forefinger as he bent his head closer to hers. His breath fanned her face when he whispered, "You look like you need to be kissed."

Yes, she had wanted him to kiss her, but she didn't know he could sense that. "I do? I mean, yes, I do."

He gently cupped each side of her face with his palms and placed a kiss on the tip of her nose and her cheek. "You need to be kissed on your cheek." He kissed each eye. "You need to be kissed on your eyes." He kissed her forehead. "You need to be kissed on your forehead and your lips."

She craved the feel of his lips on hers. "Yes, my lips, please," Sophia whispered breathlessly, unable to withstand his slow progress of kisses any longer.

"With pleasure," he answered.

With her heart pounding, she turned her face slightly, and her lips made contact with his in a long, searing kiss that was urgent from the start. It was demanding, fascinating, and desperate. Sophia felt as if she had been starving for this one moment. His hands dropped to her shoulders, and he pulled her gently—firmly—against him. Her arms slid around his neck, and her hands threaded their way through his hair. She eagerly matched his aggressiveness, opening her mouth so his tongue could slip inside, filling her and teasing her with the taste of him.

His hands slid from her shoulders to the swell of her breasts, where he cupped their weighty fullness with his palms. Sophia moaned softly at the intimacy of his touch, and her body quivered in response. Devoid of any apprehension or hesitation, she wantonly kissed him with all the passion that had been building inside her since their last embrace on the Serpentine. She was eager for the same closeness they'd shared that afternoon.

Matson's hands moved down to her buttocks. He cupped them and pressed her tightly against his hard body. His lips left hers, and he kissed his way down her neck and chest. He buried his face between her breasts, rubbing his face first over one mound and then the other. Pleasure grew inside her, spreading warmth all the way down to the center of her womanly core.

"Yes," she whispered and slid her hands down his waist to the hardness beneath his breeches.

His raspy, uneven breathing wafted past her ears as he moved to kiss the soft skin behind her ear. "You must stop, Sophia. I fear you have me on the brink of doing something foolish."

"Then do it," she whispered.

"No. That was not my intention in coming here. I wanted only to give you the brooch in private."

Her breathing slowed a little, but only a little. She knew she was asking a lot of him, but what was she to do? Soon she would have to say good-bye to

Matson and settle for a man she neither loved nor desired so she could fulfill her vow to her father. These stolen moments with Matson were all she would have.

Sophia swallowed hard. "I need to celebrate my good fortune in getting my brooch back." She kissed him again and again, and then said, "What was lost is found. Let me thank you, Matson."

He lifted his head and looked into her eyes. "You have, and you can thank me again another time, but kissing this passionately between us is foolhardy here in this place. Your aunts, Sir Randolph, or the servants could come down this path at any time."

"I know, Matson. I am desperate to kiss you. For reasons beyond my understanding, every time I see you I want to do again what we shared in the boat."

"That is a brave statement, Sophia."

"And true. If I believed in such things as spells, I might be tempted to think you had cast one on me."

He chuckled. "And I might do that if I had been blessed with such capabilities." He straightened and stood away from her. He brushed her hair behind her ear. "It disappoints me as much as it does you, believe me, but I will go before someone comes."

She felt bereft but knew he was being the wise one. She wanted him to linger, so she said, "We didn't talk about Lord Tradesforke's May Day Fair Day."

"Didn't we?" He smiled. "I wonder why. We have five days before Saturday. A perfect reason to return another day and enjoy the early morning, don't you think?"

She smiled. "I think that would be nice. Just let me know which morning you pick."

He touched her brooch, letting the heel of his hand linger against the swell of her breast. "I'm glad you got it back."

"Thank you," she said but realized the words were only mouthed, because her throat was once again too choked up to let the words be heard.

He turned away, and finding her voice, Sophia called to him, and he looked back. "What should I tell my aunts and Sir Randolph about how I got the brooch?"

"Tell them the truth. It was delivered to you by private messenger early this morning."

Nineteen

While man's desires and aspirations stir he cannot choose but err.

—Johann Wolfgang von Goethe

THE END OF THE TREE-LINED PATH CALLED Rotten Row was almost deserted. Matson saw a couple of other riders on horseback ambling along at a slow pace, enjoying the warm late afternoon, but no carriages. Dash had been restless since they entered the park. He'd stop, stomp and paw the earth, and then prance again.

"You're eager for a run, aren't you, boy?" Matson said, patting the horse's firm, warm neck. "I think we can do that. There don't seem to be any pedestrians on the pathway right now. It should be safe enough. We don't want to run anyone down, do we?"

Matson had already made one slow trot around the park, looking for Sophia. He assumed her aunt June was still refraining from her afternoon walks because of her tender ankle, but Matson expected Sophia and her aunt Mae to show. He hadn't seen

Sophia last night, though he'd made an appearance at every party he'd been invited to. After he'd given her the brooch yesterday morning, he'd forgotten to ask which parties she would be attending and at what time.

A warm, good feeling settled over him. It was no wonder he forgot about asking about the parties. They'd shared that heated kiss, which he hadn't expected and he certainly hadn't regretted. She could stir the passions in him faster than any other woman he'd ever been with.

Matson took off his hat and dropped it around the pommel, and then ran his hands through his hair. No doubt about it, Sophia had gotten to him and he couldn't get her out of his thoughts. Maybe both he and Dash needed a good run.

He replaced his hat on his head, picked up the reins, and giving them plenty of slack, he dug his heels into Dash's flanks and the horse took off. Matson leaned low and forward over the horse's neck and let the animal have his head.

Taking the freedom his master gave him, the powerful roan showed off his racing skills in fine fashion. They flew past the other horsemen before the riders knew anyone was behind them. One gentleman yelled for Matson to get control of his animal, but he just smiled and kept allowing Dash to race the wind. He didn't slow the horse until he came to the other end of the path.

Both he and Dash were winded from the exhilaration of the ride.

He patted the roan's neck after they stopped. "Well done, my boy, well done."

Dash jerked his head and snorted, as if to acknowledge Matson's praise.

While Matson let Dash cool down, he searched the park for a glimpse of Sophia or her aunt. He knew her walk and the way she carried herself so well that he could find her even at a great distance away in the park or milling among fifty other ladies on a crowded ballroom dance floor.

Matson shortened the reins. "Come on, Dash, let's walk to the gate where Sophia usually enters."

Just as Matson urged the horse forward with his knees, someone called his name. Matson looked behind him and saw Iverson riding toward him at a fast clip. Matson smiled. It was always good to see his brother.

Iverson reined in his horse beside Matson's. "That was some fast riding you were doing, Brother. I was trying to catch you, but your mount ran off and left us eating your dust."

Matson grinned. "Maybe it's time to buy yourself a new ride."

"Maybe, but if I didn't know better, I'd think hellhounds were after you."

"You don't know better. They might have been nipping at my boot heels."

"Then you're safe. I don't think the hounds can outrun Dash. Where have you been? Brent and I are beginning to think you are trying to avoid us."

"I suppose I am."

Iverson's eyes narrowed. "That's not what I wanted to hear."

"A bachelor can take only so many long conversations about happily married bliss."

Iverson laughed. "You lie, Brother. We do no such thing."

"You come close. And before you ask, no, I'm not free for dinner tonight or any night the rest of the Season. I'm otherwise engaged."

"That's good to know, even though I hadn't planned to ask you to join us for dinner." Iverson smirked in amusement.

"Then that makes us both happy," Matson said with a smile.

"I'm glad you are staying busy. Does that mean a lovely lady has caught your eye and you don't want to miss seeing her for even one evening?"

Iverson had always known him too well. Sometimes it was hell being a twin. "It means I'm busy."

"A new mistress to occupy your time?"

Matson ignored his brother's prying. "So tell me, did you just stumble upon me or were you searching for me?"

"I was looking for you," Iverson said, all teasing

gone from his tone and his features. "This letter was delivered to me this morning." He pulled a folded paper out of his pocket. "I'd rather you handle this. You have a more level head about this kind of thing than I do."

"All right," Matson said. He took the folded sheet and slipped it into his pocket without bothering to open it.

Iverson pointed to the letter. "I think that is something that needs to be handled with haste."

That piqued Matson's interest. "What's it about?"

"Sir Randolph. He wants to void our leasing agreement with him."

"What?" Matson frowned. "He can't do that!"

"Apparently he thinks he can."

"After we've paid for the space for almost six months," Matson said. "Who does he think he is? He has to know that our ships have arrived and we're unloading our machinery and materials."

"Yes, they started yesterday. And yes, I think the man knows every little thing that goes on in London. I think perhaps he just wants to stir up a little trouble and get people to gossiping about us again."

"Then he knows just how to do it," Matson grumbled.

"In the letter, he had the audacity to say that he'd subsidize our lease payments somewhere else for six months."

Matson grunted irritably. His horse stirred restlessly beneath him. "Does the popinjay think we can't pay our own way? If he's trying to insult us, he succeeded."

"I don't know his thinking, Matson, but I have a couple of theories as to what might be behind this."

"They are...?"

"The only reasonable explanation I've come up with is that he has received a better offer for the space and he'll make more money leasing to someone else."

"If he wants more money, we'll have to pay what he asks until we can get in touch with the Duke of Windergreen," Matson said.

"Agreed. We have no choice, and according to Brent, there is no telling how long it might take us to find the duke."

Matson's ire increased. "I never trusted that man to be fair about anything."

Iverson hesitated and then said, "I also have an unreasonable explanation as to why Sir Randolph might want to throw us out of his space."

Matson wrinkled his forehead. "Unreasonable? What are you talking about?"

"You and his ward, Miss Hart."

Matson went still. His horse snorted and pawed the ground. "What could Sophia possibly have to do with this?"

"So Sophia is her name?" Iverson said.

Matson realized his mistake as soon as he said her name, but it was too late to take it back. "This is business and has nothing to do with her."

"For you it's business. I think it might be personal for him."

Matson remained silent, pondering what Iverson had said.

"I hear you are her partner for Lord Tradesforke's May Day Fair Day event," Iverson said, picking up the conversation again. "Maybe Sir Randolph doesn't like the interest you've shown in his ward. Maybe he doesn't want you courting her."

Matson started to say he wasn't courting her, but he was. He just wasn't doing it openly. He agreed that Iverson had a point. A very good point. Sir Randolph was a clever and astute man. He certainly knew about seeing a lady on the sly. This duplicity could be his way of telling Matson to back away from Sophia. If it was, Matson didn't like it.

Matson knew Sophia was bound by a vow to marry a titled man. He tried not to think about that. And he sure as hell didn't want Sir Randolph trying to force him to stay away from her.

Suddenly Matson swore under his breath. Ever since their time on the Serpentine, he had felt like she belonged to him. He had tried not to get involved with her. He'd tried to forget about her, but she was constantly on his mind.

"I think I would be a little more satisfied right

now, Matson, if you were to tell me you have no designs on Miss Hart."

Matson wasn't in the habit of lying to his brother, so he ignored the references his brother made about Sophia and said, "I'll go see the man and find out what he has up his sleeve. I never wanted to lease from him, but now that we have the space, I won't have him trying to throw us out."

Iverson grabbed hold of Matson's reins. The startled horse yanked at the tight hold, but Iverson held firm and stared into Matson's eyes. "You've been with her, haven't you?" Dash yanked his head again and pulled at the short, tight hold. "Speak to me, Brother."

Matson remained calm. "I'm not going to say anything about Sophia," he said more incautiously than he intended.

"You just did."

"Let go of the reins."

Iverson dropped the leathers. "Matson, you know she's already had several offers for her hand, and from titled gentlemen."

An ache started in Matson's chest. "She's beautiful and wealthy. It's expected she will get many offers."

"And her wealth and her beauty will insure that she can pick whomever she wishes, and the rumor is that she will choose a title—Hargraves, Bighampton, or Snellingly."

His brother wasn't helping his feelings. Iverson

knew how to lay it all out with no sweet talk to soften the blow. Matson tried to tamp down the frustration building inside him.

"We both know that Londoners delight in believing rumor over truth. I'll take care of the letter. You go take care of your beautiful bride."

Matson kneed Dash and sauntered away.

———————

Matson hit the doorknocker twice and waited. He never would have dreamed that one day he'd be a regular caller at Sir Randolph's house, but ever since Miss Hart came to town, he found himself coming back to either the front door or the side of the house. He was in an unusually foul temper, and the only way he could think to change his composure was to set a few things straight with Sir Randolph.

The housekeeper he remembered from previous visits opened the door. "Good afternoon," he said, removing his hat. "I'm Mr. Matson Brentwood to see Sir Randolph."

"I'm sorry, sir," she said politely. "He isn't in, and I don't know when he's expected back. Would you care to leave your card?"

Matson smiled at her. "Thank you, no, but I would like to wait for a time, if I may, to see if he returns shortly."

She smiled at him. "Don't mind at all, Mr.

Brentwood. I remember you've been here a few times before."

"Yes, that's right," he said affably, though inside he felt far from it.

"Come in and let me take that hat and coat for you." She laid them on a side table. "Follow me. You can wait in the drawing room for as long as you want. I'll get you some tea."

"Please don't trouble yourself," he said, following the sturdy-framed woman into the drawing room.

"No trouble at all, but I can get you a glass of something stronger, if you prefer."

"No, thank you." He didn't need courage from a bottle to take on Sir Randolph. "Tell me, are Miss Hart and her aunts home?"

"The Misses Shevington went out earlier in the afternoon, something to do with having a new apothecary look at Miss June's ankle, and they haven't returned. Miss Hart is here. Should I ask if she's available to see you?"

Matson's breathing escalated. "Yes, thank you."

Sophia was home without her guards. He bet that didn't happen often. No wonder he couldn't find her in the park this afternoon. Any other day, it would have thrilled him to have a few moments alone with her, but right now he was too interested in getting to the reason for Sir Randolph's rescinding the lease. And though he couldn't put his finger on why, he was upset with Sophia too.

Matson stood in front of the fireplace and chuckled softly. Oh, no, he couldn't lie to himself, even though he wanted to. He knew exactly why he was upset with Sophia. It was her vow to marry a titled man. When he'd first heard that she was bound by such a vow, it made no difference to him. He had no plans to marry her, no designs on her; but somewhere along the way of getting to know her and making love to her in the boat, things had changed. His resolve to befriend her but not get involved with her hadn't worked. She was the most exciting and intriguing lady he'd ever met, and that included his long-ago desire for Mrs. Delaney.

Maybe he did have designs on Sophia. And if he did, he didn't want to be told he didn't measure up because there was no title connected to his name. Perhaps because of Sophia's beauty and wealth she deserved a titled husband. But a title would not make a man love her, be good to her, or watch over her fortune for her. If she wanted a title from England's peerage, she had a fop, a scoundrel and card cheat, and a tired old boar to choose from.

Matson felt like growling. He didn't even want to think about her marrying any of those men. How could she have made such a foolish vow to her father? How could he have asked it of her?

Matson heard a door close. If it was Sir Randolph, he would suggest they go into his book room. He didn't want to take the man to task with Sophia present.

"Mr. Brentwood," she said, walking into the drawing room. "Mrs. Anderson told me you were here to see Sir Randolph."

Matson looked around, and his gaze fell on Sophia. She looked like an exquisitely hand-painted doll. Her lavish golden-red hair was pulled up on the sides and hanging in luscious curls down her back. Her pale lemon-colored frock suited her coloring perfectly.

His body and his heart were telling him she was his, but his mind was telling him she could never be his, and that thought made his words clipped when he said, "Yes, but I found out he isn't here, and neither are the Misses Shevington. I'm surprised they left you alone and defenseless."

Sophia's eyebrows shot up defiantly. "You forget yourself, sir. I am not alone. The housekeeper is here, and I'm never defenseless."

"Ah," he responded. "That's right, your aunts just treat you as if you were."

Sophia eyed him suspiciously. Matson knew he was sounding like a lout, but he couldn't seem to stop himself. It was her fault. Her connection to Sir Randolph and her vow were the reasons she could never be his.

"That is their job," she said calmly. "And mine is to allow them to do their job properly, and as you know better than anyone, I sometimes acquiesce to their rules and sometimes I don't." She walked closer to him. "You are tense. Something is wrong?"

A hell of a lot is wrong.

"I need to talk to Sir Randolph," he said, sensing he needed to leave. He was fighting emotions for her that he preferred not to deal with at the moment. "I'll go to White's. Maybe I'll find him there."

"You would probably miss him. He usually comes home about this time every afternoon to rest before he gets dressed for the evening's parties." She walked closer to him, concern etched across her face. "Matson, what has you in such a state?"

He didn't want her concern. "It's a business matter, Sophia," he said irritably.

"Well, sir, I would have you know that I *know* more about business than Sir Randolph does." She gave him a teasing smile. "It's a good thing his father left him well set because he doesn't know anything about reading ledgers and looking over account books to make sure he's not being cheated."

Matson had no doubt that she was smarter than the old man. He saw no harm in telling her what a scoundrel Sir Randolph was, so he said, "He sent a letter canceling a lease agreement my brother and I have with him."

Her eyes widened a little. "Oh, is that what this is about? I can help you with the lease on the dock space. What do you want to know?"

Matson frowned. "You know about it?"

"Yes," she said confidently. "The company is actually owned by my father—that is, by me now. Sir Randolph handles everything as my trustee and guardian. It's logical that anyone would assume the company is his."

"But we are not leasing from Shevington Shipping. We would have recognized that name," Matson said, trying to make sense of this new information.

"My father had companies in many different names. Shevington is the largest and came from my mother's family."

Matson's ire grew. "My brother and I are leasing our warehouse space from you? You knew this and didn't tell me?"

A worried expression settled on her face. "I only learned that you had the lease after I found out who you were."

His eyes narrowed, and he took a step toward her. "And you didn't think that was information I would like to know?"

"I don't understand why you are upset about this," she said, lifting her shoulders a little higher. "How could I possibly know that you didn't know or that it would matter to you?"

"Did you know Sir Randolph was canceling our lease?"

"I suggested it."

Matson was stunned. He hoped he'd heard her wrong. "What did you say?"

"It was my idea. I don't understand why you find this so shocking. London is my home now. I want to move my father's company from Southampton to London. I knew we had the warehouse space to accommodate all our shipping supplies, so I talked with Sir Randolph about doing that."

This was incredible. "So you decided you'd just throw out Brentwood's Sea Coast Ship Building and take it for yourself?"

"No, it wasn't like that," she said, standing her ground. "Sir Randolph said that he thought you would be agreeable to canceling the lease because you didn't want the space. He said you had been looking for other accommodations ever since you leased it. He also added that you've put nothing in it."

"What does it matter to you or him whether or not there is anything in the space? We have paid the rent. Our ships have been in the harbor, waiting to be unloaded, and in fact that started yesterday."

He saw her swallow hard. Matson knew he was being unreasonable, but he couldn't seem to stop himself. He had expected something like this from Sir Randolph but not from Sophia.

"I thought I would be helping you. If you wanted other space, I thought the kind thing to do would be to help you get out of your lease with us."

"You did this to be kind to us? You think we need your kindness? Did it dawn on you that the reason we haven't moved is because we have been looking for other space but haven't found it?"

Sophia's shoulders and chin lifted as her eyes narrowed. "I happen to know that there are plenty of other warehouses available to lease, Matson," she said, her voice rising a little. "Perhaps you are just being too difficult to please."

Matson huffed out a laugh. If only she knew how many times they had tried to lease from someone else. If only she knew how difficult it was to find the duke.

"So you think I am being difficult?"

"Well, aren't you?"

"No, I'm not. And furthermore, we're not giving up the space, Sophia. If you want to move your business to London, I suggest *you* lease one of the many spaces available."

Her eyes flashed brightly at him. "I'm happy to find other space so I can show you just how easily it can be done."

"You do that, Miss Hart. No, wait, maybe your name isn't Miss Hart. Maybe it's Miss Heartless, or maybe it's Miss Cold Heart."

Sophia gasped. Hurt mingled with anger and filled her eyes. Matson's gut twisted.

"You are absolutely right, Mr. Brentwood. I am not often called Miss Hart by gentlemen. I am usually called Miss Sweetheart. Now, I believe it's time for you to leave."

Matson started to say he was sorry for suggesting she was heartless and coldhearted, but in the end he simply walked past her. He picked up his hat and coat on his way out the door.

It was better this way, he told himself as he hurried down the steps. Things had become too complicated between them. He knew Sir Randolph's ward wasn't the lady for him, and he should have stayed away from her.

He was glad she had vowed to marry a titled man. That was just what she needed. In fact, he'd see what he could do to help her with that.

Twenty

Some persons do first, think afterward, and
then repent forever.

—Thomas Secker

MATSON STOOD IN LORD SNELLINGLY'S DRAW-
ing room, looking out the window. How could twilight look so beautiful when he felt so wretched?
He had to do this. There was no other way.

He couldn't believe that Sophia was the one who
really owned the warehouse space, and that *she* had
wanted to kick them out of it. He had to hand it to
her. She had more nerve than most men. He had
ignored his gut feelings for Sir Randolph because
she was so charming.

Matson sighed heavily. It was downright hellish
how attracted he was to her. But he'd known from
the moment he found out she was Sir Randolph's
ward that he needed to stay away from her. He'd
allowed himself to be fascinated with her. He had
been lured by her sweet innocence and compelled
by her broken past. Ever since that afternoon in the
rowboat, he'd been haunted by the feeling that she

was his in a way that she would never be another man's. He was the first for her, and he couldn't forget that.

He'd gone to Timsford's Square nearly every day for weeks trying to recover her brooch. And how had she rewarded him? By wanting to throw him out of the warehouse. Matson shook his head and chuckled ruefully. His abominable temper wasn't because he'd learned she owned the warehouse or that she had written the letter. It wasn't even really because of Sir Randolph. It was her vow to marry a title. That was her oath, her honor. He couldn't fight that and win. Life had to be lived by a set of principles. Matson believed a person was only as good as their word.

Getting her completely out of his life was the right thing to do. The faster the better.

He thought he could handle his feelings for Sophia the way he'd handled his feelings for Mrs. Delaney all those years ago. The problem was that Mrs. Delaney played by the rules. Sophia did not. She tempted him in ways that Mrs. Delaney hadn't, and he hadn't been able to resist Sophia.

Right now, this was the only way he could think of that would make her want to turn away from him. He couldn't give her up willingly. He had to have her help, and this was the way to get it. He'd see how she liked rowing the boat while Lord Snellingly read poetry to her. She'd probably be the one pushing Snellingly in the wheelbarrow too. And she would probably never speak to him again.

"Mr. Brentwood, this is an unexpected call, but I'm always delighted when anyone cares to visit. How are you this fine spring day?"

Matson turned away from the window. "Good, my lord. You?"

The earl picked up several sheets of writing from one of the chairs and sat down. Matson hadn't noticed when he first walked into the drawing room, but it was littered with papers strewn over the settees and chairs. Quills and open jars of ink sat on every table.

"Splendidly good, sir. Sit down, sit down. I've asked my housekeeper to see that tea is brought in for us. I can put a spot of something stronger in it for you."

"Tea will be fine," Matson said, knowing that he really needed a brandy but would wait until he returned home. "I have a favor to ask of you, Lord Snellingly."

"Well"—he sniffed into his lace-edged handker-chief—"I must say that doesn't surprise me. People often want favors from me, you know. I'll tell you what I tell them all. You may ask, but I make no promises about what I can do for you."

What a fop.

"I understand that, my lord, and you will get no argument from me if you are not agreeable."

"Perfect, then, go ahead and ask."

The man sniffed again, and Matson couldn't help but think the man would breathe easier if he wouldn't wear his collar and neckcloth so high and tight on his throat. Matson had never paid much attention to the earl and hadn't noticed how much Lord Snellingly looked like a baby bird who had its neck stretched out and its mouth opened wide to receive food from its mama.

"Not long ago you asked if I would exchange partners with you for the May Day Fair Day that Lord Tradesforke is hosting in Hyde Park."

"Yes, of course, I remember. Quite well, in fact. You told me that you had no desire to give up your lovely partner. I completely understood. I wouldn't have done it either."

"That's how it was at the time, but now I find that I need to change partners with you. Does your offer still stand?"

The earl blinked rapidly. "Ah—well—yes. Yes, indeed it stands, but why would you want to?"

"I'd rather keep my reasons to myself."

"Yes, I understand that, but I'm partnered with Miss Craftsman, you realize."

Matson knew.

Lord Snellingly cleared his throat and sniffed. "I mean, the lovely Miss Craftsman. She tries hard to appreciate good poetry, but she simply doesn't have it in her soul to do so." He put his hand over his heart. "But Miss Hart. My heart. She is like a beacon of light."

One corner of Matson's mouth lifted in a half smile. "Some of us are like Miss Craftsman, my lord. It would be a great help to me if you would agree to the exchange."

"Yes, yes, I already have," he said, laughing. "I'll agree again now before you can change your mind."

"Good. If you'll send the lovely Miss Craftsman a note telling her that things have changed and I will now be her partner, and I'll do the same for Miss Hart."

"Gladly. I'll do it today. Right now. As soon as you leave."

Matson rose. "You do know Miss Hart adores poetry, don't you? She would probably love it if you recited some deep, meaningful poetry to her during the rowboat race."

Lord Snellingly's brows lifted, and his eyes shone brightly. "Yes, I think that would be just the thing to win her heart. I'll be sure to have plenty of poetry for her."

"We'll consider it done, then. Thank you, my lord."

Lord Snellingly stood up. "Don't you want to stay for tea? Perhaps you might help me pick out some poetry that will be fitting for Miss Hart."

"I'm sure you can do that much better than I, and I have other things to see to this afternoon.

I'm certain you will fill her head and her heart with your words."

When Lord Snellingly had shut the door behind him, Matson closed his eyes and took in a long, deep breath. It was settled. He was rid of her. She'd never speak to him again after this.

But for some reason he didn't feel as good as he'd expected to. There was no relief, only an empty feeling inside him. But what else was he to do? Her vow left him no choice in the matter.

He would get over her. He did what was the best thing for him and for her. And of all the titled men seeking her hand, Lord Snellingly was the best one for her. He wouldn't gamble away her inheritance like Lord Hargraves. He wouldn't bed her just once or twice, get her with child, and then send her off to live in the country the rest of her life. And Matson was sure he'd never be cruel to her.

Matson felt as if he'd been punched hard in the stomach. There was one other thing Lord Snellingly wouldn't do. He wouldn't make her feel the passion Matson had made her feel.

Matson's hands made fists at his sides as he started down the stone walkway.

God help him. Already he was wishing he hadn't made the trade.

Twenty-one

Who brought me hither will bring me hence;
no other guide I seek.

—John Milton

THERE WAS NO PLEASURE INSIDE SOPHIA AS SHE
sat at her dressing table to finish dressing for the
parties she had to attend later in the evening. She
didn't know how Matson could have misunder-
stood her so badly about the warehouse.

And why had it made him so angry?

He could have the space as long as he needed
it. Shevington Shipping had been in Southampton
for many years and could stay there until other
arrangements were made. There was no hurry to
get it to London. She wished she knew what parties
he was attending so she could find him. She wanted
to make things right with him.

A light knock sounded on her bedchamber door.
"Come in," she called and picked up a pearl earring
to fasten to her ear.

Her aunt Mae rushed in and quickly closed the
door behind her and locked it. She kept her face
toward the door and her back to Sophia.

"What are you doing?" Sophia asked when she didn't immediately turn around or say anything.

"I'm thinking."

"About what?"

"That I need to find my courage," Mae said.

Sophia smiled and attached her other earring onto her ear. "Do you think you will find it on my door?"

"No. It's inside me, but I haven't seen it in so long that I'm not sure I know where it is."

Sophia's hands stilled at her aunt's odd words. "Is something wrong, Auntie?"

Mae slowly turned around, holding her arms crossed over her upper chest with her fingers splayed. Her eyes were wild with panic.

Sophia rose from her dressing stool. "What has happened? Is something wrong with Aunt June or Sir Randolph?"

"No, it's me."

"What?"

Mae lowered her arms to her sides, and revealed the extremely low-cut gown she was wearing.

"Oh," Sophia breathed softly. The scooped neckline of the sheer, ruby-colored gown was one of the most revealing Sophia had seen all Season. The high waist fit snug under Mae's breasts, helping to lift them up to pop from beneath the neckline. Sophia was sure that only the most daring of ladies would wear a gown cut that low.

"Well, what do you think?" Mae asked.

Sophia hesitated. "I think that dress is reve— ravishing. Yes, it makes you look ravishing."

"Oh, I thought so too when Mrs. Franco first showed it to me," Mae said with a beautiful smile of relief as she rushed closer to Sophia. "Do you think it will make gentlemen finally take notice of me?"

"Yes, yes, they will notice you," Sophia agreed.

"You don't think it's too low, do you? I've seen other ladies, highborn ladies, wear them cut this low."

Sophia started to say yes, maybe it was a little too daring, but when she saw the hope for approval in her aunt's eyes, she knew she couldn't take that away from her. And after all, she was the one who had cut the lace from Mae's neckline a couple of weeks ago.

"If you want to be noticed by all the gentlemen at the parties tonight, then this is the dress for you. You look young and stunning, Auntie."

Mae beamed. "I've had a fichu made to cover it until I can get out of the house, so June won't see it. She wouldn't approve."

Sophia was certain of that. Suddenly Sophia took her aunt's hands and said, "Come sit on the window seat with me. I want to talk to you."

"All right."

They settled onto the velvet-covered seat, and Sophia said, "I've been pondering this for the past few days. I think it's time we told June that you want

Sir Randolph to make it known that you would be amenable to gentlemen calling on you."

Mae pulled her hands out of Sophia's and leaned away from her. "Oh, no." She shook her head. "I couldn't do that. You know I can't do that."

"You must, Auntie. What we have been doing is not working. We have tried to get the gentlemen who call on me to engage with you, but we haven't had much success."

"No, that's not true," Mae argued. "They all talk to me and smile at me once in a while. They all enjoy hearing the story of mine and June's birth. Well, maybe not that Mr. Parker Wilson, but he was such a stuffy prig. And he isn't that handsome anyway, is he? But all the others have been kind."

"Yes, but they came here expecting to call on me. Not you. They won't develop designs on you because they don't know that you are available to be courted."

"It may not be working yet, but it can. It will," she said enthusiastically.

Sophia smiled indulgently at her. "Look at how splendid you look in your opulent red dress, Aunt Mae. With your three strings of pearls around your neck and the lovely white feathers in your hair, you will be the belle of the ball. You have lived June's life for years, and it's time you came out and lived your own life."

"Oh, I want to," Mae said excitedly. "I just don't want her to know."

Sophia decided to try a different tactic. "What

would you do if you found a beau? If he came to call on you, June would know. You couldn't hide him from her."

"Hmm. I hadn't really considered that." She seemed to think on it for a moment and then said, "I know. I could meet him in the park."

"You know that won't work. June walks with you to the park each day."

A knock sounded on the door. "Sophia, dear. Are you dressed?"

Mae jumped off the seat fearfully and whispered, "Shh. Don't answer her."

"I have to answer," Sophia whispered. "She knows I'm in here."

"No, she can't see me in this dress. You must do something."

"Sophia." The doorknob turned, and then the door rattled. "Sophia, is your door locked? Sophia?"

"Don't," Mae mouthed.

"Just a minute, Aunt June," Sophia called. She turned to Mae. "It's time you found that courage you were looking for earlier."

Sophia walked over to unlock and open the door.

"What are you two doing in here with the door locked?" June asked, relying heavily on her cane as she walked into the room.

Sophia turned back and saw that Mae had grabbed a pillow from the window seat and clutched it to her chest.

"We were just having a chat about gentlemen," Sophia said, hoping to encourage Mae to be truthful with her sister.

"And you needed to lock the door for that?" June asked and then made her clucking sound.

Clearly June was thinking there was more to the story. Sophia looked at Mae, who stood wide-eyed and rigid with fear.

"You look lovely, Sophia," June said. "I approve of the dress you chose. And what do you have on, Mae? I don't recall seeing that shade of red among your gowns."

"No, it's new," Mae said, her eyes looking glassy with guilt.

"Then let me see it."

Mae timidly walked around in a tight circle to show June the back of the dress, but she didn't lower the pillow.

"It's lovely. I wouldn't have chosen that dramatic ruby shade for you, but I think it goes well with your coloring."

"Thank you," Mae said stiffly.

"Since I'm not going tonight, why don't you wear my black velvet cape. The one with the velvet ribbon and jeweled neckline."

"That would be nice. I think I'll do that. I'll go get it right now."

Mae walked past June, and as she did, June reached out and grabbed the pillow, saying, "Don't take Sophia's pillow with you, silly— Good heavens, Mae! What do you have on?"

"I don't know," Mae said, seeming terrified.

Sophia wanted to stay out of the conversation, knowing it was really between her aunts, but felt compelled to say, "Tell her, Aunt Mae."

Mae remained mute and shook her head.

"Tell me what?"

"Nothing. I'll just go to my room and change."

"Aunt Mae wants a beau," Sophia said, not knowing if it was her place to say it, but June had to know.

"A what?" June asked and wrinkled her nose as if she were looking at a soiled piece of laundry.

"She wants to be courted by a gentleman, Aunt June."

"Well, she can't," June said, lifting her chest, her shoulders, and her chin defensively. "I won't allow it."

Sophia looked at Mae, wondering if she was going to bow to June's commands once again or stand up for herself.

"Sister," Mae said quietly, "in this you have no say."

"Of course I do," she said emphatically, clearly affronted Mae had the gall to question and defy her. "Now go take off that dress and put on something appropriate for your age and place in life to take your niece to the parties."

Mae promptly stomped toward the door, and Sophia's heart dropped. But all of a sudden, Mae stopped and turned back to June. "No, not this time, Sister. Tonight I will wear what I want, and I want to wear this gown."

June's bottom lip quivered. "You can't wear that. It's…it's too revealing and downright scandalous. That gown won't get you courted, it will get you bedded."

"Then that will be all right too," Mae said.

June gasped.

Sophia felt triumphant.

"No," June demanded. "I can't allow you to be hurt that way. You don't know how painful it is."

Mae looked confused. "I don't intend to get hurt. I intend to enjoy myself."

"But you will be hurt. Men will tell you how beautiful you are and how much they want to kiss you and touch you, and then when you let them, they won't ever call on you again."

Sophia saw tears gather in June's eyes, and her heart broke for her strong, unbending aunt. So there was a man in June's past.

A faraway expression settled over June's features, and Sophia knew the years were rolling back for her.

"It was our first Season. You remember Mr. John Phillip Bailey, don't you, Mae?"

"Yes," Mae whispered softly, inching closer to her sister.

"He was so handsome, so dapper, so dashing.

And he thought I was the most beautiful young lady he'd ever seen. And I was beautiful, wasn't I?"

"You were gorgeous, Sister."

June smiled sadly. "We danced and chatted at every party. And when we went into the garden, I let him kiss and touch me so many times. And it was so wonderful." June closed her eyes for a moment, and slowly the expression on her face changed from serene into a bitter frown. "But after all we had shared, he decided he wanted someone else."

"Why did you never tell me?" Mae asked affectionately.

"I couldn't. No one ever knew, but when he rejected me and told me he was going to marry someone else, a titled man's daughter, I almost ended my life that night."

"No," Mae said in earnest, her gaze never leaving her sister's face.

"Yes, I did. I thought long and hard on it, but I didn't end my misery and heartache. I suffered through it, and I still endure it every day—because of you."

"Me?" Mae asked.

"Yes, I lived so I could keep you from making the same mistakes I made. All these years I have shielded you from the hurt and the anguish of being used and rejected." She pounded her fist over her heart. "I did that for you."

Mae stepped closer to June. Sadness clouded

her eyes. "And I appreciate all you have done for me."

"Then prove it," June demanded harshly. "Take off that dress!"

"No, June, that time has passed." Mae inhaled deeply. "I might be hurt. I might even be deeply wounded one day, but I can't be hurt until I have loved. I want to know what it's like to love a man."

June huffed bitterly. "Then go and wear your revealing gown and have all the men gawking at you—and at your age! It's shameful. But don't come running home to me when your heart is broken, because I won't be here for you."

June turned and hobbled from the room. A few seconds later, Sophia heard a door slam down the corridor.

"What have I done?" Mae said.

"You helped your sister face a past she didn't ever want to see again."

"Do you think she will ever forgive me for making her tell that story?"

"Of course," Sophia reassured her aunt. "I think she will pout for a few days, but she will come around. I'm willing to bet she loves you more than she hates her past."

"I wonder why she never told me she had been hurt so badly that she almost ended her life. I thought we shared everything."

"It was obviously something that was very hard for her to bear."

"But I could have helped lighten the load for her," Mae said sympathetically.

"And you will. You already have. She no longer has to carry that burden alone now that you know."

"I hope you're right."

"Do you think we should pass on the parties and stay here with her tonight?" Sophia asked.

Mae studied over her suggestion. "No. That might make her think I have weakened. I must admit I am tempted to take off this gown and stay here with her. But I need to go out tonight and wear this dress for me."

"All right." Sophia smiled. "I'll meet you downstairs in a few minutes."

Mae kissed her cheek and hurried out the door.

Sophia sat back down at her dressing table and smiled. Mae certainly knew how to get Sophia's mind off her troubles with Matson. She was even more eager to find him and clear up their misunderstanding.

"Miss Hart?"

Sophia looked up and saw the housekeeper standing in her doorway.

"This was just delivered, and the man said he was told it must be given to you straightaway."

"Thank you, Mrs. Anderson."

Sophia waited until the woman was gone before she opened the card and read:

Miss Hart,

I have spoken with Lord Snellingly. He and I have agreed to change partners for Lord Tradesforke's May Day Fair Day alfresco event on Saturday. He will meet you at the park at the appointed hour and be your partner for the day.

Mr. Brentwood

Sophia's heart broke.

Twenty-two

The course of true love never did run smooth.

—William Shakespeare

IT HAD TAKEN SOPHIA TWO DAYS, BUT SHE HAD finally gotten mad at Matson.

How dare he trade her for the beautiful Miss Craftsman, with her clear olive skin and hair as dark and shiny as a raven's feathers. And of all the gentlemen in London to trade her to—Lord Snellingly!

If Matson hadn't wanted to attend May Day Fair Day with her, he could have at least changed with the younger, stronger Lord Hargraves so she would have had at least a chance of beating him in the rowboat race. The only way Sophia could imagine Lord Snellingly in a rowboat was with a servant doing the rowing while he read poetry. The only other worst possible choice would have been the amorous Lord Bighampton.

She had tried to refrain from wondering if Matson had taken Miss Craftsman for a practice session on the Serpentine. The only thing she could hope was that there hadn't been enough time.

Sophia took out the last dress hanging in her wardrobe, looked it over, sighed, and then threw it on top of all the others she had piled high on the bed. She had morning dresses, day dresses, and carriage dresses, but none of them seemed appropriate for the kind of dress Matson had described for a day of excitement and activity in the park. Her aunts had successfully seen to it that every piece of clothing she had was adorned with lace, ribbons, bows, or buttons, with many of them having a combination of all four.

She knew Matson was right when he'd told her that dresses adorned with elaborate sewing notions were simply too fancy for outside games and frolic. Sophia was strong and determined, and even with Lord Snellingly as her partner, Sophia planned to be respectable competition for Matson and all the other people in the rowboat race. And she intended to enjoy herself and not even look at Matson should he dare come near her.

Standing with her hands on her hips at the end of the four-poster bed, she studied the mountain of garments in front of her. The May Day Fair Day was tomorrow. She had to make a decision. She would go through them all again and decide which one would be easiest to remove the trim, and then do it herself. If she mentioned it to her aunts, they would surely insist that Mrs. Franco should come and do it for her. Sophia couldn't bear the thought of more endless hours standing on that woman's seamstress stool.

Sophia started her search again and finally picked up a dark gray morning dress with short, puffy sleeves. The black bows on the hem of the sleeves and at the jewel neckline should be easy enough to remove, and so would the wide sash that tied in the back. She held the dress up to her. She also needed to make the hem of the skirt shorter, and that would be the difficult thing for her to do, but do it she would.

"What are you doing?"

Sophia turned toward the doorway and saw her aunt June, leaning on her cane and staring at all the dresses heaped on the bed. Sophia moved in front of the pile of clothing in hopes of keeping it from looking so rumpled.

"Good morning, Aunt June. You're up early."

"That's because I've been going to bed earlier since I haven't been able to attend any of the parties due to my ankle."

June hadn't lost the sauce in her voice since she had revealed her past to Sophia and Mae two nights ago, and she hadn't softened her stern expression any either.

"I'm trying to decide what to wear tomorrow for the May Day Fair Day in the park."

"Why didn't you tell me you need a new dress? I'll call for Mrs. Franco to come at once. She can make the dress just the way you want it. She is a wizard with patterns, and her workers are fast."

"There really isn't time for that, Aunt June. I'm sure this dress will be perfect if I take off the bows and shorten the hem. I'm used to doing the finer stitchery with an embroidery sample, but I think I can handle a sturdier sewing needle."

June walked farther into the room. "Well," she said cautiously as she looked over the dress in Sophia's hands, "I could help you with that if you would like. I have the time."

Surprised, Sophia said, "That would be lovely." Sophia didn't mind her aunt helping, she just didn't want her taking over. She explained to June what she wanted done to the dress.

"Give the dress to me. I'll do it for you."

Sophia continued to hold the dress in front of her. "I don't want to bother you to do all of it. I can help."

"Don't be ridiculous," she said, taking the dress from Sophia. "It's never been a bother for me to do anything for you. Besides, it will make me feel useful. I used to be quite handy with a sewing needle."

"You did?"

"Yes. You know when your mother, Mae, and I were young girls, we only had one maid, not three or four like most homes have today. Our maid had all she could do just taking care of the cleaning and cooking. We girls, your mother included, had to take care of our own mending."

Sophia felt a quickening in her stomach. "I would like to hear more about that time, Auntie."

June's shoulders relaxed a little, and Sophia saw a hint of a smile. She saw a softening in her aunt, and she was drawn to it. Suddenly Sophia knew that her aunt was going to be fine.

"All right. I'll do this for you right after breakfast. You can watch me to make sure it's done just the way you want it, and I'll tell you more about your mother's childhood."

"Thank you, Auntie."

"I'll go put this in my room and meet you below stairs in a few minutes."

Sophia walked down the stairs and into the breakfast room. Sir Randolph was sitting at the head of the table, reading his newsprint. "Good morning," she said.

He folded the paper and laid it aside. "Is that a smile I see on your face?"

Sophia showed him an even wider smile as she walked past him and over to the buffet. "You sound like that surprises you."

"It does. The last two days, you've been walking around here like you'd lost your best friend."

"I woke this morning and decided I was not going to let Mr. Brentwood keep me from enjoying the day tomorrow."

THE ROGUE STEALS A BRIDE

"That's the way to be."

"Will you be going to the May Day Fair Day?" Sophia asked, helping herself to scrambled eggs, cheese, and scones.

"I wouldn't miss it. I'm sure Lord Tradesforke has worked hard to make it very entertaining. Though, you know members of the *ton* don't need much of a reason to have a party or a good time. Tell me, did you ever find out if Mr. Brentwood was the one who found your mother's brooch for you?"

A pang of sadness and regret stabbed through Sophia. She was glad her back was to him, because the smile quickly faded from her face. She couldn't let him know how deeply she felt about what Matson had done. She couldn't let anyone know.

"Yes, but he didn't give me any details."

"You know what Mr. Brentwood did was the best thing for you. He needed to step aside and let you continue with what you need to do. The Season is more than half over."

Yes, she knew, but she didn't want to face it. She would put on a happy face as she did this morning and be brave for all to see, but she felt wretched and empty inside.

Sophia placed her plate on the table and saw an envelope with her name on it. For a fraction of a heartbeat, she thought perhaps it was from Matson, telling her he was sorry and she would be his partner after all. A closer look at the writing told her it wasn't from Matson. The large fanciful script writing was from Lord Snellingly's hand. She pushed the note aside and sat down.

"Aren't you going to open your letter?"

"No," she said. "Lord Snellingly sent me three notes yesterday and all of them were filled with poetry he'd written for me. I can't read any more of it."

"You know the earl will be the best one for you to make a match with, don't you?"

Sophia's stomach tightened as she looked up at Sir Randolph. She didn't want to think about the fact that she needed to decide on a man to marry, so she remained quiet.

But Sir Randolph didn't. "I know Lord Hargraves is younger, more handsome, and probably more to your liking, but I would have doubts about his handling of your inheritance."

"Why is that?" she asked, pouring herself a cup of hot chocolate.

"I'll just say that he's known to be free with his own inheritance, so I wouldn't want to trust him with yours. He gambles without setting boundaries or control. I fear the bigger his pockets, the bigger his borders will be, if you know what I mean."

Yes, she knew what that meant, and that wasn't the kind of person she wanted to be in control of her father's company.

"You know, Sophia, your father didn't want me

picking a husband for you, he wanted me only to guide you. He wanted the man to be your choice. He never wavered on that point."

"My choice as long as he is titled, Sir Randolph," she said.

"Yes. He never wavered on that either."

"Good morning, Sir Randolph," June said when she walked into the breakfast room.

"Miss Shevington," he said and picked up his newsprint, stuck it in front of his face, and went back to his reading.

"Would you like me to help you with your plate, Auntie?" Sophia asked.

"I'm crippled, not helpless. I can manage it."

Sophia spread butter and plum jam on her scone while she thought over what Sir Randolph had said. There was no way she was going to consider Lord Bighampton. She didn't want to spend her life being chased around the settee, or being isolated at his country estate. She agreed with Sir Randolph. Lord Snellingly would be the most likely husband to give her the freedom she desired so she could continue to help oversee her father's business. But could she live with his incessant need to write and read his poetry to her?

And what about his touch? He had never tried to kiss her, and when he touched her hand while they were dancing she felt no spark of desire, no craving to see him or touch him or to be with him like she felt every time Matson crossed her mind.

She laid her scone down without having taken a bite. Lord Snellingly's poetry was the least of her worries. Could she ever let him touch her after Matson? Her only hope was that she could find some measure of solace in Shevington Shipping.

"You have a note by your plate, Sophia," June said when she took a seat at the table. "Aren't you going to read it?"

Sophia sighed. "I can tell by the writing that it's from Lord Snellingly, and I don't want to read more of his poetry right now. I will let Aunt Mae read it. She seems to be enthralled with every word he writes."

"May I?" June asked.

"Of course," Sophia said and pushed the card toward her.

"Sophia, this isn't poetry," June said. "Something has happened."

Sir Randolph lowered his paper. Sophia's heart sped up again. "What? Did Matson ask for me to be his partner again?"

"Matson?" June and Sir Randolph said at the same time.

"Oh, I'm sorry, Aunt Mae, Sir Randolph. I think of him by his first name sometimes. Just tell me, am I to be his partner?"

"No, but neither will Lord Snellingly be your partner. Shall I read it to you?"

"Yes, please," she said, wondering if the entire event had been canceled.

June read:

My dearest and most lovely Miss Hart,

I regret having to tell you that I cannot partici-pate in the eagerly awaited May Day Fair Day games and alfresco entertainment with you at Hyde Park tomorrow. I have had the unfortu-nate displeasure of being stricken with a pain-ful uprising of gout, and the beast has laid me low. So it is with great sorrow that I have had to ask my cousin, who's just arrived for a visit from Cornwall, to act as my proxy. He will arrive in my carriage precisely at half past nine in the morning for you and the Misses Shevington so that you might be on time for the festivities start-ing at ten. I'm sure he will make a good show-ing for me.

I am with all due respect yours very truly,
Snellingly

Sophia put her elbows on the table and dropped her forehead into her hands. "Oh, Aunt June, what am I to do? I will have to spend the entire day with a stranger. I could just—"

"What, dear?"

"Oh, I don't know. Maybe I could scream at Mr. Brentwood for putting me in this position."

"Sophia, you know what he did was the best thing for you," Aunt June said. "I've said this before. You can't marry him."

A deep longing stirred inside Sophia. "I have not lost sight of what I need to do, Auntie."

She just wished she didn't have to do it.

Twenty-three

Love is a second life; it grows into the soul,
warms every vein, and beats in every pulse.

—Joseph Addison

SATURDAY DAWNED WITH BLUE SKIES AND A BIG
yellow sun heating the air.

Matson had dressed in his lightest shirt, waistcoat, and coat. He had loosely tied his neckcloth
and made sure his collar wasn't too tight. He knew
the day was going to be long and, if the sun was any
indication, very warm for the last Saturday in May.

Lord Tradesforke's people must have worked all
night to set up the fair. They had roped off a large
section of the park near the Serpentine to keep out
the uninvited. But plenty of onlookers were already
crowding the edges of the ropes in hopes of getting
a glimpse of all that would be happening.

There were booths laden with food, drinks, and
games. The cubicles that housed puppets singing
and dancing were drawing the largest crowds. Card
tables had been set up at various places around
the ringed area, and some eager souls were already

playing loo, piquet, and commerce. Another section had been roped off separately, where there were monkeys, bears, an elephant, and other animals caged for everyone to see. As Lord Tradesforke had promised, there would be no lack of entertainment.

Matson had arrived at the park early to pick out which boat he wanted for the race. There were several different races to participate in throughout the day, but he wanted only to compete in the rowboat race, and then only if Lord Snellingly and Sophia participated in it. Outwardly, he was making a good show of looking forward to the day, speaking to gentlemen and tipping his hat to the ladies. He would do his job and see to it that Miss Craftsman had a lovely time, but as for himself, he would only be pretending to enjoy himself.

Once he had picked the one he wanted and put a flask of water in it, he then looked at the watch he'd stuck in his coat pocket. He'd told Miss Craftsman to be on the banks of the Serpentine by ten, but she had already missed that by thirty minutes. The race wasn't until half past one, but he'd wanted to go over some of the instructions with her that he had covered with Sophia.

It didn't matter what Matson was doing, his thoughts always drifted back to Sophia. He had often been hit with mild interest in young ladies, but he'd felt stirrings of lust the first time he saw Sophia. There was no doubt he wanted her. But

over the weeks he'd known her, those rash feelings
had changed to something more reverent than lust,
and he was still trying to recognize, understand,
and accept them.

His mind took him back to that day on the
Serpentine with Sophia. He would never forget
how fragile she was when she was reminded of the
fire. He would never forget how right she felt in
his arms, how satisfying she felt beneath him, or
how sweet she tasted to his tongue. He squeezed
his eyes shut for just a moment and imagined his
lips on hers. He heard her soft sounds of passion
and felt her fingertips on his bare skin. He would
always remember her willingly giving herself to
him with such innocence and eagerness to know
what being with a man was all about. And he
couldn't shake the feeling that she belonged to him
and no one else.

When Matson looked up, he saw Sophia walking
in his direction. His heartbeat slowed and started
thumping hard and determined. He couldn't help
but smile. She was dressed perfectly for the day
in a dark gray dress that wouldn't show soil easily.
There were no bows, lace, or ribbons adorning it,
and it was just the right length. On her feet were
safe, comfortable boots. Her hair was tucked under
a short-brimmed oval bonnet, perfect for protec-
tion from the sun but would not impair her vision.
Matson smiled. She'd listened to every word he'd

said, and he didn't think he'd ever seen her look more beautiful.

He had an overwhelming desire to rush to her, pick her up in his arms, and swing her around until she was dizzy with delight. He wanted to hold her, kiss her, and touch her. He wanted to ease the ache in his chest.

He knew the moment she saw him. Her steps faltered slightly. She blinked and quickly looked away from him. His gut wrenched. He didn't blame her, only himself. This was what he'd wanted. The turn of events for this day were all his own making, but looking at her now, he wished like hell he could go back and change what he'd done. But he couldn't. No matter the feelings eating away inside him, they didn't belong together.

Matson didn't see Lord Snellingly walking with her. Where was the fop, and who was that young buck walking beside Sophia? Why was he talking to her on such friendly terms? And why was she smiling and laughing with him?

Matson studied the man, certain he hadn't seen him before. He was about Matson's height and almost as broad in the shoulders. He supposed the man could be considered handsome by the ladies. Matson figured the blade looked to be about six or eight years younger than he was.

Where was the earl? Matson grimaced. He scanned the crowd that had grown quite large over the past half hour but didn't see him. He followed Sophia and the man to a gaming booth, where the buck easily knocked over all the bottles with a ball and won Sophia a little doll not much bigger than her hand, but it certainly put a smile of appreciation on her face.

Matson was suddenly plagued with huge bouts of the green-eyed jealousy Shakespeare so cleverly wrote about in *The Merchant of Venice*. He couldn't stop following them. They left and walked to another booth, where the man purchased her a sugared tart. It drove Matson crazy watching her eat it while she conversed with the man, who appeared to be trying to charm her out of her chemise.

Finally, when Matson could no longer stand watching the buck make her laugh with such ease, he walked over to them and said, "Good morning, Miss Hart."

Sophia turned toward him. She was still holding the doll in her hand. Matson had a sudden urge to rip it from her and throw it in the Serpentine.

The smile on her face dried up instantly when she saw him. "Mr. Brentwood," she said, and turned to the man beside her. "Have you met Mr. Adam Beckett?"

The men greeted each other coolly. "No, I don't believe I have."

"Perhaps you know Mr. Beckett's father, Viscount Rosenwall."

Matson scoffed a bitter laugh under his breath. He should have known. The man would have a title one day. Why didn't that surprise Matson?

"I've heard of him."

Sophia smiled at Mr. Beckett before looking at Matson again and saying, "Mr. Beckett is Lord Snellingly's cousin and my partner for the day."

Shock registered on Matson's face before he could stop it, so there was nothing to do but admit it. "That surprises me."

Sophia gave him a look that seemed to say *I bet it does.*

Matson's jaw tightened. The reason he'd traded Sophia to Lord Snellingly was because she was safe with the earl. He envisioned the man reading poetry to her while she rowed the boat. It never dawned on Matson that she might somehow be put into the hands of another man—a much younger, stronger, much more handsome, and soon-to-be-titled man.

"What happened to the earl?" Matson asked.

Sophia said, "Lord Snellingly took to his sick bed with an affliction that comes on him from time to time. It's nothing serious, and it seems to pass in a few days."

It was Matson's turn to give Sophia a look that said *I bet it does.*

"It's gout," Mr. Beckett said.

"How fortunate it is for Miss Hart that you were

able to step in and fill his shoes for today's events," Matson said.

"Isn't it, though? I just arrived in London a couple of days ago to enjoy the last two weeks of the Season." He looked down at Sophia. "I had thought about not coming. Now I'm glad I did."

"And do you write poetry like your cousin, Mr. Beckett?" Matson asked.

Beckett wiped the corner of his mouth with his thumb. "No."

Matson smiled. "That's too bad. Miss Hart loves poetry."

"Look, Mr. Brentwood," Sophia said, "here comes your partner for the day, Miss Craftsman. And see how lovely she is."

Matson looked behind him and swallowed hard. Miss Craftsman was dressed as if she were going to a dinner party rather than a fair day in the park. Her dress was not only sweeping the ground with every step she took, it was ballooned with lace-trimmed flounces and ribbons streaming from her cuffs and the waistband. Her bonnet looked to be the size of a washing tub, and still she carried a parasol decked with ribbons.

The tables had turned on Matson, and he didn't like it. He had hoped to see Sophia stranded in the middle of the lake while the earl read poetry to her, and instead he was the one with the alba-tross in his boat. Damn that Snellingly. Why did the man have to get sick and turn Sophia over to Mr. Beckett?

Hadn't it been punishment enough that he'd verbally lashed himself over and over again for the foolish move of exchanging Sophia for Miss Craftsman?

"Hmm." Sophia said. "It looks like you didn't have any rowing practice with Miss Craftsman."

"No, I didn't," Matson mumbled tightly, but looked directly into Sophia's eyes. "There's only one person I want to be in a rowboat with."

He saw her swallow hard.

"Are you a betting man, Mr. Brentwood?" Mr. Beckett asked.

"As much as any man," he answered without taking his gaze from Sophia's. He had a feeling she knew she was torturing him.

"What about a friendly wager between us on who wins the rowboat race on the Serpentine? I think I can beat you."

Matson forced himself to take his eyes off Sophia. The man looked strong, capable, but Matson had done a lot of rowing when he was in Baltimore. Many times their ships wouldn't have docking space at the harbor, so they would anchor offshore. He'd never minded rowing out to the ships. He was confident he could take this young man.

"All right," Matson said. "If I win, I get to be Miss Hart's partner the rest of the day, and you take mine."

He heard Sophia's intake of breath.

Mr. Beckett looked from Sophia to Miss Craftsman, who was walking delicately toward them, and he said, "That's not what I had in mind. I was thinking we'd lay down a little blunt to make the race interesting."

"I don't care if it's interesting, and I don't want your money. If I win, I get Miss Hart. I'm a shipbuilder. If I lose, I'll build and present you with a small ship."

Beckett grunted.

"That's my wager. Take it or leave it."

Sophia gasped. "Matson, have you lost your mind?"

"I have no use for a ship," Mr. Beckett said.

"Thank God," Sophia whispered.

"But I accept your bet," Mr. Beckett added.

"No," Sophia whispered, and then said, "Stop this madness, both of you, right now. There will be no betting on this race. How dare you suggest a wager, Mr. Beckett, and how dare you offer such a prize, Mr. Brentwood."

Matson stared at Sophia. She was outraged, but she would get over it. He was determined to right the wrong he'd done. He wanted her back, and he'd risk everything to get her.

"It's a deal," Matson said, reaching out his hand to Mr. Beckett.

Mr. Beckett snorted a laugh and folded his hands

across his chest. "Not so quick. How do I know that you will build me that ship when you lose?"

Matson spread his arm out toward the crowd. "Ask any of the gentlemen you see here. They know me as a man of my word."

"Don't be foolish, Mr. Beckett," Sophia said. "And take my word for it that you cannot trust Mr. Brentwood's word." She turned to Matson. "He says no, Mr. Brentwood. Now, if you'll excuse us, we have other people to see."

Mr. Beckett stuck out his hand and said, "I accept that you are an honorable man, and I accept your terms."

"But you can't," Sophia said, looking from her partner to Matson. "This is outrageous."

Yes, but you are worth it, and I will win you back!

Sophia stared at Matson. "What if you lose?" she continued.

"I will pay my debt."

Her eyes softened, and she implored him, "Don't do this, Matson."

"I have to," he said and turned toward Miss Craftsman.

───────

It was half an hour before the rowing would begin, and Matson had left Miss Craftsman in her parents' care so he could have a few minutes of quiet before the race started. The lady was lovely to look at, but she never stopped talking. He did his duty as her partner for the morning and walked around the fair with her, buying her sweets and flowers, winning her a lace handkerchief, and telling her more than once how lovely she looked.

He'd walked quite a distance away from the crowd and found a place where he could take his coat off and stretch his arms and shoulders. It wouldn't do to get a cramp while he was rowing. He had the opportunity to get Sophia back, and he didn't intend to lose. Lord Snellingly would never have agreed to such a wager.

Matson had to be at his best. He wished he could row without having Miss Craftsman in the boat with him. At least Sophia knew how to row— but would she? She was upset with him for more than one reason, but was she angry enough to help Beckett win?

"What in the bloody hell have you done?"

Matson turned at the sound of his brother's voice. "Plenty, but what specifically are you talking about?" Matson said. He wasn't sorry about what he'd done, and he wasn't going to let his brother change that.

"Is it true that you bet a man a ship that you would win the right to spend the afternoon with Miss Hart? A ship?"

"Yes."

Iverson shook his head in disbelief. "A ship? Have you gone completely mad?"

"I don't think so."

"Of course you have. You just bet a ship, Matson. A ship for a partner you had and traded her away."

"I know all the details, Iverson."

"I—I don't know what to say. What could possibly have possessed you to make such an outlandish wager? You don't look that deep in your cups."

"I'm not."

"You don't look jug-bitten either, and I know you haven't been to a smoking house, so what in the bloody hell is wrong with you?"

"All right," Matson said angrily. "I spoke before I thought things through. I let my temper get the best of me."

"Then let's go get you out of this wager before it's too late."

Matson's brow wrinkled. "I'm not talking about the wager. I'm talking about trading Sophia to Lord Snellingly. The wager stands, Iverson. I made a mistake and I'm rectifying it. That's all there is to it."

"No, that's not all there is to it. Not when it concerns our business and you giving away a ship."

"A small ship, and that's only if I lose. I'm not going to lose, Iverson."

"You can't be sure of that, Matson. Things happen, and that was one big wager you made."

"It was a big mistake."

"But a *ship*!"

"You've said that five times or more."

"Because I can't believe it, and I'll keep saying it until you come to your senses."

"You know I'll pay for the ship if I lose. It won't cost you a penny."

Iverson swore and shook his head. "Bloody hell, Brother, you know it's not the ship or what it costs."

"You could have fooled me, with all the blustering you're doing," Matson said as he shrugged back into his coat.

"It's who she is. You're doing this for Sir Randolph's ward."

Matson had only one answer. "She's worth it."

Iverson took off his hat and ran a hand through his hair. "Then why the hell did you trade her in the first place?"

"I was angry over a little thing."

"This was a hell of a time to start acting like me."

"I agree, but nothing you can do or say will change my mind about this. I'm going to get her back."

"For how long? Just for the afternoon? You've known almost since you met her that she will marry a title."

Matson hated the truth of his brother's words.

He heard a bell ring, summoning the racers to their boats.

"I've got to go."

Iverson shook his head again and fell into step beside Matson. "You have surprised me, Brother."

"I surprised myself."

"In one way, it's about time you got passionate enough about something or someone to get damned outraged, but did it have to be over a woman you can't have, and did you have to bet a ship?"

"You're a bloody nuisance," Matson said.

"Yes, I know, but you have me worried."

"There's no cause for it. This is my fight."

"I'll be the judge of that. Now, go show that young blade how a man rows a boat."

Matson left his brother's side and headed toward the water's edge to find Miss Craftsman. From the corner of his eye he caught sight of Sophia. She was hurrying toward him. Seeing her caused the tightness in his shoulders and jaw to loosen.

"It's not too late for you to stop this madness," she said, stopping in front of him.

"The only thing you need to do, Miss Hart, is your best. I know you don't like to lose any more than I do. I'll expect you to do all you can to see that your partner wins."

"You don't mean that."

"I do. I expect no less of you, but I don't intend to let you and the future viscount win."

"How can you possibly win with Miss Craftsman? She's dressed as if she's going to a cotillion."

He looked over at Miss Craftsman, who stood with her parents. "Yes, she looks very pretty today."

Sophia jerked her hands to her waist. "Oh, you miserable beast! Do you think I care if you lose a ship? I don't. You tossed me aside like a piece of unwanted baggage. You deserve to lose your ship."

Matson gave her a teasing smile. "Now that is the Sophia I want to see. Did you know your freckles get bigger when you get mad?"

"What?" She touched her cheek. "They do not."

"Well, maybe not bigger, but they do turn a lovely shade of pale copper. Do you know how very attractive that makes you and how kissable you look?"

Sophia glanced around. "You can't talk to me that way. Look how close those people are to us. Someone might overhear you."

He stepped closer to her. "Right now, Sophia, I don't care. But I do see your partner is looking for you. You'd better go to him. But don't worry, I'll be back to claim you at the end of the race."

Matson walked away from Sophia and headed toward the water's edge where Miss Craftsman stood with her satin slippers. She didn't look happy with him, and neither were her parents, but Matson didn't give them time to say anything. As the second bell rang, he offered Miss Craftsman his arm and said they must hurry to get in place. Courtesy of Mr. Beckett, the news of their bet had spread through the park like a fire through dry brush. Almost every gentleman was making his own wager on who would win.

There were five boats between Matson's and the boat Sophia would be in. Matson knew he couldn't let her distract him. He had to keep his mind on winning.

Remembering that Sophia already knew how to row, he said to Miss Craftsman, "Do you know how to row?"

She laughed. "Of course not, Mr. Brentwood. Why would I need to know how to row when I have a strong, handsome gentleman to row for me?"

"So true," he said more under his breath than to Miss Craftsman.

Matson had picked a boat on the end of about twelve that were lined up on the shore. He didn't want to get stuck in the middle and have to deal with someone who couldn't row his way out of the cluster. When the whistle blew, they had to get in the boat and row down the lake to where there was a barge they had to row around. Then whoever was the first gentleman with his partner's feet touching the ground would be declared the winner.

"Mr. Brentwood?"

"Yes, Miss Craftsman."

"Is it true? This wager I've heard about a ship and Miss Hart?"

Matson felt a tinge of remorse for entangling her in his machinations. "Yes."

Her lips formed a pout. "But I thought you traded with Lord Snellingly because you wanted to be with me today."

"What I realized was that I did a disservice to Miss Hart when I asked Lord Snellingly to exchange with me, and it's only right I should try to make amends. May I take your parasol and put it in the boat for you? It will make it quicker for us to get in the boat. You can open it again once we start rowing."

Miss Craftsman smiled sweetly at him. "Oh, I couldn't possibly do without my parasol for even a moment, Mr. Brentwood. The sun burns my skin so easily."

Matson looked at her lovely olive skin and smiled. He could see now he wasn't going to get any help from her. She didn't want him to win. He just hoped she didn't try to do anything to stop him from winning.

He looked up and down at his competitors. He guessed that by the time they made the turn, there would be about four or five of them in the running to be the first back to the shore.

Matson moved closer to Miss Craftsman. The whistle blew, and he grabbed her arm. Her parasol knocked his head, and she deliberately tried to delay stepping into the boat by stumbling. He tried not to look at others who had already pushed off and were rowing.

"Sit down, Miss Craftsman, or you will land in the water," he said tightly as he started gently pushing the boat.

By the time he put his oar in the water, most of the boats had already turned and were headed toward the bridge where the barge was anchored just on the other side. He would have to stay focused and row hard and quick to catch and then pass them.

"Mr. Brentwood?"

Matson took a quick glance behind him at the same time Miss Craftsman leaned forward, and one of the tips of her parasol caught the corner of his eye. A pain shot through him, and he winced as his eye watered.

"Oh, I'm so sorry, Mr. Brentwood. I didn't mean to hit you with my parasol."

He blinked rapidly, trying to clear his watering eye. "Don't worry about it, Miss Craftsman, just please stay seated, still, and quiet, or I fear you will land in the middle of the Serpentine. You can swim, can't you?"

"No, of course not," she said, sounding a little wary.

"Then I must ask again that you stay still and quiet until we get back to shore. If the boat tips over, your skirts would probably drag you to the bottom before I could get to you."

"I'm not sure I like being out on the water like this. It looks dark and deep."

"It is, Miss Craftsman," he said, slicing the oars through the water.

Matson heard her gasp. He didn't like using a scare tactic on a young lady, but maybe this was his chance to keep her in line. He didn't intend to let her make him lose the race.

By the time Matson made it to the center of the lake, more than half of the boats were ahead of him. His eye continued to ache and water, but he didn't take the time to wipe it. He hadn't counted on Miss Craftsman's antics of taking her time getting in the boat and getting seated, or being struck in the eye with her parasol either. It hadn't dawned on him that Miss Craftsman might hear about his wager and try to sabotage him. But all he could do was continue to row.

As soon as he made it to the open water, he saw that at least eight boats were in front of them. He knew all he had to do was set a fast pace and keep to it. One by one he passed the boats, and by the time he rowed around the official barge, he saw only three boats were ahead of him. Sophia and Beckett were in the lead and a good three boat lengths ahead of him and the other two boats. Matson picked up his pace.

Another thing he hadn't counted on was the heat of the midday sun beating down on him, draining his energy faster than he'd anticipated. The muscles in his arms burned, but Matson didn't let up. He struggled for deep breaths and kept pushing the oars harder and faster into the water with each stroke. The minutes seemed like hours, but Matson passed first one boat and then the other, leaving no one between him and the shore but Sophia and Beckett.

It surprised Matson that Sophia had taken him at his word and was helping Mr. Beckett row. He didn't blame her for wanting him to lose, after what he'd done. But what he told his brother was true. He'd made a big mistake, and it was going to take a big effort to set it right.

Beckett was strong, but Matson could see he was tiring, and slowly Matson was gaining on him. The problem was that with each slice into the water, they were getting closer and closer to shore. Matson felt a little safer when, at last, the front tip of his boat came even with the back of Sophia's boat. Sophia looked back at him, and seeing her face gave Matson the surge of energy he needed to dig harder into the water. He heard the roar of the crowd on shore, some urging him to win and some urging Mr. Beckett to be the winner.

In a last hard, sweeping push of the oars through the water, Matson caught Beckett and Sophia; their boats hit the shore at the same time. Beckett reached back for Sophia's hand to help her step out of the boat. Matson knew he had only one chance to win, and he took it. With arms weak and trembling from exertion, he reached down and picked up Miss Craftsman in his arms. She gasped as he swung her around and quickly set her feet down on the shore just before Sophia's feet touched the ground.

Matson heard cheers and clapping. He also heard jeers, which obviously came from the gentlemen who'd bet against him winning. Iverson bolted down to the shore and patted him on the back.

Beckett quickly turned angry eyes on Matson and said, "You cheated."

The crowd fell silent. "Watch your accusations, Beckett," Matson said, stepping closer to the man. "I don't cheat."

"You picked her up"—he pointed to Miss Craftsman—"out of the boat."

Matson's breathing was labored. He looked at Sophia. She was his.

"I don't recall there being any rules about how our partner's feet made it to the ground, only that she be the first to touch it for the win."

Beckett looked up into the crowd and asked, "Who's in charge of this race?"

"I am, I am," Lord Tradesforke called, waddling down to the water's edge. "Hold on, hold on. I'm on my way."

Matson's gaze didn't waver from Beckett's while

he waited for the earl to get to them, but he knew Sir Randolph and the Misses Shevingtons had crowded around Sophia.

"He cheated," Beckett said when Lord Tradesforke was close enough to hear him.

Rumblings of discontent came from the crowd. Matson's eyes narrowed, and his hand made a fist at his side. He was prepared to fight over this if need be. He didn't like his honor being questioned, and especially in front of more than half the *ton*. He didn't want to have to defend himself with his fists or swords after he'd just rowed like the devil himself was after him, but damnation, he'd do it if Beckett persisted in this false claim.

"That's a serious charge, sir," Lord Tradesforke said, wedging his large body between Matson and Mr. Beckett.

"He picked up his partner out of the boat and set her feet on the ground."

Lord Tradesforke looked up at the crowd and asked, "Did Mr. Brentwood's partner's feet touch the ground first?"

Shouts of yes, absolutely, and clapping flowed from the crowd.

"Then there is no problem of cheating. I didn't stipulate how the lady's feet should touch the ground, sir, only that she be the first to do so. If you had picked up your partner, perhaps you would have won. As it is, you lost fairly."

A roar of support went up from the crowd, and Matson took in a deep, satisfying breath. Mr. Beckett turned to Sophia and continued to complain that the rules were unclear and therefore he hadn't truly lost the race.

Matson turned to Miss Craftsman, who was scowling at him. He really couldn't blame her. This was the second time she'd been handed off to another man. "Miss Craftsman, it's been a pleasure to be your partner this morning."

She looked at him for a moment as if she were trying to decide if she should pout and be remorseful or slap him. Matson was so tired and so happy at the moment, he really didn't care. "Would you allow me to see you back to your parents?"

Obviously the nicer side of Miss Craftsman won out. She sucked in a deep breath, smiled unconvincingly sweetly, and said, "I would not care for you to do another thing for me, Mr. Brentwood. And please don't call on me the next time you want to make Miss Hart jealous. This is really not a role I'm suited to play." She turned and stomped away.

Matson walked over to Sophia and greeted her, her aunts, and Sir Randolph. He ignored Beckett, who was still at her side.

"You almost lost a ship today, Mr. Brentwood," Sophia said.

"I admit I was worried for a short time. You never gave an inch."

Smiling, she said, "You didn't expect me to, did you?"

"Nor did I want you to. It made the win all the sweeter."

"It was very clever of you to pick up Miss Craftsman."

He fought to suppress a victorious grin. "I had no doubt it would be the quickest way to get her out of the boat."

Sophia turned to Mr. Beckett. "I'm sure you made Lord Snellingly very proud of you today."

"I'm sure I didn't, Miss Hart." He nodded to her and walked away.

Matson looked at Sophia. Her aunts and Sir Randolph stood behind her. His brother was behind him. "It appears we are partners once again, Miss Hart. You look like you could use a cup of tea or chocolate, or something stronger, if you prefer. May I?" He held out his arm.

For a long time, Matson had felt like Sophia belonged to him, and at that moment, with his brother, her guardian, and her aunts looking on, Matson knew he loved Sophia.

The problem was that he wasn't at all sure he had her heart.

Twenty-four

Two souls with but a single thought, two hearts
that beat as one.

—John Keats

INHALING DEEPLY, SOPHIA SOFTLY OPENED HER bedchamber door and stepped out into the darkened corridor. Silently and slowly she pulled the door shut behind her. All was quiet except for her own excited breathing huffing in her ears. The rug beneath her bare feet kept her footsteps soundless as she hurried toward the stairs.

She had never before had a reason to slip out of the house and into the night. Her heart pounded, and her throat felt tight. Fear of getting caught rippled through her. Sir Randolph had been good to her, and she didn't want to bring shame to him. But she was willing to risk everything to be with Matson again.

She picked up the hem of her cloak and night rail as she descended the stairs and quickly headed toward the back of the house. Once at the exit, she leaned her cheek against the cool wood and tried to still her rapid breathing.

It had been almost midnight before she'd made it home from the park. The afternoon and evening with Matson had flown by as they visited all the booths at the fair, and later danced under the stars until the orchestra had stopped playing and Lord Tradesforke bid everyone good night. Just before they had parted, Matson asked her to meet him in the garden after everyone had gone to bed.

As quietly as possible, she opened the door and stepped out onto the landing. Anticipation and excitement grew inside her. There was only a slight chill to the air, and a thin slice of moon hung in the sky. It was barely enough to light her way, but bright enough that she needed her black cloak to hide her white cotton nightgown.

The steps and stone-covered pathway were cold to her bare feet as she fled to the end of the garden. When she made it to the gate, she took hold of the handle and looked back at the house to see if any lamps or candles had been lit. The house was dark, quiet. She breathed a sigh of relief.

"Sophia."

Startled, she spun and saw Matson step out of the shadows. She looked into his eyes, and he smiled at her. Her heart melted for the second time that day.

She had never seen him dressed so casual or look so handsome. He wore only a white shirt and dark trousers. He had discarded his coat, neckcloth, and waistcoat. Her heart overflowed with love for him.

He slipped his hand around to the back of her neck, pulled her gently to him, and lowered his head to hers. His soft, moist lips brushed over hers, teasing her with the lightest contact.

Sweet contentment settled into her soul.

"You are late again," he whispered against her lips.

"And you are early again." She smiled. "I wanted to be sure everyone had time to get to sleep after retiring."

She stepped into his arms, and they circled her. She loved the comfort and safety of his embrace. Matson covered her lips with his, drawing her closer to his chest. He kissed her reverently at first, but quickly his kisses turned impatient and passionate. His hands moved over her unbound breasts, down her waist, and over her hips.

Her arms slid around his broad back and gloried in the feel of the strong muscles that had helped him win the boat race. She had been hurt and angry that he had deserted her, but he had come back for her. All was forgiven. She wanted to be here with him like this. She loved him with all her heart, and though she could never tell him, she could show him.

They kissed with all the passion they were feeling for a few more moments, and then he hugged her close, kissed the warmth of her neck just under her ear, and whispered her name.

"Come," he said huskily. "I've laid down my cloak for us in the corner behind the table and chairs."

"I thought we were to meet outside, between the hedges."

"I was too fearful someone might use the pathway as a shortcut to the mews and disturb us. We are safely secluded here in this corner of the garden. No one can see us from the house because of that tree. No one can enter through the gate because I locked it."

Matson took her hand and led her to his cloak, where they sank to their knees as their lips met once again. She leaned sensually into him. Her lips parted, and his tongue swept inside her mouth slowly, delicately. His tongue played with hers as they tasted, teased, and tempted each other. He untied the ribbon at the base of her throat, and her cloak fell to the ground. Her long hair spilled down her back. He caught it up in his hands and crushed it in his gentle grip.

"I've dreamed of seeing your hair spread across your shoulders like this," he said against her lips.

"It pleases you?" she asked.

"Very much," he answered and cupped her cheeks with his hands and pressed his forehead against hers. "There is much I need to say to you, Sophia. I'm sorry I—"

Her fingers pressed against his mouth, stopping him. "Later," she whispered. "Right now I want to kiss you, to touch you, and to taste you again. We'll leave words between us for another time."

He raised his head and looked into her eyes. "How can I not tell you how beautiful you are and how good you make me feel inside?"

She laughed softly. "You can tell me wonderful things."

His hand combed down her hair. "I wish I could see you better."

"It would be dangerous for us out here tonight if there were more moonlight."

"I know." He grinned. "But I can still wish."

He bent his head and slanted his lips over hers in a slow, tender kiss. His hand left her hair, and his fingers floated down her neck to her chest, and on to the firm swell of her breasts nestled warmly beneath the cool cotton fabric of her night rail.

Sophia's breathing increased. His hand felt strong, tender, and sure. Matson's thumb brushed against the taut tip. Her nipple grew hard and erect under his ardent touch, and she moaned softly with pleasure.

She wanted their time together to be slow so she could enjoy every touch, every kiss, and every breath. Their coming together in the rowboat had been exciting and eager but too cramped and rushed to be savored.

"Sophia," he whispered into her mouth, "lie with me."

That was what she was waiting to hear. She had yearned for his touch again. She sank from her

knees to her buttocks, and Matson gently tumbled her onto his cloak. He bunched her wrap
behind her head. He then stretched his long, lean
body beside her as his lips sought hers again. He
kissed her passionately as his hand eagerly caressed
her shoulder, down her arm and over her chest to
fondle her breasts. Occasionally he would stop and
tease the nipple with his thumb and finger, which
sent shivers of delight shooting through her.

His lips left hers, and his tongue swept down her
neck, tasting her skin, and back up to her mouth
again to devour her lips. She pulled the front of his
shirt from his trousers and slid her hands beneath
it to feel his warm, firm skin. She let her fingertips
glide softly and tantalizingly slowly over his chest
and down his midriff. Her hand slipped lower to
the hard swell beneath his trousers. She heard his
soft moan of satisfaction, and it pleased her that her
touch could make him feel so good.

Matson's lips left hers, and he rose up over her.
He untied the bow that held the front of her gown
together and slowly slid it off first one shoulder and
then the other. He gazed lovingly at her breasts.

He then looked into her eyes and said, "You are
as beautiful as I knew you would be."

She shivered. "Touch me."

He lowered his head and closed his mouth over
the tip of one breast and tasted her hungrily. A
whisper of need eased past his lips as he cupped,

lifted, and caressed her breast as if he were feeding an insatiable desire to possess her with all the hunger he was feeling.

Sophia threw her head back and lifted her chest to him. She took pleasure in the earth-shattering sensations spiraling through her body. She cupped his head to her while her fingers played in the warmth of his thick hair. She stroked the line of his shoulders and muscled arms and then all the way down his wide back and straight spine, before sliding her hands up to sensuously tangle again in his dark hair.

She gasped and sighed softly as one sensational feeling after another shot through her. His hand cupped and molded the swell of her breasts as he gently teased her nipples with his tongue. With loving caution, his hand slid down her rib cage, over her abdomen, and to her lower, most womanly part. She sucked in her breath at the feelings. His touch sent rushing, delicious warmth sizzling through her. She lifted her body toward him. Her erratic breaths quickened, and so did his.

He rose, and in one fluid motion he ripped his shirt over his head and off his arms, dropping it to the ground beside him. A smile spread across her face. She wound her arms around his strong back, leaned up, and kissed his neck, letting her lips skim along his shoulders and across both nipples on his chest.

Her hand raked down his thigh, over his buttocks, and then around to the thick shaft between his legs. She fumbled with the buttons on his trousers. Matson helped her slide them down his hips and off his legs. He grabbed her night rail and pushed it up and over her head, and bunched it with her cloak to make a soft pillow for her.

Sophia lay completely nude before him, with the pale moonlight shining down on her.

Matson smiled at her. He ran the palm of his hand and tips of his fingers over her naked shoulders to her breasts, to her waist and abdomen, down the slim plane of her hip and over to her inner thigh, before going back to her face to lovingly caress her cheek.

"You are gorgeous, Sophia. Perfectly shaped, beautifully soft, and yet womanly firm."

She smiled. "I'm glad I please you."

He looked at her for a moment or two longer before his lips, tongue, and hands once again started working their magic on her senses. His open palm slid down and cupped the curve of her waist before tenderly sliding to the warmth between her legs.

The slow movement of his fingertips created an intense fire of desire burning inside her. She rotated her body in movement with his fingers.

"I am so eager for you, Sophia," he whispered huskily.

"Then don't keep us waiting."

He rose over her and covered the length of her body with his, settling his weight on her. Her hands were free to comb the solid, muscled wall of his back, hips, and thighs. His body was firm, his skin smooth.

All her senses burst to life when he pressed his manhood against the softness between her legs, and slowly, deliberately, continuously pressed into her, joining his body to hers. She felt him tremble, and she gloried in the power she had to give him such pleasure.

Matson stopped moving and sighed contentedly. "You are mine once more, Sophia," he whispered against her lips. "You are mine."

Her pulse beat loudly in her ears, but she heard him whisper her name over and over as he kissed her lips, her eyes, her ears, and her neck.

She felt full, complete. She pressed against him, rocking in motion with his movement. His thrusts became fast and sure. She rose up to cup his body to her. With uneven breaths, she stroked down his back, across his buttocks, and up to his shoulders again with loving hands.

With his thighs wedged between hers, they moved together, engulfed in the exquisite, luxuriant sensation of pleasuring each other. She clung to him and rode the waves of delirious desire with him until they both silently cried out in fulfillment. She fell limp with contentment. Matson's body shuddered as he buried his face in the crook of her neck and inhaled deeply. She realized he hadn't rolled away from her before completing their union, as he had when they were in the boat. That pleased her.

They lay quietly for a few moments before Matson lifted his weight from her and quickly took the sides of his cloak and wrapped it around them like a cocoon. Sophia snuggled tightly to him, fitting her body perfectly against his, with her head nestled on his arm.

Matson propped on his elbow, lifted her chin with the tips of his fingers, looked into her eyes, and said, "Sophia, I know you're going to find this difficult to believe, but I'm in love with you."

Sophia held her breath, trying to keep the pain of his words from penetrating to her heart.

"I want to marry you, Sophia."

She let out a sighing breath. "You know that's not possible."

He looked down into her shimmering eyes. "No, I don't know that, and if I did know it, I wouldn't accept it."

She moved to rise, but he touched her arm. "I won't let you run away from me."

Sophia stared deeply into his eyes, aching with the pain of loss. "You can't stop me, Matson."

"I must. I love you. I want you to be my wife."

She tried to look away from him. "I can't marry you."

"Do you love me?"

"After what we just shared, how can you ask that?"

"Because you haven't said the words to me that I long to hear."

She withdrew farther from him. "I won't say them. I can't."

"Sophia—."

"Matson, you know this barrier has always been between us. If I could change taking that vow, I would." She slowly shook her head and cringed as she looked up at him sadly and said, "No, that's not true. I don't think I would change it if I could."

A deep frown of confusion marred his face, and she knew he didn't understand what she was saying.

"You weren't there, Matson. You didn't see my father struggling and gasping for every breath. I would have promised him anything to ease his suffering."

"But he is gone, and you are here. This is your life we are talking about, not his."

She shifted and rose on her elbow too, facing him. "No, this is about me. It's about who I am. It's the only way I know how to absolve myself of the guilt I have lived with for so long. I must do this for him."

"Sophia, any father would have risked his life to save his child from a burning house. It was his duty to save you and everyone else in the house. You don't owe him anything for that."

She closed her eyes. Deep sorrow filled her. "You don't know. It was more than that."

"More than what? Open your eyes, Sophia." He touched her shoulder softly. "Tell me."

That time in her past came rushing back, and it pained her. "No," she whispered earnestly, "I can't bear it. Don't make me tell you what a horrible, selfish child I was."

"Sophia," he said huskily, "look at me."

She opened her eyes and realized they were clouded with tears that wanted to spill, but she refused to let them.

"First, I don't believe you were horrible or self-ish, and second, if you were, do you think it matters to me what kind of child you were?"

"You don't understand."

"Tell me so I can."

She swallowed past an aching throat. "You know the fire was about six months after my mother died."

With a loving hand he brushed a strand of hair away from her face. "Yes."

"What you don't know is that about six months after the fire, my father came home jubilant one day. He told me he was going to marry the most beautiful woman in the world. She was a noble-man's daughter and had him feeling young and more alive than he'd felt in years. She would come live with us and be my mother. My mother! I remember I just started screaming at him. I still hear my screams in my dreams sometimes." Her hands balled into fists.

"Sophia, you were a child."

"Yes, but I continued to scream, and I hit him over and over again, telling him he couldn't marry her. I ran out of the house, and Papa had to chase me down. I wouldn't stop screaming until he promised me he wouldn't marry her, and he didn't. As I grew older, I realized what a selfish thing that was to have done to him. I've often wondered if I thought maybe my mother would come back if he didn't marry her. Maybe I thought that woman was the reason I had nightmares of my mother being consumed by the fire until there was no trace of her left. I don't know why I behaved as I did. I only know I have to make amends."

"Did your father ever tell you he held your actions at that time against you?"

"No. And I often tried to get him to talk about it with me when I was older, but he wouldn't. When I tried to apologize, he wouldn't even discuss her with me."

"I don't like seeing you in such anguish." He touched her cheek with the backs of his fingers, wanting to comfort her. "I'm sure he didn't blame you for his not marrying that woman."

"But it was the last time I ever saw my father truly happy. I had cost him his healthy lungs when I left my room and he couldn't find me in the smoke, and I cost him the woman he loved and wanted to marry. I did owe him my vow. I still do."

"This is madness! You were seven. You had been anguished. He couldn't possibly hold that childish behavior against you."

"No, he didn't. He would never, but I fault myself. That is why I made the vow to him to marry a title. Don't you understand, Matson? I need the redemption and forgiveness for what I did to him."

"Sophia, no."

"Yes," she pleaded. "He called her name on his deathbed. Not my mother's name, not my name, but her name, and I kept him from her. I don't deserve happiness."

"You can't believe that," he said, looking into her bright eyes.

He reached for her again, and again she pulled away from him. "I have to do this so I can be free of the guilt," she said, pushing him away. She reached behind her and grabbed her nightgown and yanked it over her head. "The only thing my father ever asked of me is that I do for him what he could never do for himself, and that was to have a title connected to my name." Her voice cracked. "I will do that for him."

Matson threw the cloak aside and grabbed his trousers and started shoving his legs into them. "Do you want to spend the rest of your life bearing the touch of a man you don't love?"

"No," she said, tying the ribbon at her throat. "But I will. I must. I can't live with this guilt."

"Sophia, you are making me crazy."

"Have you ever made a vow?"

Matson thought for a moment as he pulled his shirt over his head.

His eyes turned guarded. "Yes. I have vowed that I will never forgive Sir Randolph for having an affair with my mother and fathering me."

"Do you know of anything I could say that would make you change your mind so you would forgive him?"

"No," he answered quickly.

"Yet you ask it of me."

He hesitated. "I must. Sir Randolph is not keeping us apart. You are. Sophia, what do you want from me? Am I to be your lover while you are married to Snellingly, Bighampton, or someone like Beckett?"

"No, of course not," she whispered earnestly as she gathered her hair underneath the hood of her cloak. "Once I am married, I will not betray my husband."

Matson put his hands on his knees and clasped them together and shook his head. "So what are we to do then, Sophia? Look at each other from across the room at every ball and dinner party and wish we could touch and kiss like we have this night?"

"After tonight, nothing else is possible between us. I must choose a husband."

Sophia rose and ran across the lawn. She had to get to her room before the tears started flowing.

Twenty-five

Love is light from Heaven; a spark of that
immortal fire.

—Lord Byron

THERE WAS NO PUBLIC ROOM IN LONDON AS OPU-
lent as the Grand Ballroom, with its gilt moldings and
carved fretwork. There was hardly an evening of the
year that the baroque chandeliers were not lit with
burning candles that threw colorful prisms and dancing shadows of golden light across the large room.

Tonight was no exception.

Matson leaned against a column where he could
watch the dance floor. Sophia had been on it three
times since he'd been standing there. He'd seethed
with that rotten, green-eyed beast called jealousy,
watching her glide easily through the steps, turns,
and twirls with Lord Hargraves, Mr. Beckett, and
the rapidly recovered Lord Snellingly. The hell of it
was that all three men measured up to what Sophia
wanted; Matson didn't.

No, he thought, she didn't want them, she
wanted him but was going to settle for one of them.

Matson tried to stay away from the party, telling

himself that he didn't give a damn, but the problem with that was he did. He'd spent the entire day at his home, replaying his time with Sophia last night in her garden with the moonlight shining on her delicate white skin. He remembered every kiss, every caress of her rounded shoulders, swelling breasts, curved waist, and the soft flare of her shapely hips. He remembered every detail of making her his and then her refusal to accept him.

He didn't know how long he'd sat in her garden after she'd left him. He was too stunned to move at first. Sophia would rather live with a vow than give it up for him. A thousand thoughts had crossed his mind, including one he'd pondered long and hard today. His heart was telling him one thing, but his honor was telling him another.

He had a ship heading back to America at first light. He'd seriously considered kidnapping Sophia and sailing away with her on his ship. She loved him. He was convinced of that, and felt in time she would forgive him for forcing his will on her. But that contemplation had lasted only as long as the afternoon. If anyone had forced him to give up his vow, he would have never forgiven them. Honor was a matter of personal choice, not someone else's choice.

The cold, unmasked truth of what Sophia made him face last night rang in his mind. He was asking her to do something he wasn't willing to do himself, until now.

It took a lot of soul searching to realize that he wasn't going to let his hatred for Sir Randolph keep him from Sophia. He didn't want to spend the rest of his life hating a man and defending a mother who'd said yes to the very kind of passion he'd shared with Sophia that afternoon in the rowboat.

He had to tell Sophia that.

He watched her leave the dance floor and be escorted back to her aunts. Matson pushed away from the column and headed toward them.

As he waded through the crowd, Matson smiled and accepted words of congratulation, hearty claps on the back, and nods of admiration for winning the race yesterday.

"Good evening, ladies," he said, stopping in front of Sophia and her aunts.

"Delightful to see you, Mr. Brentwood," Mae said with a beaming smile.

"That's a lovely dress you have on, Miss Shevington," he said to Mae. "And you, too, Miss Shevington."

"Good evening, Mr. Brentwood," June said tightly and then lifted her chin and looked away, as if she were searching for someone in the room.

"How are you this evening, Mr. Brentwood?" Sophia said.

Her eyes seemed to be caressing his face as he spoke to her. "I'm well, Miss Hart, and you?"

"I'm—I'm still trying to get over the events of yesterday—and last night."

So am I.

"I've never seen a lady row a boat as well as you," he said.

"And you, sir, are by far the strongest gentleman I've met," Sophia said.

"Mae," June said sharply, and Matson and Sophia looked at her. "Is that man smiling at you?"

Mae turned to her sister. "Why, yes, Sister. Yes, I believe he is."

June clucked. "It's disgraceful for an old spinster such as yourself to be flirting with a gentleman, and one who appears younger than you too."

Mae smiled at the man. "Oh, I know it's absolutely scandalous, Sister, and I'm enjoying it so much."

Sophia looked at Matson and gave him a weak smile. A waltz was announced. "Are you free for this dance?" Matson asked her.

"Yes," she answered quickly.

"You don't mind, do you, Miss Shevington?" he asked Mae, deliberately not looking at June.

"No, of course not."

As Matson and Sophia started to walk away, the gentleman who had smiled at Mae walked up to her and asked her to dance. She accepted. Matson smiled to himself. Perhaps Miss Shevington was finally going to get a beau.

Matson led Sophia to the far corner of the dance

floor, where they would wait for the music to start. He looked at her face for a long time before finally saying, "Has anything changed?"

She shook her head as if she didn't trust herself to speak.

"You have a past, Sophia, but so have I."

She cleared her throat. "What do you mean?"

The music started, and Matson took Sophia's hand with his left hand and placed the other high on her back between her shoulder blades. Her body was warm. He stepped forward, and she slid her foot back, starting the box step.

"My first love was a married woman," he said to her as they danced.

"Oh," she said, clearly surprised. "I didn't know you had a first love."

"I was only twenty when I met her and didn't know she was married until a few nights later. My heart was already involved by then. At every party I went to, I had to watch her with her husband, knowing I could never touch her. It was hell for a couple of years, but I managed."

"I don't know what I can say to that."

"You don't have to say anything. I watched you dance with other men tonight, Sophia, and I knew that what I felt for Mrs. Delaney doesn't compare to what I feel for you."

Sophia missed a step, but Matson made up for her error. "Matson, don't."

"You asked me last night if I could think of a reason that would make me give up my vow to hate Sir Randolph, and I realized today I have a reason. You. You are that reason. Marry me, and I will deny my vow and welcome Sir Randolph into our home."

Tears pooled in her eyes. She missed another step. Matson quickly corrected for her again.

"There is a difference."

"No."

"Yes," she whispered earnestly. "Your vow was made in hatred. Mine was given in love. I can't break it."

He swallowed hard and looked around the dance floor for a moment, trying to handle her rejection. Finally he said, "I can't stay here and watch you marry another man. When I was in love with Mrs. Delaney, I could stay in Baltimore, see her, talk to her, and put my desire for her aside. I know myself and what I'm capable of, and I can't stay here and watch you going home with another man, to his bed for his kisses and touches, and not mine."

"No, don't." She looked away.

"I have had you, Sophia. I had you first. Marry me," he said as his hold on her tightened.

"You know I can't. Don't ask me again."

Matson felt as if a knife sliced through his heart, but he managed a nod, and they finished the waltz in silence. As the crowd left the dance floor, he held back and said to Sophia, "You know I thought about kidnapping you and taking you away with me on my ship. I wanted to steal you from the titled men pursuing you and force you to be my bride."

She gave him a sad smile. "Perhaps you should have and left me with no choice."

"I won't dishonor you by forcing you to give up your vow. I wish I could. And I know if I stayed here, I would ask you to betray your husband. I can't watch you live with another man. I want you to have a good life. I have a ship leaving at first light for America. I'll be on it. Good-bye, Sophia."

Matson turned and walked away.

―――――――

On what felt like wooden legs, Sophia followed her aunts and Sir Randolph into the house later that night. She had been in a stupor since Matson left her on the dance floor.

She stopped in the foyer and gave her wrap to Mrs. Anderson. Ever since Sophia had watched Matson walk away, she'd felt as if her heart had shriveled into a cold, hard knot. She kept hearing him say that he would give up his vow for her, but he couldn't dishonor her and take her vow away. Sophia had thought of nothing else since he left. Her guilt over what she did to her father had always been great, but through his actions, she knew he had forgiven her.

Now she had to forgive herself.

"Sophia, aren't you coming up?"

Sophia looked up the stairs and saw June, Mae, and Sir Randolph at the top of the stairs. "No, I'm not. I'm going to pour myself a glass of port."

"Port? You don't drink port," June admonished.

"Tonight I do."

"What's wrong with you?" Mae said.

Sophia paid no mind to her aunt. She walked down the corridor and into the drawing room. She was pouring from the decanter and into a glass when her aunts and Sir Randolph walked in with worried expressions on their faces.

"Tell us what is wrong, Sophia," Sir Randolph said, coming to her side.

She took a sip of the deep-red wine. "I had decided earlier tonight that I was going to marry Lord Snellingly."

"Oh, how wonderful," June said. "Sir Randolph, did you hear that?"

"Of course, Miss Shevington. I might be old, but I'm not deaf."

"No wonder you want a port. This calls for a celebration. We need champagne, Sir Randolph."

"There is no cause for celebration, Auntie. After I decided on Lord Snellingly, a man I didn't love and could never love, I realized I would probably cringe every time he touched me, because I love another man."

"Sophia!" June exclaimed.

"Oh, Sophia," Mae whispered softly. "It's Mr. Brentwood, isn't it?"

Sophia looked at Mae and nodded sadly. "I was barely seventeen when I made that vow to Papa. How could I know about true love and the unrelenting desire for a man? I wanted to redeem myself for costing my father the woman he loved. I now know the only way to redemption is forgiveness. I have forgiven myself. Perhaps I could have married Lord Snellingly if I hadn't fallen in love with Matson, but now I can't. I know all of you will be disappointed in me, but I can't live without Matson. I must go to his ship now and stop him from sailing away."

"We are not disappointed in you, dearest," Mae said. "Would your father really want you marrying a man you don't love? It won't change the past and what happened to him. Besides, if he had truly wanted to marry that lady, he would have sent you to your room for the disobedient child you were and married her anyway. Don't give that vow another thought. If you love Mr. Brentwood and he loves you, marry him."

"Mae!" June said harshly. "Just because you have completely lost all your common sense is no reason for you to encourage Sophia to do away with hers."

"No, Miss Shevington, Sophia is right," Sir Randolph said. "It's time she knew the whole truth."

"What truth?" June asked.

A faraway look settled in Sir Randolph's eyes. With an expression filled with contrition, he said, "I always agreed with your father's obsession for you to marry a title. It seemed the right thing to do. I lost the woman I loved to a title too. I had more money than we could have ever spent, but money meant nothing to her. She wanted a title. When her first husband died, I thought now Lady Elder will finally marry me, but she didn't. She married four times and always for a title. Sophia, it's true your father loved Miss Hamilton, but she never loved him."

"What?" Sophia whispered. "I don't understand."

"Your father saw her and fell instantly in love with her. He assumed she would marry him. He was young, healthy, and wealthy. He didn't not marry her because of you. Miss Hamilton wouldn't marry him. He asked her and she refused him. She told him she intended to marry a gentleman with a title, and she did. Your father and I concluded that if titles meant that much to the two ladies we loved and wanted to marry, then you must marry a title too. We've always wanted the best for you. You don't need redemption, Sophia. You did nothing wrong."

Sophia felt as if a weight had been lifted off her shoulders, and her knees went weak.

"That's all well and good for you, Sir Randolph," June said, "but Sophia is not absolved from keeping her vow. I don't intend to let Sophia go back on her word. I won't hear of—"

All of a sudden, Sir Randolph grabbed June by her upper arms and kissed her hard and quick on the lips.

She gasped, and so did Sophia and Mae.

He looked down into June's wide eyes, and then he kissed her open mouth again. He then turned her loose, stepped back, and said, "Now, Miss Shevington, I think you should consent to be my wife."

Sophia's gasp was muted by her aunts' gasps.

"What did you say?" June asked.

"Marry me, Miss Shevington. I've only ever found one other woman who tries my patience, challenges me on every issue, and provokes me to madness like you have. Because of that, I think we will suit."

More gasps were heard.

"When I asked Lady Elder to marry me over forty years ago, she turned me down for a man with a title. So, Miss Shevington, what do you say? Will you marry me or refuse me?"

June turned a stunned face to Mae. "Sister?"

At first Mae's eyes were full of questions, but slowly a smile eased across her face. "I think you should say yes."

"But what about you?" June asked.

"I can't marry him, too, June. It's time we have our own lives. It's time we part."

"Part?" Sir Randolph said. "What are you talking about, Miss Shevington? You'll live with us. I need you here to help me keep her straight when she gets crotchety."

"Crotchety?" June said, jerking her hands to her hips in indignation. "I'll have you know I have never been crotchety in my life."

"See what I mean," Sir Randolph said and then smiled. "I can't even get her to say yes to my proposal."

"Then I'll say it for her," Mae said. "Yes, Sir Randolph, June will—"

"Wait," June interrupted. She ran her palms down her sides. "I'll take care of this myself, Sister." June turned to face Sir Randolph. She relaxed her shoulders and lowered her chin a fraction and smiled. "Yes, I'll marry you."

"Good. We'll make plans over breakfast tomorrow morning, but right now I have to get Sophia to the docks. I am an honorable man. I am partially responsible for keeping them apart. I must help them get back together. I pray we can get there before the ship sets sail." He looked at Sophia. "You get our cloaks and meet me out front. I'll go to the mews and get our carriage before the horses get unharnessed."

A few minutes later, when Sophia and Sir Randolph were settled in the carriage, he told the driver not to spare the horses on his way to the docks. Sometimes they took the corners so fast Sophia thought the carriage would topple. Thankfully, Sir Randolph knew exactly which ships were Matson's, and he had the carriage pull them right up to the ship. When she stepped out of the carriage, Sophia saw three huge ships at the dock.

"This is the one that will be leaving," Sir Randolph said. "See the smoke rising from it?"

Sophia's heart pounded, and she looked about the dock. She wanted to board and find Matson but realized the gangplank had been removed to get ready for their departure.

"Matson," she called. "Hello! Can anyone hear me?"

A light lifted above the hull of the ship, and a small face came into view. Sophia blinked, thinking her eyes were deceiving her. It was the boy thief who had stolen her brooch.

"You!" she said. "What are you doing on the ship?" she called up to him.

"Doing me job, lady," he called back. "What can I do for ye?"

"You're working? On Mr. Brentwood's ship?"

"I 'ad no choice. 'E told me I could go to an orphanage or take a job learning to be a sailor. I took the ship."

Sophia's heart swelled even more. Matson had taken care of the little boy. "That was very kind of Mr. Brentwood. Do you know where he is?"

"'E's standing right behind you."

Sophia spun and saw Matson. She rushed into his arms, and he caught her up to him and swung her around. "Don't leave, Matson, I will marry you. I love you. I will marry you. Please don't go."

Matson set her on her feet and looked at Sir Randolph.

"I'll wait in the carriage," Sir Randolph said and turned away.

"Do not tease me about this, Sophia."

"I'm not. I don't want to live without you. I've forgiven myself, my father, everyone. I have to live for me, and I want to live with you."

Matson pulled her up against his chest. "Sophia, I have been waiting here, hoping you would come so I wouldn't have to get on that ship and sail away. Let me hear you say it again."

"I love you, and I will marry you if you still want me to."

"You know I do."

Matson looked up at the boy on the ship and said, "Henry, tell the captain to prepare to sail without me."

"Aye, sir."

Suddenly there was a loud bang, and bright lights filled the sky.

"Look." Matson smiled. "Beautiful fireworks from Vauxhall Gardens."

"I see fireworks every time you kiss me," Sophia

said, looking up at Matson with all the love she was feeling for him.

"So do I, my love."

Matson pulled Sophia into his arms again and kissed her as the sky rained lights.

Sophia thrilled to his touch.

Epilogue

Where love is concerned, too much is
not enough.

—Pierre de Beaumarchais

SOPHIA WAITED ANXIOUSLY FOR MATSON TO
come home. She had donned a light turquoise-blue
dress and fastened her mother's brooch to it. A fire
had been burning all day, and the drawing room
was warm and inviting.

It was her first dinner party in their new home.
It had taken them six months to find a house and
furnish it, but now they were happily settled. They
were having his brothers and their wives, her aunt
Mae, and newly married Sir Randolph and Aunt
June for dinner. They couldn't have been coming at
a more perfect time.

Finally, Sophia heard Matson come in the front
door. She moistened her lips and walked to the
doorway of the drawing room to meet him. He
smiled when he saw her. Matson wrapped her in his
arms and kissed her lovingly.

"You're late," she whispered seductively.

"Hmm, had I known such sweet kisses would be waiting for me, I would have hurried to get home."

"You did know," she teased him. "Now tell me, did you have a good day, my love?"

"No, I missed you. How was your day?"

She smiled. "I missed you too, but I found the perfect place for the offices of Shevington Shipping, and I sent a letter to Mr. Peabody telling him to start making arrangements to move everything to London. Thank you for letting me continue to oversee my father's company."

"It makes me happy that you are so happy." He kissed her again.

"Come and sit down," she said. "I have something to discuss with you before our guests arrive."

"If we haven't much time, I think I would rather kiss you and then talk later," he said, not letting go of her.

"There will be plenty of time for that after our guests leave, now sit."

"Yes, Mrs. Brentwood," he said and made himself comfortable on the settee.

Sophia poured him a drink, and when she handed it to him, he promptly placed it on the table in front of him. He pulled her onto the settee with him and kissed her again.

"Now, tell me what it is you want to discuss."

"I know you told me you would not touch Sir Randolph's estate when it is passed on to me, but what about your sons? Will you let them have it?"

Matson gave her a curious look. He shrugged. "Maybe, I don't know. I haven't even thought about that. We have plenty of time to discuss that. Last time I saw Sir Randolph, he looked younger and happier than ever."

"But there is another reason we might want to talk about it now."

"Why?"

"You are going to have sons or daughters in about six months."

Matson's eyes widened. "I—you—we will have sons, as in more than one?"

Sophia smiled. "The midwife is certain I am carrying more than one baby. She says she has never been wrong in predicting two, but she doesn't predict whether boys, girls, or one of each."

"I don't know what to say."

"Maybe that you are happy?"

"Happy?" He looked into her eyes. "I'm elated, Sophia. I can't believe I will be having sons or daughters before either of my brothers."

"And do you agree that we will tell them tonight at dinner?"

"Yes." He laughed and hugged her close. "I can't wait to see the expressions on their faces when we tell them there will be another set of twins in the family. I love you, Sophia."

"And I love you, Matson. I always will."

About the Author

New York Times and *USA Today* bestselling author Amelia Grey grew up in a small town in the Florida Panhandle. She has been happily married to her high school sweetheart for more than thirty years. Amelia has won the Booksellers Best Award and Aspen Gold Award for writing as Amelia Grey. Writing as Gloria Dale Skinner, she has won the Romantic Times Award for Love and Laughter, the Maggie Award, and the Affaire de Coeur Award. Her books have been sold in many countries in Europe, in Russia, and in China, and they have also been featured in Doubleday and Rhapsody Book Clubs.

Amelia loves flowers, candlelight, sweet smiles, gentle laughter, and sunshine.

Follow Amelia on-line at www.ameliagrey.com and on Facebook at FaceBook.com/AmeliaGreybooks.

Also by Amelia Grey

For more thrilling Regency romance,
check out *The Duke in Question*
by Amalie Howard.

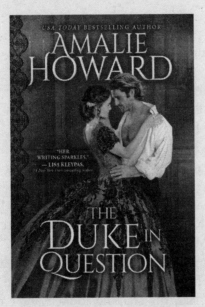

Available now from Sourcebooks Casablanca.

One

The SS Valor, *Atlantic Ocean, 1865*

LADY BRONWYN CHASE GASPED FOR BREATH, tucking her body into the narrow alcove and not daring to breathe. *He* was here. On her brother's ship. She had only met the Duke of Thornbury once, during her stepbrother's wedding ball last season in London, and it had been enough to make a lasting impression. He'd struck her as sharp and intelligent, a man whose piercing gaze missed nothing.

And handsome too, she reminded herself.

Her memory wasn't wrong. In the year since she'd seen him last, his striking looks hadn't changed. They'd grown more pronounced. Or maybe that was because she'd idolized him in her dreams... an unreachable fantasy lover with tawny hair and citrine eyes. Bronwyn let out a silent breath to calm her racing heart that was pounding for a variety of reasons—fright, fatigue...and pure womanly fascination. *He should not be here.*

Why was he here?

Had she made a mistake? Perhaps she'd mistaken him for someone else. But even as she thought it, she discarded the notion. It was him, no doubt of that. That thick, sun-gilded, tawny-brown hair still curled around his angular face in unruly locks, a jewel-gold stare and a hawklike nose combining to make most people wary of the hunter prowling in their midst. The duke was attractive in a throat-drying, fierce way; everything about him made her silly heart thrum. Even dressed in formal evening wear, he stood out like a tree in a field of pretty flowers.

Most steered clear of him.

Not her, obviously, because she had rocks in her head. Too bad he was taken, though like everyone else in the *ton*, she'd heard the whispers of estrangement, if they were to be believed. Bronwyn hadn't seen anyone resembling his wife before fleeing the salon earlier, however. Then again, she'd run at the first sight of him. The girlish infatuation she'd quashed a year ago had returned in full force. The urge to throw herself in his path, look up into that sultry stare, and offer herself up like a too-willing Andromeda displayed on a rock for his pleasure had been too compelling.

Good gracious, her thoughts were absurd.

Not that she hadn't dreamed of being swept off her feet and shamelessly seduced by a man who greatly resembled her pursuer. Bronwyn scowled.

Now was not the time to be reminiscing about *private* fantasies that had nothing to do with *him* whatsoever. The dratted duke was here to arrest her or worse. What were the odds that he was on *this* ship while she was in possession of documents that could get her thrown into jail?

Or executed for treason.

Perhaps Thornbury had only seen her in the dining room and recognized her as Ashvale's sister. Perhaps he only wanted to say hullo. Then why were her nerves on edge as though she were teetering on the edge of a dangerous precipice? Her instincts were screaming at her to flee. Not that she could jump off the side of a massive ship and swim to safety. She would have to act, pretend to be taking a pleasure cruise or some such. And hiding in an alcove off the main salon only made her look guilty.

Sucking a breath into her tight lungs, Bronwyn eased from the space, peering up and down the corridor. He hadn't followed her, thank God, though she'd felt the visceral tug when he'd set her in his sights in that room, eyes lighting with *something*. Recognition? Suspicion? She was letting fear get the best of her, and that was never good.

With a toss of her head, she smoothed her skirts, lifted her chin, and walked down the hallway. She wanted to run, but she cautioned her trembling legs to take a pace that didn't stamp her as someone suspicious, just in case the duke was watching. The hairs on her nape stood on end at the thought. She walked until she came to a door that led to one of the main decks, her lungs filling with salty chilled ocean air and her gaze greeted by a twilight sky with stars beginning to glimmer in the distance. The endless horizon over the dark, white-crested sea was beautiful in a stunningly vast way, one that made her feel small.

Insignificant.

Bronwyn wanted to make her mark. A mark… *any* mark that would deem her worthy, that would be a reminder that she had been here on earth at this time. It was perhaps what had pushed her to agree to this whole scheme. Using the nom de guerre "the Kestrel," at first she had done small tasks in London. A delivery here, a word there, all with the goal of helping the oppressed to lift the yoke of subjugation. She had started out fighting for women's rights with the suffragettes, but the world was so much bigger and broader than England.

Her brother, Courtland, and his wife lived in Antigua.

His duchess's best friend hailed from India.

There was more she could do…a better way she could make a difference with her time and her efforts. Despite the stringent rules impressed upon her as a woman in England, Bronwyn was acutely aware of her own privilege and the fact that she held power that others might not have. While she could not own property or vote, she still had *some* self-governance. Little actions, no matter how small, could have big ripples. And so, here she was, en route to Philadelphia with sensitive documents.

Bronwyn had known what she was getting into when she had agreed to ferry the packet across the Atlantic. She did not know what was in the letter, only that it would aid in the cause of the Northern states during the American Civil War. Seeing some of the opposition her brother had endured as a man of mixed heritage in England, despite his status as a peer, a fire had been lit beneath her to *do* something.

But unlike her brother who was the Duke of Ashvale, Bronwyn did not have a seat in the Lords. She wasn't a *man*. She might not have the power he had at his fingertips to effect change, but she wasn't incapable, and so she had agreed to hand-deliver the package, despite the personal risk to her person, her reputation, and her family name. Though right now, the thought of being caught and imprisoned by a man rumored to be the greatest spy in London left her cold.

Should her mission be compromised or the documents fall into the wrong hands, lives would be endangered and innumerable losses encountered. The packet was safe in her stateroom, thank God, hidden where no one would find it, but she felt the weight of her choices with every breath.

Bronwyn swallowed, resting her fingers on the metal railing.

You're doing the right thing.

She hoped.

"Lady Bronwyn, I thought that was you," a low voice said.

Bronwyn didn't have to turn to know who had found her, even as that lush baritone shivered over her senses like raw silk gliding over bare skin. The greeting wasn't untoward, considering they'd been properly introduced in town, but her heart kicked against her ribs all the same. She'd been wrong to come out here alone. At least in the dining room, there were other people.

Other *barriers*.

Scolding herself silently, Bronwyn lifted her chin. She could do this. She wasn't some ingenue fresh out of the schoolroom. She was a woman grown and more than capable of handling a simple gentleman. There was only one problem with that logic—the Duke of Thornbury was hardly *simple*. No, he was highly intelligent, distressingly alert, and nobody's fool. Least of all hers.

Act natural, Bee.

Pasting a demure smile on her lips, she turned and took him in up close. Fitted bespoke clothing, tremendous height—he practically towered over her smaller form—those angular cheekbones, hooded golden eyes, and lush mouth all conspired to make her lungs squeeze. His pale skin took on the silvery gleam of the moonlight, making him appear more chimerical than he should be…some fantastical sultry specter from her imagination come to taunt her. She'd take that option if it meant she didn't have to speak to him, but alas, he was indeed real.

"Your Grace, what a surprise."

A thoroughly unwelcome one.

He leaned against the railing and perused her. "It is, isn't it? Fancy seeing you here. I thought I had been mistaken in the dining salon, but here you are…in the flesh. Are you alone?"

"My chaperone retired with a headache," she replied, thinking quickly. Her flighty lady's maid, Cora, who was prone to the vapors and disappearing at the most inconvenient times was hardly a proper chaperone, but beggars could not be choosers. Particularly beggars turned international spies. Though Bronwyn wasn't a spy, per se; she was more of a discreet informant. "Is your wife here as well?"

He cleared his throat. "The lady is, though we are no longer married."

Goodness, her heart shouldn't have raced so violently at that, but Bronwyn could feel it hammering like a bird about to take flight. His marital state had nothing to do with her. He was her brother's friend! And a former British undercover agent. A man who would put her in handcuffs without blinking. A different scenario involving restraints—a much naughtier one with rather less clothing—crept into her mind, and she felt her face flame. *Did* he carry handcuffs?

Stop it, stop it, stop it.

"I'm sorry to hear that," she managed to say.

The duke nodded. "Where are you headed?" he asked. It was a casual inquiry, and yet, Bronwyn recognized that nothing was casual for this man. A seemingly basic question could lure out secrets, ferret out clues. He was a master at interrogation and artifice...while she was a mere novice.

She feigned a coy look and fluttered her eyelashes. "Did the Duke of Ashvale send you to follow me, Your Grace? Very well then, I am visiting an aunt in Philadelphia."

Speculation gleamed in that shadowed gaze. "I didn't realize that you had family in America."

Gracious but he was quick. Bronwyn shook her head, smile pasted on firmly. "On my mother's side, I fear. She is ill, and Mama thought I would be able to offer some comfort."

Now, *that* was a mistake. She almost kicked herself when those heavy-lidded eyes narrowed.

"Lady Borne sent you to play nursemaid to an ailing relative," he murmured slowly. "Unless she has changed in temperament, that is a rather surprising kindness."

Bronwyn stopped herself from gritting her teeth in frustration. A man like Thornbury, an expert in body language and human behavior, would not miss it. Her mother was not known for being the most generous or *kind* of ladies. In fact, she was a terrible person to her core. It still astounded Bronwyn that her mother had attempted to oust Courtland—the legitimate heir to her dead husband's estate—by sending him away from England in hopes of elevating her own son. Perhaps that was another reason why Bronwyn felt so compelled to do what she was doing…to make up for the grievous wrongs within her own family.

"Surprising or not, Your Grace, it is the reason for my journey. Now if you'll excuse me, I must check on Cora." She moved to walk past him, only to be stopped by a firm grip on her elbow. Heat spread across her skin at the contact, even though he wore gloves and she wore long sleeves. Bronwyn couldn't help the gasp that passed her lips, nor the instant tightening of her belly. A wild gasp throttled in her throat, the sensation of his grasp almost too much for her wayward brain to handle. She glanced up, and the moment their eyes collided, something all too visceral shot between them.

"Does Ashvale know you are here?" he asked.

No, because her brother would hardly approve if he knew she'd name-dropped him to commandeer one of the owner's suites onboard. Hiding out in a common stateroom would not have been ideal—what if she'd been recognized?—so she'd elected to travel in plain sight. A loud and obnoxious heiress was dismissible. She had no doubt that Courtland would hear about the incident, but she hoped to have delivered the packet and be on the return voyage by that point. As far as anyone was concerned, Lady Bronwyn Chase was a vapid nuisance, abusing her brother's connections and wealth and visiting an ailing family member.

It was a thin camouflage at best, but the only one she could come up with.

"Ashvale doesn't keep track of my every step, Your Grace," she snipped, her stare dipping pointedly to the long fingers still pressed in the crook of her elbow. He did not take the hint, damn the man, one corner of that indecent bottom lip kicking up in a way that suggested he was well aware of what his touch was doing to her. Bronwyn pushed a haughty smirk to her lips. "And besides, it's not as though everyone onboard doesn't know who I am. My brother owns this vessel, after all."

Distaste flickered across his face, and she winced. Better he think her a shallow, frivolous excuse for a chit who was using her brother's title and property than the reality. Still, something inside of her rebelled. She *wanted* him to keep her in some esteem.

Duty won out over pride, of course, as she

widened her coy smile. "Don't tell anyone, but I cannot wait to see Philadelphia. Do you know how much they fawn over aristocrats? As if our blood is so blue, it's gold. Perhaps I shall find myself an obscenely rich husband for my efforts. I suppose that's why Mama agreed to let me go. Fatten the coffers and all that."

"Indeed." The word dripped with derision.

Heavens. She almost loathed herself in that moment, but the unguarded disgust blooming on the duke's countenance was like a blow. She ignored it…his instant and unguarded contempt. Bronwyn felt her cheeks heat, but played into her performance. Her gaze canvassed him in an almost covetous way, lashes dropping bashfully. "I hope you don't think me forward, Your Grace, but perhaps we should have dinner one night. For my brother's sake."

The hefty flirtation worked like a charm.

He released her like a hot coal and bowed, the slightest dip of his head as though he couldn't muster much more than that, his face going studiously blank. Cold. Untouchable.

"Perhaps. Enjoy your trip, my lady."

———

God but she was a spoiled, abominable brat.

Valentine couldn't fathom how the girl who had

so courageously helped the Duke of Ashvale and his duchess claim his birthright had turned into this…this avaricious nitwit who'd looked at him like a spider eyeing her next meal. The expression of greed on her face as she'd contemplated her marital prospects in Philadelphia had sickened him. Perhaps he'd become too jaded in life.

He pinched the bridge of his nose between his thumb and forefinger as hard as he could until spots danced in his vision. He had a job to do, and babysitting the younger sister of one of his friends was not in the cards. Valentine hadn't expected her to be on the ship, and he was certain Ashvale would be surprised to learn that she had bandied his name about to secure passage.

He wondered if the ailing relation was real, or whether that was some pretext to leave her mother's clutches. He shook his head—that adder of a woman wouldn't let her spawn go far, not if it endangered her chance to make an exceptional match. Her young, nubile daughter was much too valuable a commodity for that. Then again, money was as attractive a lure as a title these days.

Valentine recognized the initial pulse of interest for what it was. Lady Bronwyn was a comely girl, there was no denying that. Ash-brown hair with hints of rich chestnut was coiled into an artful arrangement that framed her oval-shaped face to perfection. Darkly lashed crystalline blue eyes were the jewels of a creamy porcelain countenance, overshadowing the small bow-shaped mouth that resided below a sloping nose.

She wasn't even his type. He preferred his women bashful, buxom, and brainless.

While she had the last going for her, Valentine couldn't explain the vexing pulse of attraction. Thankfully, the early spurt of it had evaporated the moment she'd opened her mouth. And he had more important things to do than worry about some silly chit, though he did feel a beat of responsibility to his friend, the duke. Ashvale would pummel him to a pulp if he found out that Valentine had left his friend's younger sister in a compromising situation.

He palmed his face and frowned. So *was* she lying?

No. She had likely used the Ashvale connection to occupy the owner's accommodations onboard. He sighed, rethinking his early thought that she was the shallowest sort of woman. A pity, really. Or perhaps a blessing in disguise. Not that he required any temptation while he was working. He had one job—he needed to find the rogue operative known as the Kestrel.

And his prey was on this ship.

From his years in covert operations, Valentine was well aware that a handle could by definition be anyone. The Kestrel could be a man or a woman,

THE DUKE IN QUESTION   403

but they had intelligence that it was most likely a man. Though never apprehended, the Kestrel had been seen and described once or twice—a narrow-faced, rangy man of average height with a sparse beard and mustache—and a passable sketch had been rendered.

Halfway into the voyage, however, Valentine had been unable to unearth any more clues as to the man's identity or find anyone matching the likeness. He'd perused the ship's manifesto, but of course no names had jumped out at him. Criminals rarely did.

He blinked. Come to think of it, Lady Bronwyn Chase hadn't been on there either.

The cheeky little liar! Spotting her in the dining room had only been by chance, and though their eyes had met, she hadn't seemed to recognize him at first. And then she'd run off toward the necessary. Valentine went over the names in his memory, stopping at a Miss Bee Chase. It was a common enough last name, but he should have paid it more attention. In truth, he'd been more concerned with the men onboard. A mistake a novice would make. Now, he'd have to go over the list again with a more discerning eye. Still, it had to be a nickname so he couldn't fault her for using it to assume some clandestine deception.

Lady Bronwyn was much too on the nose for that.

Dinner, indeed. He'd stay a far step from the twit

if he could help it, or he'd find himself leg-shackled by the end of the journey. Lord knew the grasping Lady Borne wouldn't turn her nose up at the title of duchess for her daughter.

Making his way back inside, he had just entered the vacated salon when footsteps tapped on the polished wooden floors toward him.

"There you are, my darling. Thought I'd lost you."

His fake former countess when he'd been earl and an operative like him fastened herself to his side. While Valentine was officially retired, she was not. In fact, Lisbeth was the one who had asked him to take on the assignment. She was convinced that the Kestrel was a peer, and the only way to uncover a peer was to be part of aristocratic circles.

A year ago, they had started the rumor that they were estranged and a fake divorce to a hitherto fake marriage had been procured and granted by the Home Office, but now she needed him and his connections. It was no hardship. In truth, he'd been bored out of his skull playing duke these past few months, thanks to Uncle Bucky's sudden demise. Valentine had yet to visit the ducal seat in Scotland—a task he hoped to put off for as long as possible.

"Lisbeth, dearest. Weren't you supposed to be playing cards?"

Her lips curled, her eyes flashing with chagrin. "It was a bust."

Damn. He felt his frustration rise. They were both sure that the mysterious Lord Kestrel would show his face after being at sea for three days. Dinner, a dance, or a hand of cards, but no, nothing. Peers, even treasonous ones, enjoyed their entertainments.

"Everyone in the cardroom has been cleared," she said. "Did you find your little diversion? You took off like a bat out of hell when you saw that chit. Who is she?"

"It's Ashvale's sister," he said in a dispassionate tone.

Her brows rose in surprise. "Lady Borne's daughter?"

"One and the same, and suffice it to say that that apple is firmly still part of that beetle-bitten tree."

"Wasn't she the one who helped the duke?" Lisbeth frowned. "She seemed to have a good head on her shoulders despite her sorry parentage."

"A year is a long time to change a person," he said, lip hooking in a repulsed sneer.

"*That* bad?" Lisbeth asked.

"Worse, if you can imagine it."

"I cannot."

Passing another couple and exchanging pleasant nods, Lisbeth hooked her arm in his and peered up at him. It was all a farce, of course, but it was like walking in a worn, comfortable shoe. The pretense came easily to both of them. Though they had been lovers in the past, that had been a long time ago. Valentine kept his liaisons short and detached, while Lisbeth preferred female company these days. Still, they remained close friends, and he suspected that that would never change.

"She wants us to dine together," he said.

Lisbeth grinned as he led her back to their adjoining chambers. "Will you?"

"I'd rather take my chances with the sharks, thank you very much." He shook his head and scowled. "It's only because of Ashvale that I'm even considering it. She claims to have a sick aunt in Philadelphia, but I expect it's more than that. She could be running away the way the Duke of Embry's sister did."

"Do you blame her?" Lisbeth asked when they stopped at her door. "With a mother like that threatening to marry her off to the highest bidder, if I were her, I'd slip away too the first chance I got. Leave her be, Val. You remember what it was like to be young once, don't you?"

"She'll only ruin herself," he said.

His partner patted his shoulder with a laugh. "I think you gentlemen put too little faith in us women. If she's anything like her elder brother, that girl won't allow herself to be ruined. Or perhaps she's the sort who doesn't put much stock in ruination—we're quite a popular set, you know. Keep an eye on her, if you must, but I suspect that Lady Bronwyn might be made of much sterner stuff than we know."

"I won't hold my breath," he said drily. "The chit's head is full of matrimonial ribbons and conceited delusions of grandeur."

Lisbeth laughed at his droll reply. "She sounds delightful! I could do with some entertainment after the last few days. Invite me to your little dinner and I'll be the judge. Twenty guineas says you're overreacting."

He entered his room and nodded just before closing the door. "I'll take that wager. Don't blame me when your ears start to bleed, and remember that you brought this on yourself."

A pair of limpid crystal-blue eyes formed in his head with a face like an angel. She had the body of a siren and the wits of a gnat. Despite the former, Valentine felt a beat of distaste. He'd never been a man ruled by base passions. He wasn't about to start now. Lady Bronwyn might be beautiful, but she was a pest and a grasping sycophant just like her mother.

He scowled with dispassion. He would not allow her to filter into his thoughts…or his dreams. Some strong physical activity was in order so that he could work himself to exhaustion and fall into a dreamless sleep. After putting his body through a grueling bout of exercises that left his muscles weary and shivering, he was finally fatigued enough to crawl into bed.

He needed rest.

Hopefully, one unplagued by blue-eyed angels intent on wedlock.

UP ALL NIGHT WITH A GOOD DUKE

A new sparkling and sexy Regency romance series
from award-winning author Amy Rose Bennett

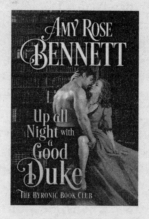

Artemis Jones—"respectable" finishing-school teacher by day and
Gothic romance writer by night—has never lost sight of her real dream:
to open her own academic ladies' college. When Artemis is unexpect-
edly called upon by a dear friend to navigate her first London Season,
she comes at once. Perhaps she can court the interest of a wealthy
patron for her school. As long as she can avoid her aunt's schemes to
marry her off. Little does she realize she's about to come face-to-face
with a Byron-esque widowed duke determined to find a bride...

"Infused with heat, energy, and glamour."
—Amanda Quick, *New York Times* bestselling author,
for *How to Catch a Wicked Viscount*

For more info about Sourcebooks's books and authors, visit:
sourcebooks.com

LORDS OF THE ARMORY

Escape into the passion and adventure of the Lords of the Armory series from award-winning author Anna Harrington!

An Inconvenient Duke

Marcus Braddock, Duke of Hampton and former general, is back from war and faced with mourning the death of his beloved sister. He's sure Danielle Williams knows something about what happened, and the only option is to keep Danielle close...

An Unexpected Earl

Brandon Pearce, former brigadier and now the Earl West, is determined to help the girl he once loved save her property and the charity she's been struggling to build. But he'll have to deceive her first...

An Extraordinary Lord

Lord Merritt Rivers has dedicated his life to upholding the law, but when he meets a female thief-taker who takes his breath away, he'll have to decide what's worth saving—the life he's always known or the love that made him yearn for more...

LADY EVE'S INDISCRETION

Captivating, steamy Regency romance from *New York Times* and *USA Today* bestselling author Grace Burrowes

Lady Evie Windham has a secret to keep, and a wedding night would ruin everything. She's determined to avoid marriage, but with her parents pushing potential partners her way from every direction, she needs a miracle. Perhaps old family friend Lucas Denning, the newly titled Marquis of Deene, could be the answer to everything.

"Grace Burrowes is terrific."
—Julia Quinn, *New York Times* bestselling author of the Bridgerton series

For more info about Sourcebooks's books and authors, visit:
sourcebooks.com